Praise for *Clear My Name*

"A sixth winner for Daly . . . Fans of revelations about families and the len ters go to protect one another both du

—*Booklist*

"Paula Daly's *Clear My Name* is yet another terrific page-turner, to coin a phrase, from one of the finest of the U.K.'s emerging authors." —*Winnipeg Free Press*

"Daly's thrillers are engaging and well plotted; there is a nice mix of investigative process . . . as well as character development." —*Kirkus Reviews*

"Superbly character-driven, with a sharp plot and a terrific sting in the tale." —*Sunday Mirror* (UK)

"Exquisite pacing . . . The last quarter of this mystery doesn't so much as unfold as it explodes; the tension is at a fever pitch and the final revelations are genuinely surprising. With a wonderfully executed mystery and two unreliable narrators, *Clear My Name* straddles the line between psychological thriller and good old-fashioned whodunit." —*BookPage*

"Gilroy investigates the serpentine twists and turns of the evidence, proving how spectacularly talented Daly is as a weaver of intensely compelling contemporary tales." —*Daily Mail* (UK)

CLEAR MY NAME

PAULA DALY

CLEAR MY NAME

Grove Press
New York

First published in Great Britain in 2019 by Bantam Press
an imprint of Transworld Publishers

Published simultaneously in Canada

First Grove Atlantic hardcover edition: September 2019
First Grove Atlantic paperback edition: September 2020

Library of Congress Cataloging-in-Publication data available for this title.

ISBN 978-0-8021-5731-7
eISBN 978-0-8021-4784-4

Grove Press
an imprint of Grove Atlantic
154 West 14th Street
New York, NY 10011

Distributed by Publishers Group West

groveatlantic.com

20 21 22 23 10 9 8 7 6 5 4 3 2 1

For my family, with love

Now

T ESS GILROY CRADLES her coffee cup in her hands and watches
the small television on the kitchen counter. This morning,
the screen is filled with a familiar face. It's a young face. A young
man. And he is speaking directly to camera. He has tears in his
eyes and his hands are shaking as he reads from a sheet of paper –
it's a prepared statement.

The camera pans out and now the court is visible in the background. Surrounding the man is his family. His mother is at his
side, weeping silently, and she looks as if she's had something
pulled from her. This whole process has been hardest on her, Tess
thinks. It's as if she's lost something along the way, something
essential and life-giving.

'It has been a living nightmare, not just for me, but my entire
family. If it wasn't for their support—' The young man breaks off,
overcome, unable to read for a moment. 'If it wasn't for their support,' he continues, 'and the tireless work of Tess Gilroy, as well as
the people at Innocence UK, I would not be standing here now.'

Tess takes a swallow of her coffee. She glances at the clock and
realizes she should already have her coat on by now, but she continues to watch. The camera pans left and it's now that Tess sees
herself on screen: head down, avoiding, camera-shy as ever, as his
voice continues to be heard over the image. 'I'd like to put this
behind me and would ask that my family and I are afforded some
privacy as we try to move forward with our lives.'

Then we're back to the newsreader in the studio. 'Warren Douglas,' the newsreader says, 'who was freed from prison yesterday, after his sentence for rape was overturned.'

Tess takes this as her cue to leave.

She pulls on her coat, picks up her briefcase as well as the stack of envelopes ready for posting, and she's on her way.

Tess likes this little town. She lived here before – way, way back – when she was straight out of college. She shared a one-bedroom flat above the betting shop with a Bangladeshi girl. The girl has since moved to New Zealand – according to Facebook anyway – and the betting shop is long gone too. Tess likes it when she knows her way around a town; she likes it when she knows how the one-way system works, the filter lane at the traffic lights. This time, Tess managed to move house in four trips, her car stuffed to bursting with heavy-duty black bags, which has to be some kind of record. Perhaps she's been losing belongings along the way? she muses. Tess imagines her clothes, dotted in ditches, strewn along the highways and byways of England's northwest. She imagines her underwear caught in hedgerows, her scarves fluttering at the tops of trees.

Tess has spent most of her adult life moving from small northern town to small northern town, where she finds, despite the borderline poverty, the people to be unwaveringly friendly, the old men comedic, and the rents reasonable. She also never tires of being addressed as 'love' by complete strangers.

She has only been at her current address for a few days but already her clothes hang neatly in the wardrobe, the freezer is fully stocked with food, and her home office is organized just the way she likes it. She has even managed to rig up the bird-feeding station in the back yard to see the local wild birds through the late-autumn lean stretch, and she gets a small thrill from knowing she is providing them with a new feed source.

This is simultaneously counterbalanced, however, by a feeling of remorse and regret, as removing the feed source from her previous address means those poor birds are now going without.

She heads down the hill now towards town. She takes it steady, keeping in second gear, as a heavy snowfall two days ago means the West Pennine Moors are flooding the roads with their meltwaters. She checks her watch again and chides herself for remaining at home for the extra five minutes watching Warren give his statement. How did it feel to sleep in his own bed last night? she wonders. Good, she hopes. It can be strange, but people do miss different things. For most, it's their family they miss, rather than freedom, and it can come as quite a shock when the people they've spent their lives bickering with turn out to be the ones they find themselves aching to see.

There's a parking space a little further along from the post office and Tess grabs it while she can. The pavements are empty of pedestrians, the weather putting people off from venturing out, she presumes, so Tess is optimistic of getting back on the road fast and reckons an hour is probably enough time in which to make it to Manchester city centre for the meeting. But when she pushes open the post office doors, she whispers an emphatic '*Fuck*' under her breath, because the place is filled to the brim with pensioners: all chatting amiably, all with surely not much on in the way of work today.

Tess tries to swallow down her frustration. Tells herself to be patient and a little more generous as she, too, will be old eventually. And she can understand how leaving the house early, heading out, can give a person's day purpose and structure . . . perhaps even stave off the loneliness and isolation the elderly can be so susceptible to.

When it's her turn to be served, when the room has completely emptied of bodies, Tess approaches the glass wall which separates the postmaster from the communal space and places a Jiffy bag on the weighing scales.

'I'd like to send this first class, please, it doesn't need to be signed for . . . and can I collect the forwarded mail from my last address you've been holding for me? It's in the name of Tess Gilroy.'

Tess looks up at the postmaster expectantly.

No response.

She waits. But there is nothing. No response from him at all.

Tess feels mildly uncomfortable as she examines the postmaster's blank face. He's not young, nearer to seventy than sixty, and now that she looks more closely, his skin does have a clammy pallor to it. 'Are you OK?' she asks.

Again, there is no reply, and Tess glances behind to see if anyone else has entered the post office in the time she's been engaged.

She's alone.

'Do you want me to call someone for you? Get you some help?' she asks.

And it's only when she's surveying the contours of his face again, for signs of palsy, a stroke, that he raises his right hand slightly and gestures to a sign, high on the wall, over to Tess's left.

The sign reads: 'Wait behind white line until called'.

Tess looks behind her and sees the white line painted on the floor.

She looks back to the postmaster and his face is still without expression, and so, dutifully, she picks up her Jiffy bag and returns to the queuing area, making sure the rounded toes of her boots are positioned neatly behind the white line.

Once there, the postmaster calls out, 'Good morning!' and beckons for Tess to approach the glass. She does this and suddenly he's all smiles. He says, brightly, 'And what can I do for you today?'

Tess just looks at him.

Outside, Tess is holding an envelope in her hand. It has her name on it; it's part of the batch forwarded on from her previous address. She recognizes the sender instantly and toys with the idea of putting it straight into the nearest bin, but she can't quite bring herself to do it this time, for a reason she doesn't comprehend. Instead, she takes a pen from her handbag and scores through the lettering, before writing 'NOT KNOWN AT THIS ADDRESS' across the front. Then she drops it into the post box with the rest of her outgoing mail.

Now

WHEN SHE JOINS the motorway, Tess heads south, not encountering any heavy traffic until the M60, where each branch of the network converges. From then on, she drives at a stop start, stop start, until finally she reaches the car park on Bridge Street in the city centre. There is no snow here. Manchester rarely gets snow because of the urban warming effect and Tess can perform a kind of half-run, half-walk, whilst laden with her briefcase, case files and handbag, without risking serious injury.

She clatters into the conference room at exactly 10.04 a.m. and is quietly pleased with herself as Clive hasn't yet got his coat off.

Tom Robinson has his laptop fired up and is chomping at the bit, so Tess clears her throat. 'Before you get started,' she says quickly, addressing the room, 'can I just congratulate everyone on a job well done? I spoke to Warren last night, when he'd got himself settled at home, and he's doing well. Thank you, thank you again ... Over to you, Tom ...?' she prompts.

Tom stands. He is early thirties, slim and geeky-cool. Tess has a soft spot for him, not least because he's confided in her over the years when his relationships have begun to sour. Once, he told Tess he thought of her as a mother figure, and Tess didn't know whether to be flattered or not. She is only forty-five after all, eleven years older than Tom, but she reminded herself that a lot of men remain in adolescence until well into their thirties now, or at least that's what she's been told.

Tom pushes his glasses into place and smiles at his audience. They are all professionals, all – with the exception of Tess – volunteering their time and expertise for free. Together they make up the advisory panel of Innocence UK. It's a charitable organization which relies solely on private donations. Its purpose? To overturn wrongful convictions.

The panel comes together for a few hours once or twice a month, or as the case necessitates. Tess is the only full-time employee, and the only person in the room who is paid by the charity. The rest provide advice and guidance, and serve as a kind of back-up for Tess, which allows her to get on with the nuts-and-bolts work of investigating – and, with any luck, *overturning* – alleged miscarriages of justice, unhindered.

Before working at Innocence UK, Tess was a probation officer. It was a job she enjoyed; something she could do that made a difference, she liked to think. For the most part, Tess forged good relationships with her clients and their reoffending rates were substantially lower than the national average. But it was the ones who Tess *knew* were never guilty in the first place that kept her awake at night. The ones who'd been let down by the system. And it was because of those clients that Tess ended up here.

'Good morning, everyone,' Tom says. He's a solicitor and has volunteered at Innocence UK for around six years. It's his job to sift through the many enquiries that come their way, decide which cases have merit, and present them. The team will then take a vote, agreeing which they will investigate next, and this case will be passed on to Tess. It's Tess's job to coordinate the investigation and examine the crucial points of the prosecution's case, retesting their theories and so forth, to see if they still hold up.

As well as Tom and Tess, the rest of team is comprised of:

Vanessa Waring – Home Office pathologist
Chris Pownall – forensic scientist (special interest in fibre analysis)
Dr Fran Adler – Professor of Forensic Science at Manchester University (special interest in blood)
Clive Earle – ex-Detective Inspector with West Yorkshire Police. Pensioned off after fracturing two vertebrae on a job, and now advises Innocence UK on all matters relating to the police.

'If I can start by introducing you all to Avril Hughes,' Tom says, and Tess's eyes flick to the young woman to Tom's immediate right, who she assumes is here to take the minutes. Tom brings in a temp sometimes at the beginning of a difficult case to document the initial stages. 'Avril will be joining us as another full-time member of the team and will start by shadowing Tess. At least for the first couple of months anyway, or until she's learned the ropes.'

Tess frowns.

She looks directly at Tom and frowns again.

Tom won't meet her eye, however, and so she looks at Clive. Clive is now smiling at her broadly, raising his eyebrows, as if finding Tom's disclosure the funniest thing he's heard all week.

Frantically, Tess begins scrolling through the emails on her phone. Has Tom informed her of this and she failed to see his message? Surely he wouldn't dump someone on her without asking first? Tom wouldn't do that. Not out of nowhere. Tom knows Tess works alone. Has *always* worked alone.

'I'm new to this,' Avril is saying to the group. Her voice is soft and breathy-sounding and Tess looks up from her phone to examine her briefly. Avril appears to be around twenty-four, twenty-five at the most, but her plump frame has rendered her features childlike. She has round, rosy cheeks and big, trusting eyes. Apart from the high colour of her cheeks, though, the rest of her skin is beyond pale. And her bobbed hair is nearly black. Tess thinks Avril is like a lovely, plus-sized Snow White, but she's not at all right for this job, she decides instantly. She has no sharp edges.

'I don't have any special skills as such pertaining to this type of employment,' Avril continues, 'so I'm just going to have to try and learn from Tess, and hopefully I'll—'

'Nonsense.' Tom cuts her off. 'Avril' – he turns to the group – 'comes to us highly recommended. She has spent her time as a legal secretary, where she assisted some of the area's leading figures in family law. So she is not *completely* unfamiliar with our world . . . Avril, welcome,' he says, warmly. 'Now, shall we get to it?'

Tess opens her mouth to say something and then closes it again.

She can find no message from Tom on her phone.

'Right,' Tom says, still avoiding Tess's glare, 'as ever, we're indebted to you all for giving up your time and services, et cetera . . . We have three new cases to consider today. The first is another from the balls-up that was Operation Swallowtail. Like many of the others, Terry Carmichael's credit card was used to purchase indecent images of children online. There were never any images found on his *own* computer, but he's been serving a three-year sentence for possession of child pornography, and it's the usual scenario: his family have disowned him, his kids won't see him, he's lost everything . . . He's eager to clear his name before his release, try and build bridges and so forth.'

'How many of these Swallowtail cases have we covered now?' asks Tess.

Tom checks his notes. 'This would be the fourth.'

'And how many suicides, to date, as a result of Operation Swallowtail?'

'Seven,' he replies.

'Is Terry Carmichael a suicide risk?' she asks.

'Hard to say. If I had to call it, I'd say no. But you know how it is. Often it's when they get out that the wheels really fall off.'

Tess considers this.

'Next up is Ryan Green,' says Tom. 'He was convicted of rape but claims he wasn't in the right county at the time. He was four hundred miles away in Aberdeen. There's a good case for lab cross-contamination with this one. Especially with all the lab blunders we've heard about of late. Might be good timing, what with the press jumping all over the forensic screw-ups?'

'Who did he rape?' asks Clive.

'Allegedly, a young woman. A twenty-two-year-old on a night out. She was grabbed from behind as she walked home.'

Tess glances around the table. Everyone is taking notes. She'll be surprised if they vote for Ryan, as the last case – Warren Douglas – was a rape case too, and Tom likes to mix things up a bit. He has to answer to the charity's board members, and they don't like it if the team are seen to be favouring one type of mis-carriage of justice case over another.

'The last,' Tom says, 'is Carrie Kamara. She was imprisoned for murdering her husband's lover. She's served three years of a fifteen-year sentence. This one was brought to my attention by her barrister.'

'Her *own* barrister?' asks Clive, sceptical.

And Tom replies, 'I know, right? Like, when does that ever happen? He wrote to me quite adamant she's innocent. He really wants us to take a look. She's not doing too well inside appar-ently. Her daughter's very supportive; I've spoken to her on the phone – Mia – she's articulate, cooperative, very sincere. She's not typical of the usual family members we find ourselves dealing with. She's in . . . hang on—' Tom clicks his trackpad a couple of times. 'She lives in Morecambe . . . Isn't that where you're from originally, Tess?'

Out of nowhere, Tess feels faint, light-headed, as if she's stood up too quickly.

'What?' she says weakly.

'Morecambe,' replies Tom. 'Didn't you grow up there?' and Tess nods. 'Well, it'll certainly be useful if you know your way around the place.' Tom waits for Tess to say something more, but when she doesn't speak, continues on. 'Well, basically, what I can gather is that there was no money for Carrie Kamara's defence. Her husband, Pete, turned his back on her the second she was arrested for murdering his girlfriend, and she was left completely to her own devices. Her barrister feels she's been let down by the criminal justice system – his words. He said there just weren't the resources to go out and gather the necessary evidence to counter the prosecution's claims. I've had a look at it and I think this could be another example of a wrongful conviction because evidence wasn't made available to the defence.'

'Was the husband investigated?' asks Fran Adler.

'His alibi checked out,' replies Tom.

'Potential pitfalls of the case?' asks Clive.

At this, Tom shifts his weight to his other foot. 'Carrie Kamara had no alibi,' he says carefully, 'and there was also DNA found at the scene.'

'*Her* DNA?' asks Tess, taken aback.

And Tom nods solemnly. 'They found a blood smear on the internal handle of the victim's front door. The prosecution claimed Carrie left it when exiting the house. But her barrister feels this is an anomaly. Carrie was not found to have any open wounds at the time of her arrest and he says the rest of the prosecution's case was purely circumstantial, farcical even. But, as you would expect, the jury totally ignored all that. They convicted entirely on the strength of the DNA.'

'I remember this case,' Vanessa Waring says, looking at the ceiling as if casting her mind back. 'Wasn't the victim stabbed repeatedly?'

'Yes,' replies Tom. 'Victim's name was Ella Muir. Thirty years old.'

The room is silent as the panel absorbs Tom's information.

'I really think this one might be worth a shot,' Tom adds after a moment, hopefully.

But still no one speaks.

Blood? Tess thinks. On the door handle? She'll be surprised if they go for it.

'OK,' says Tom, 'I know you're probably thinking this is going to be difficult. Risky, even. But the fact of the matter is, in the nine years that Innocence UK has been investigating wrongful convictions, we haven't looked at any cases involving female prisoners. And it's been noted.'

Tess can feel her fellow professionals shifting uncomfortably in their seats. Tom's right, of course. They should have taken on a woman's case before. Way before now. In fact, it's such an outrageous blunder that she's about to voice her support because this needs rectifying immediately.

But then she remembers. She remembers *Morecambe* and the contents of her stomach roil.

She closes her eyes, thinks back. She feels as if a large wave is being swept over her head. She can hear Tom's voice, faintly, as if she's being pulled out to sea. 'A show of hands please for Terry Carmichael and Operation Swallowtail . . .' Tess can hear him say, and she lifts her hand, weakly. She is the only one who votes for Terry.

'Next,' Tom continues, 'Ryan Green and the potential lab cross-contamination,' and his voice is further away still.

Tess is vaguely aware of Avril raising *her* hand, and of Avril dropping it again quickly, embarrassed she's made a mistake.

'Lastly then,' says Tom, his voice coming into sharp focus and Tess is now suddenly aware of everything: every sound, every person's breath, the temperature of the air on her skin, 'Carrie Kamara.'

Tess looks around the room and each person's hand is raised. Including, inexplicably, her own.

So they spend the next hour talking strategy. The panel decides that Tess and Avril should first look at the CCTV footage from the night of the murder as well as rechecking the one recorded witness statement, as it was these two pieces of evidence which formed the bulk of the prosecution's case, along with the DNA.

When they file out later, everyone on their way to lunch, Tess hangs back as she needs to speak to Tom privately.

'I know what you're going to say,' he tells her with an air of resignation. He's packing away his laptop.

Tess gathers up her things and approaches Tom's side of the desk. 'You think I'm going to try and persuade you not to take this case,' she says. 'You *think* . . .' She pauses for greater emphasis. '. . . I'm going to tell you that the DNA is too much of a stumbling block.'

'I think you don't want Avril shadowing you,' Tom replies bluntly. 'And I *know* you're going to spend the next five minutes trying to get me to change my mind. Well, let me save you the trouble, Tess. I won't.'

'But—'

He turns to face her. 'We can't get through our current work-load as it is. You know how stretched we are. And the legacy fund's been bolstered, which of course is fantastic, but there's only one of you, Tess, and you can only do so much. With Avril, we can get through twice as many cases as we do right now. And the only way to train her to do that is to have her follow you around learning what it is that you actually do.'

'No one trained me,' Tess argues, but Tom doesn't reply. Instead, he shrugs on his coat and gestures that he is leaving, discussion over.

They walk along the hallway together, side by side, making their way towards the lifts. Once inside, Tess turns to him. 'Look,' she says, in one last-ditch attempt to sway him, 'Avril is very young. Very young and immature.'

'She's not immature, she's gentle. She has a softness to her that could be valuable.' Tom smiles. 'She could be the yang to your yin, Tess.'

'What's that supposed to mean?'

'Nothing at all.'

Tess is put out. 'OK, so she's gentle,' she says, 'but this is a difficult job, Tom. I see stuff that isn't for everyone. It can be upsetting. It can be scary. Are you completely sure about this?'

And Tom sighs. 'All right,' he says, 'I concede, yes, Avril is very young . . . and that's entirely the reason we're getting away with paying her so little. But she's not immature, Tess. She's keen. So play nice, will you?'

Four Years Ago

CARRIE IS THE first to arrive on the day that will change everything. She's always the first to arrive. She's the type of person who would rather be an hour early than five minutes late. She waits in the hotel lobby in one of the low-slung leather chairs, and has to plant her feet firmly lest she slide off the thing and become a puddle of a woman on the tiled floor.

She checks her phone to determine if her friend is running late – she *is* running late, clearly, as it's now seven minutes past – but not so late that an apologetic text is warranted.

Could Carrie have got the wrong date?

Wrong venue?

Wrong time?

Could her friend have got the wrong date? Wrong venue? Wrong time?

These are the things that run through Carrie's head as a matter of course these days. She frets about the smallest of things. She read recently that women become more anxious as they get older (is forty-three older?) whereas men become more miserable. Not depressed kind of miserable, but more cantankerous, more everything's-suddenly-a-problem kind of miserable.

Carrie lifts her head and spots her friend. Helen is hurrying across the car park, trying to stuff her keys into her handbag as she walks. The heel of her right shoe catches on the tarmac and momentarily Helen is sent off balance.

'Hi-yaaa!' Helen shouts as she enters the lobby, spotting Carrie. 'Am I late? Have you been waiting ages? Sorry, I got caught up at work. I had my coat on and was halfway out the door and that sly bitch Marianne *knew* I was coming out to lunch, so what does she do? She starts rearranging the holiday rota so I have no choice but to stand there and make sure I get the weeks I want.'

'You're not late,' replies Carrie just as Helen is leaning in for a hug.

'Can't believe it's been a month already,' Helen says.

It's actually been two months since they've last done this but Carrie doesn't correct her. Helen cancelled last month's meet-up but Carrie didn't mind. She rarely minds if people cancel. She would never admit to it of course, but it's usually the outcome she's hoping for. Carrie will commit to a lunch, or dinner, or a shopping trip, or a girls' night out, something to give some shape to her life, something to make her feel as if she's *participating*, something to tell her other friends about when she meets up with them, and then when the event itself is cancelled, and she doesn't have to go through with it, she is hugely relieved.

Her friends speak of FOMO – Fear Of Missing Out – whereas Carrie thinks she's more WINJI – Wish I'd Never Joined In.

'How's work?' Helen asks.

'Great,' replies Carrie.

'And Mia?'

Carrie drops her gaze. 'She's great too.'

They make their way into the restaurant and Carrie feels Helen pull her shoulders back and adjust her expression into that of not a mere dentist's receptionist, but of someone altogether more successful and power-wielding. 'Yes, we have booked,' she says snippily to the young man in the waistcoat and polished shoes. 'It's in the name of Carter. And I hope you won't be sticking us over by the piano. My friend hasn't dined here before and I'm keen she has a good view of the bay.'

Carrie *has* dined here before. With Helen. Two months ago, in fact. And Carrie's pretty sure that the young waiter served them on that occasion too, but she says nothing.

They are shown to a table with a *good view of the bay* and Helen tells the waiter that this will be suitable, before shooting Carrie a look, as if to say, *If you don't ask, you don't get,* and they remove their coats and sit. 'Are you having wine?' asks Helen. 'I'm having wine. They've a strict no-drinking-on-duty policy at work but sod that. I never get out. I never treat myself.'

This is what this lunch is all about. Treating themselves. For the past however many years, women such as Carrie and Helen have put their children's needs, their husbands' needs, way above their own, and this is their attempt at reclaiming those little pieces of themselves that disappeared along the way. Carrie might even buy a new lipstick or a new scarf to mark such an occasion, as it's these small things which all add up to make her feel as though she's back in charge of her life.

Carrie has a number of acquaintances – she refers to them as 'friends', but they're not really that. Most, like Helen, are the wives of Pete's buddies and, over the years, it just became easier to fall in with these women – 'the girlies', Pete calls them – rather than to try and revive long-finished friendships from before she had Mia. There was no real reason for losing the friendships of her youth. Carrie was not the kind of sociopathic friend that everyone was keen to drop; it was more to do with the fact that she had Mia at twenty-five, which was younger – quite a bit younger – than her contemporaries, and so they'd tended to fall by the wayside as the demands of motherhood took over. When she *was* ready to jump back into the world of lunches out and girls' weekends away, Carrie's friends were burdened with young children of their own.

Carrie examines the menu. There are no surprises with regards to the main dishes: beer-battered cod, speciality sausages with herby mash, a vegetarian pasta dish that will be laden with too much double cream, butternut squash risotto. Carrie thinks she'll probably opt for two starters and forgo a main course altogether.

She peers over her menu and turns her head to the left. Surveying the room, she sees the tables are filled with women just like her: all over forty, all with freshly coloured hair, all wearing outfits that for now will only be used for special occasions, but next year will be relegated to everyday use. Carrie hears snapshots of conversations. She hears them discuss which universities their eldest children are applying to; where, as a family, they have been to, or will be going to, on holiday this year; she hears how tired/stressed/busy/under-appreciated they are; she hears discussions about books, decorating, self-tanning, weight loss, the John Lewis sale.

Helen signals to the waiter. He wends his way between the tables, taking out his notepad ready to transcribe their requests, but before he's managed to utter, *Are you ready to order?* Helen has issued him with instructions to bring two large glasses of Pinot Grigio.

'So, what's your news?' Helen asks, removing her mobile phone and placing it next to her napkin. She scrolls through the screen, saying, 'Don't mind me, I know this is rude, but I just need to check Finn's school hasn't been on again.'

'Nothing much to report,' replies Carrie.

She knows Helen is not really listening. Something on her phone has caught her attention and she is tapping out a response. Carrie's eyes slide to the left again. A woman on the next table is loudly reminding her dining companions that her family has been touched by cancer not once, but twice, and is handing out sponsorship forms. She's running a 10K. The forms are pink and the women search their handbags for pens and ten-pound notes with lacklustre enthusiasm.

Helen finishes typing and raises her head, aware, suddenly, that she took an unauthorized leave of absence there for a minute, and now she's not really sure where she was in the conversation. 'So, what's your news?' she asks again brightly.

'Nothing much to report,' repeats Carrie.

Their drinks arrive. 'Rob's being a dick,' says Helen.

Rob is frequently being a dick according to Helen. It's the usual stuff that crops up in the long-term marrieds: the unfair division of labour, domestic duties landing more in Helen's lap than his. Helen would like Rob to help out more around the house, whereas Rob would rather forgo the housework and have more sex. Helen thinks his mother speaks down to her. Rob thinks Helen spends too much time on the phone to her sister. Helen is frustrated by his lack of career drive. Rob thinks she should be happy with what they have and stop comparing him to her friends' husbands (who are not in as good physical shape as he is). Rob would like to spice things up in the bedroom. Helen is more tired than she's ever been in her entire life.

None of this is new. And Carrie quite happily listens to Helen complain about Rob, as Helen is often amusing as she re-enacts their latest run-in, and Carrie can see how Helen benefits from getting it off her chest.

When Helen has finished – when she's come to the conclusion that yes, Rob is substandard, yes, she wishes he were different, but she's stuck with him, and really, he's not that bad, all things considered – she drains the rest of her drink. And for an extended moment she lets her eyes rest on almost everything in the room except for Carrie. When she does finally turn her attention back to Carrie, Helen has an almost crazed look in her eye. 'So, what's Pete up to these days?' she asks.

'Pete?' Carrie responds.

'Yeah.'

And Carrie frowns. Because here's the thing: they don't discuss Pete. Not ever.

'Why do you ask about Pete?' Carrie enquires carefully.

Helen is arranging her napkin on her lap and is going to great pains to smooth out the creases. 'I just wondered if he was OK,' she says.

'He's OK.'

'Good. That's good then.'

'Helen,' Carrie asks levelly, 'what is going on?'

Helen swallows. She signals to the waiter for another glass of wine. She picks up her phone and puts it down again. And when, finally, she can't put it off any longer, she meets Carrie's gaze, and says in an urgent whisper, 'He's seeing someone.'

Carrie studies her friend. Her acquaintance. Whatever. She studies her and she's not sure what to say. Then she looks out of the window. The sea is teal green, the sky an unremarkable grey. The clouds are so thick and heavy that they appear as one bulbous entity.

Carrie clears her throat. 'This is something Pete does from time to time, Helen.'

'I know.'

'So then you also know that this isn't something I tend to . . .' Carrie pauses, searching for the right words. 'You understand this isn't necessarily something that would force us apart . . . as a couple, I mean. It wouldn't mean the end for us.'

'I understand that,' replies Helen softly.

'So . . . I'm sorry, Helen, but I'm struggling to see why you would think I needed to know this.'

'Because this time it's different. At least I think it is. I don't know, you tell me. He's started seeing Ella Muir.'

'Ella Muir? As in the girl from the barbeque?'

Helen nods. 'Yeah. The drunk one. You remember? Young. Pretty.'

Pete has never done this with someone she knows. Someone their *friends* know.

'Have I done the right thing by telling you?' Helen asks.

Now

CLIVE IS AT the bar ordering drinks. Tess watches him as he glances over his shoulder before speaking to the barmaid. He's up to something. Tess knows that look. Tom has disappeared to the loos which means she is alone with Avril for the first time, who is asking question after question about Tess's job description and nattering on enthusiastically about someone named William. Avril hasn't referred to him as her boyfriend but Tess can't think who else he could be and so she nods and smiles as Avril paints a picture of domestic harmony and romantic fulfilment.

'What's your cheapest lager?' Tess can hear Clive saying to the barmaid in the background. The barmaid gestures to a pump at the far end of the bar and Clive looks over his shoulder once more, furtively checking Tom is not in earshot, before saying, 'Do me a favour, will you, love? Put a pint of that cheap stuff in a Peroni glass . . . and finish it off with a Peroni top.' The barmaid agrees to this and is smiling conspiratorially at Clive, charmed, Tess supposes, by Clive's impishness, his roguish good looks, rather than his tight-fistedness. 'A pint of John Smith's Smooth as well, love,' Clive adds, 'and two glasses of white wine . . . small 'uns.'

This city-centre swanky bar is Tom's choice. Tess doesn't mind coming here as it's a short stroll from where they're based, and she enjoys the opportunity to look upon Manchester's well-heeled in their lunch hour. The place is all glass and chrome and the patrons seem impossibly young in their slim-legged suits and thick-rimmed spectacles.

Tom returns from the loos and takes his seat next to Avril, just as Clive is wending between tables, balancing the drinks on a small circular tray, trying not to spill any of his pint.

'One Peroni,' Clive says to Tom, setting it down in front of him with a flourish.

'Very generous of you, Clive.'

'Not at all,' he says, and he winks at Tess.

Five minutes later and Tess is becoming quite animated as she explains to Avril the ins and outs of, and very real need for, Innocence UK. It's been a while since she's been questioned about the charity's purpose, its mission, and whenever this happens, it's as if a kind of dam releases within her. The words come rushing out, not always in the right order, or the way that she intends, and she's sometimes left feeling mildly shocked by what has just occurred. 'It's a shitty combination of factors,' she's saying. 'There've been significant cuts to the legal-aid budgets, which means there's no one looking out for the interests of the defendant . . . Cases are built from the perspective of the prosecution, but who looks out for the innocent? No one. And the defence has no money to test their own theories, so even if they *know* the client is innocent, they can't go out and prove it. I mean, who's going to be interested in gathering evidence which does not support the prosecution's hypothesis? Certainly not the police.'

'Tess thinks most coppers are crooks,' Clive says.

'No, Clive, I think most coppers are stupid. But if I'm being generous, then I'd say the police have a difficult job to do, and they're at the mercy of budget cuts just like everyone else. So, are they going to go out of their way to gather evidence that could exonerate a suspect, if they already have enough evidence to charge that suspect? Of course not. Particularly if they have DNA.'

'Juries love DNA,' Tom says.

'Yes,' agrees Tess, 'they do. Even if all the other evidence is to the contrary, even if the suspect couldn't possibly have committed the crime, if the DNA says the suspect did it, juries will ignore every other piece of evidence and convict.'

'Which is exactly why I felt so strongly about taking on Carrie's case,' Tom declares, and Tess has to cast him a sidelong glance because they all know *exactly* why he was so keen to take on Carrie Kamara's case, and it wasn't to do with that. The fact is they'd be named and shamed if they didn't. Twenty-three wrongful-conviction investigations, and not one of them on behalf of a female prisoner? Diabolical. Even if she says so herself.

'But isn't DNA indisputable?' asks Avril.

Tom's shaking his head. 'Perhaps it used to be,' he says. 'But there've been a whole series of fuck-ups since the collection and storage of forensics has been managed by private companies.'

Avril is openly shocked by this. And Tess can't help but wonder why she doesn't know at least a little about this issue. Just what *did* Tom ask her during her interview process?

'So how does a prisoner get you to take on their case?' Avril asks Tom.

'They write a letter.'

'And how many letters do you get?'

'About four thousand a year.'

At one o'clock they get ready to leave, all slightly jollier than they were when they arrived. Avril is clearly not a daytime drinker and gets tangled up in her scarf and handbag when trying to put on her coat. Tom has to step in to prevent serious injury from occurring. In fact, Avril is *still* fairly giddy as they exit on to the street, where the blast of cold air makes Tess's eyes water; Avril tries to tag along with Tess and Clive, asking them what they're doing for lunch, telling them she knows of a great authentic tapas bar not far from here, and again, Tom has to step in and gently shepherd Avril away in the opposite direction, allowing Tess and Clive to proceed unaccompanied.

Though it has never been formally discussed, Tom, along with the other members of Innocence UK, are aware that Tess and Clive have an understanding. An agreement, so to speak. No one has ever voiced disapproval or condemned what goes down after each meeting – they're all too professional for that. And they seem to understand that sometimes, a lot of the time perhaps, people have complicated personal lives. Lives that don't always make sense. Lives that might be viewed by others as chaotic. Improper. Amiss.

Clive is married to another woman. Rebecca is her name. But no one at Innocence UK speaks about Rebecca. Not to Tess anyway.

Now

CLIVE PULLS TESS into the hotel room before turning around and pressing her up against the wall. As he kisses her neck, and then her mouth, Tess is aware of the soft thud the door makes as it closes itself, of the maid's trolley clattering along the hallway outside.

She tries to ease him away from her body so that she can get to his belt, but Clive steps away. 'Let me,' he says, and within the blink of an eye he's stripped himself fully naked, his clothes lying in a pool around his feet.

Tess laughs. She's still got her coat on.

Clive looks good without his clothes, as she had always known he would. There's something about the way a man carries himself, a confidence, she supposes, that meant Tess was not surprised by what she found under there.

Clive slides his hands beneath her skirt and hikes it up above her waist. She feels his fingers inside the elastic of her tights, working them down. Then he's on one knee, struggling with the zip of her boots, and she catches sight of herself in the bathroom mirror opposite. She'll have to move from here, she decides. She can't watch them fucking. It's off-putting. Too ridiculous to observe.

Quickly, she unbuttons her shirt, takes off her bra and steps out of her knickers, while Clive pulls the covers from the bed in a frenzied fashion, making her laugh again.

If Clive hadn't made his intentions clear to her, back when he did, she might have made the first move herself – eventually. She'd thought he'd know his way around a woman's body better than most, and it turned out he did. Clive clambers on the bed and holds out his hand. She takes it and lies down next to him. They're face to face. Eyes open. Breathing each other's breath. He wriggles towards her even more, so that the entire length of his body is now pressed upon hers, skin on skin, and he runs his hand over her hip, her belly, her waist. Tess closes her eyes and exhales.

They've been doing this every few weeks for the past eighteen months and the sex is always good. But it's not what Tess would call an affair. They don't have a second life together or anything like that, whereby they go to the cinema or take off for the beach when the weather is good. They don't write each other letters or texts filled with longing. They don't make plans for their future. Tess is not exactly sure what it is that they *do* have but, simply put, she likes Clive. She likes having sex with Clive. And she enjoys having him in her life. He's a good fit. He fills up a small but essential part of her and she is content with what they do here together.

Clive, however, does not always see things this way. And afterwards, as he lies prone across the foot of the bed, watching Tess as she steps into her tights, as she rebuttons her shirt, he says, 'Don't go.'

'I have to.'

'No, you don't.'

'I need to, and besides, you'll not make the school run if you don't get a move on.' Since his back injury and subsequent police pension, Clive acts as chief caregiver to two children under the age of six. Clive tells her that Rebecca is picking the kids up today. 'How'd you manage that?' she asks, averting her eyes. She always feels a stab of guilt whenever Clive mentions Rebecca.

'I told her the case meeting was at two and I expected it to run on.'

'She didn't mind?'

'Course she minds. She always minds. But I told her those poor bastards in jail really need my expertise, and that giving back to society provides much-needed nourishment for my soul.'

Tess smiles. Clive's Yorkshire accent is as broad as they come.

Tess checks her reflection in the mirror. Her hair is in a state, so she takes a comb from her handbag and pulls it through the ends. When she's done, there's no great improvement, but Tess has never had what the advertisers like to call soft, manageable hair. She steps into her boots and it's when she is straightening up that she notices Clive's expression has changed for the worse and she knows what's about to come next. Her heart sinks a little.

'Why won't you let me leave her?' he asks.

'You don't *want* to leave her.'

'I do. Every day, I do.'

'Well, if you really want to leave, leave.'

'Just don't include you in my plans, eh?' he says sadly and Tess shrugs helplessly.

Picking up Clive's underwear from the floor, she throws it softly towards him on the bed. He ignores it.

'I don't want it to be like this every time,' he tells her. 'I want you in my own bed. I want you in my own house. *Our* house.'

'What?' She laughs gently. 'So I can be a mother to those kids of yours?'

'You'd be a great mother.'

Tess drops her gaze. 'I'd be a shitty mother.'

Clive now has the expression of a whipped pup and Tess thinks, as she has done before on occasion, that she might be doing more harm than good in allowing things to continue as they are. She walks over and sits down beside him, kissing the top of his head. 'You OK?'

He nods. 'I just miss you, that's all. When I'm not with you, I want to be with you. I want to be with you all the time. I want more. I want more than this.'

'I know.'

'And?'

'And – what?'

'And – can you see things ever changing? Do you think there'll come a time when—'

She puts her hand on top of his. 'Don't.'

'I can't help it.'

'I know.'

'I want to look after you,' he says, and he looks up at her, eyes searching, needing an answer.

Tess sighs. She doesn't have an answer. None that would satisfy him anyhow.

A little later, they leave the hotel together, embracing cautiously before heading off in separate directions. And if Tess's head hadn't been full of thoughts about the trip north to Morecambe the following morning (the trip that she's dreading to the point that she can now feel the beginnings of a migraine about to take hold), if she hadn't been feeling bad about Clive's longing for them to set up home together, if she hadn't been ignoring a call on her mobile from a caller whom she doesn't want to speak to, then maybe she might have been aware of the car in the side street opposite.

She might have been aware of the driver of the dark-green Subaru Forester watching her carefully, and of that driver pulling out and following Tess at a discreet distance as she makes her way back to her own car, alone.

Now

Tess and Avril are somewhere around Preston when Avril finally pauses for breath. They're heading north on the M6, towards Morecambe, and the road is a filthy black. Every time Tess passes a heavy goods vehicle she has to clear her windscreen; she's just hoping there's enough screen wash to make it all the way there or they'll be driving blind. Tess can't remember the last time she refilled the screen wash; in fact, now that she thinks about it, she's not sure she ever has. 'But he really doesn't mind sharing the domestic duties,' Avril begins – but it occurs to Tess that Avril hadn't actually stopped talking at all. Rather, Tess's mind wandered, and so she heard silence instead of Avril's chatter. 'William's so good like that,' Avril continues, oblivious to the fact that Tess is not partaking in this one-sided conversation, 'even though he works really, really long hours, he's totally committed ... He puts more into his work than most of his colleagues, but he's still happy to share the cooking when he gets home, which is an absolute godsend; it makes life so much easier. I don't know what I'd do if I had one of those men who didn't know how to boil an egg, I think I'd have to—'

Silence again . . . and Tess realizes she's getting quite good at this. She's vaguely aware of Avril's lips moving, her hands gesticulating, but it's as if there is nothing coming out of her mouth. By the time they reach Morecambe Tess thinks she'll be able to do this magic trick at will, and silence Avril whenever she likes.

They pass the exit for Blackpool and the traffic thins out – as it always does – and Tess can almost feel the other drivers breathing a collective sigh of relief. The nitwits tend to head off towards Blackpool. The people (men) who think eighty-five is unreasonably slow for the middle lane, who insist on under-taking on the inside just to prove a point. Tess has a way of dealing with such drivers. She watches them moving along on her inside and, just as they disappear into the blind spot of her wing mirror, she'll flick on her indicator and begin drifting across into their lane as if she has no idea that they're there. They don't like it when she does this. Sometimes they can get rather cross.

Another ten minutes and the sign for Morecambe looms ahead. Tess observes her heart and is unsurprised to find it now palpitating wildly. She has not been back to Morecambe for twenty-six years and she supposes her heart will remain on its most rapid setting for the entire length of time she's there. Morecambe's a small town. Families have lived there for gener-ations. When Tess was young, she couldn't walk for four hundred yards without bumping into someone she knew. She wonders if that's still the case. She hopes not.

They exit the motorway and, after a couple of minutes, rural Lancashire gives way to an A road lined with 1930s semi-detached houses, and shortly after that, Tess gets her first faint whiff of the sea. 'And what's weird,' Avril is now saying, 'is I've never really got along with mothers-in-law in the past per se. There's always been, like, a conflict of interest? But William's mum's different. It's as if she sees that he's happy, so, naturally, because *he's* happy, that makes *her*—' Avril pauses, noticing the change in landscape. 'You used to live here?'

Tess nods.

Avril looks around, first out of the passenger side window, and then almost swivelling in her seat to the right to observe the view from Tess's window.

They're close to the promenade now and Avril takes in the faded grandeur of this old seaside town. Perhaps she's thinking, *What a shithole*. Tess has no idea what she's thinking, because for the first time in the last fifty minutes, Avril really has stopped talking.

'Do you get back here much?' Avril says eventually.

'Never,' replies Tess.

Tess gets out and the salt tang in the air settles on her tongue. She's parked on a street which runs parallel to the promenade, or, to give the prom its proper name, Marine Road. Tess can't remember if she's been on this particular street before. She must have, she decides as she looks first left and then right, but all of these streets look alike. There are runs of four-storey terraced houses, the brickwork painted white or cream or pale grey, built, Tess supposes, to cater for Morecambe's holidaymakers of yesteryear, back when the place was thriving. Now they're no longer guesthouses. There are no signs offering bed and breakfast, or family rooms with a shared bathroom, and looking at the lines of doorbells next to each front door, Tess assumes each house has been split into individual units.

'It's quite nice here, isn't it?' Avril says, surprised. And Tess has to agree that it is. The pavements are clean, the homes tidy, the air has a freshness to it that feels good inside her lungs. She thinks what a shame it is that no one comes here any more. Back in its heyday, Morecambe drew people from all over the north: millworkers, coal miners, foundrymen. Folk whose chests were full of dust and purulent secretions, folk who believed that a week spent in the restorative sea air could save their ruined lungs.

'It's this one,' Tess says, gesturing to the flat in front, number 78A, and she ascends the steps. She presses the doorbell. As they wait for Mia to answer, Tess watches a large crow strutting about on the pavement, immensely proud of the empty crisp packet he holds in his beak. She considers taking it away. His plastic trophy is no use to him, after all. But then she wonders: When *is* a trophy of any use? And decides to leave the bird to enjoy himself.

Inside, Mia's flat is modest – third-hand furniture, woodchip walls – but it's spotlessly clean. Tess and Avril sit drinking strong tea from hefty mugs, given to them by a very pregnant Mia Kamara. Mia herself is tiny. She's perhaps twenty-two and, apart from her fantastically rounded tummy, she has the body of a teenage boy: arms like broom handles, legs not much thicker. She is delicate, breakable.

'Is this your first baby?' Tess asks.

Mia nods repeatedly. 'Do you have kids?' she asks, and Tess tells her she doesn't. 'Do you?' Mia says to Avril, and Avril kind of snorts before answering.

'I can barely look after myself,' Avril replies. 'I'm only twenty-five. I couldn't even *think* of having kids until I'm at least—' But then she shuts up. She swallows, realizing her gaffe, because the woman in front of her is of course younger than that.

'Shall we start?' says Tess brightly. 'If it's OK with you, Mia, Avril will record our conversation to make sure we don't miss anything.'

Mia agrees and Avril sheepishly starts the recording.

'OK,' begins Tess, 'it's probably best that I be upfront from the off. It's not our job to prove your mother's innocence. If we do take on the case, and I must stress that at this stage it's still an *if*, we'll follow the trail of evidence wherever it leads. Do you understand what I'm saying?'

Mia sits up straighter in her seat. 'I do, but she's not guilty.'

Tess smiles the well-meaning smile she reserves for these occasions. 'But are you prepared to deal with the fact that she might be?'

'She's not!'

Avril shoots Tess a worried look as if to say she might want to go a little easier on Mia, just as Mia turns her head away and begins to cry quietly.

'I promised myself I wouldn't do this,' Mia is saying, reaching inside her sleeve for a tissue. 'I promised myself I'd hold it together. It's the pregnancy, I think. I'm already emotional, but it makes me cry more easily.'

'Have you ever asked your mum about what happened?' Tess asks. 'Have you ever actually asked her straight out if she did murder Ella Muir?' and Mia shakes her head.

'No.'

'It never came up?' Tess presses. 'Not even once?'

'No. Never.'

Tess always finds this a little hard to believe. Surely it would be one of the first things out of your mouth? It would certainly be the first thing out of Tess's mouth, but maybe that's just her. 'Look,' Tess says, softer now, 'people have a hard time admitting their guilt. If they didn't, we wouldn't need a judicial system. So I'm not saying your mum is odd in any way, I'm simply suggesting that this lady, who naturally loves you a great deal, might find it hard to tell you what she did, because she couldn't stand the thought of you knowing she has this other side to her.'

'She doesn't have another side to her.'

'Everyone has a side that they don't show the world. Even parents.'

'But she's not *capable* of doing it,' Mia stresses. 'And she had no reason to do it. That's what nobody seems to understand.' She says this through her tears, and Tess thinks that of course nobody will understand, because, well, why should they? It's hardly proof, is it?

Claiming your mother is innocent because she isn't *capable* of murdering your father's lover is all very well in theory, but how does anyone know what another person is capable of? We don't. We have no idea. And therein lies the problem.

'My dad'd had affairs before,' Mia says.

'OK,' replies Tess.

'Ella Muir wasn't the first woman he'd been with. And no, my mum didn't like it, but she accepted it.'

This gets Tess's attention. 'Accepted?'

'Yes. Accepted.'

Tess considers this. An unusual arrangement, for sure. After a moment, she says, 'Do you think your mum loved your dad?'

'Oh no. Not at the end anyway. Her priority was me . . . that's why I'm sure she didn't do it. She wouldn't leave me. Not on my own.' Mia holds on to the sides of her belly with both her hands, supporting her bump firmly. 'I miss her,' she says. 'I miss her every single day.' And if Tess hadn't been through this before, many, many times, she might have found herself more affected by Mia's words, by her situation. But crying about your incarcerated mother won't get her out of prison, so Tess hands Mia another tissue from her bag, as the one the girl is wringing in her hands has all but disintegrated, and she rechecks her notes.

'It says here you're not in contact with your dad.'

'I've not seen him since the trial,' replies Mia, blowing her nose noisily. 'He deserted Mum, so . . .' And she shrugs as though she had no other choice.

Tess makes a note of this and when she lifts her head, she sees Mia is examining her, as though trying to figure out what Tess might be thinking.

Mia surely has to be aware that her own words here today count. If Tess doesn't believe Mia's version of the events, then this investigation will stop right now. If Tess gets a whiff of being played, even slightly, she will put on her coat, pick up her bag, and tell Mia she's sorry but she believes this case to be a non-starter, and she's not able to help her. Mia probably knows this.

There are online forums covering Innocence UK's work after all: chat rooms populated by the prison community and their relatives, where Tess's name often comes up. She's read a few entries and wasn't surprised to find herself described as intimidating, nobody's fool, sometimes even a hostile bitch.

'Nobody knows what this is like, you know?' Mia says quietly, holding Tess's gaze. 'Nobody understands that having your mum convicted affects every single aspect of your life. And I've done all that I can do. I've written to councillors, to my MP, to every newspaper that I can think of, but they all say the same thing: they can't help. The papers are not interested in running a story about injustice because this story doesn't have a happy ending for its readers.' She looks at Tess, her eyes imploring, now brimming with tears again, and says, 'Can *you* help us?'

And Tess tells Mia she will continue to investigate her mother's case and will get back to her when she has a firm decision from Innocence UK as to whether they will be proceeding.

She promises Mia nothing except this: 'I will do my very best to uncover the truth.'

As they head away from Mia's house, towards the promenade, Avril appears slightly shell-shocked by the whole thing. 'You don't exactly sugar-coat it for them, do you?'

Tess pulls a right, driving on to the prom. The tide is out. She sees a man throwing a ball for an Irish setter, sees two toddlers bundled up against the November weather in their coats and hats, squatting with sticks, poking hard at the grey shingle. She sees the Lake District fells rising as if directly from the sea, out across the bay, their peaks capped with snow.

'How do you know if they're innocent?' Avril asks. 'The defendants, I mean. How do you know if they're lying?'

'I assume they're *all* lying,' replies Tess. 'And then I take it from there.'

Four Years Ago

CARRIE MOVES AROUND the kitchen smoothly, silently, as if on wheels. Pete will be home soon and she will remain calm, she will present her best self.

Carrie picked Mia up from school at the later time of four thirty today because it's Wednesday and on Wednesdays Mia stays for an extra hour. Mia's biology teacher is a greying, bearded gentleman, who cycles to school with his lunch, Thermos and student homework contained in an olive-green pannier strapped to the back of the bicycle. Each Wednesday, he very generously makes himself available to those students finding themselves struggling, and who would benefit from some one-on-one tuition. It is because of this, and the many other small sacrifices those around Mia have been willing to make, that she's been able to get through this year unscathed and is now upstairs memorizing the function of the human kidney. Carrie is immensely grateful to Mia's teacher because A level Biology has been a constant struggle, and Carrie will be glad when it's all finally over.

After her lunch with Helen, Carrie went back to work. She is employed at a small accounting firm on Central Drive, opposite the library. For three days each week Carrie sorts through boxes of discarded receipts from Morecambe's many sole traders – electricians, hairdressers, window cleaners, pest controllers – and tries to get them into some sort of order in the hope that the

Inland Revenue won't send out a letter with those scariest of words: 'Full Audit Pending'.

Carrie enjoys her work. It's mindless and repetitive. But it gives a structure to her days and when she leaves, at three fifteen on the dot to collect Mia, she feels a sense of pride that she has used her time productively and has contributed to the weekly household expenses in her own small way. Her employer, Eddie, keeps asking Carrie to increase her hours but she flat out refuses. 'What do you want, more money?' he says, exasperated. 'If you want more money, I can arrange more money.' But it's not the money. Carrie is happy with what she earns. She tells Eddie that the hours suit her and she'd like to leave it at that, thank you, and this is when Eddie – who is the gentlest of men and the last one to make a person feel uncomfortable about their life choices – will ask Carrie if she doesn't think Mia is old enough to make her own way home by now?

'I like to collect her,' Carrie will say simply in response, smiling, brushing it aside, and Eddie will want to say more on the matter, because Mia is eighteen after all, but he will stop himself because he knows it won't get him anywhere even if he does.

Collecting Mia from school is just one of the things Carrie must do to keep Mia 'on track'. She doesn't mind. It is a small price to pay.

Mia pokes her head around the door. 'What time are we eating?'

Carrie glances at the clock. 'Six fifteen-ish. We're having enchiladas, are you hungry?'

'Not massively. Just give me a bit?'

'Course.'

'And don't put a ton of cheese on mine.'

Carrie tells her she knows how she likes them and so she'll keep the cheese to a minimum.

It's a perfectly normal exchange. The likes of which Carrie has become quite the master of. Even on a day such as today, when her own inner emotions are in danger of derailing all that she holds dear, she can converse with her daughter. She can do it whilst removing items from the fridge, whilst chopping, sautéing, stirring, tasting; she can continue the conversation whilst pulling a balanced, nutritious meal together. And Mia will chat along and have no clue that what is going on behind her mother's eyes, her smile, is anything other than orderly.

'I'll shout when they're ready,' she says, and Mia plucks three large green grapes from the bunch inside the fruit bowl before disappearing upstairs to continue with her work. She's a fragile girl, both in looks and in temperament, certainly not the robust child Carrie expected would come from the combination of Pete and herself. But she has an elegance that both she and Pete lack: her neck is swanlike, her limbs thin and long, and when she walks into a room people take notice.

Carrie opens the oven and turns the tray of enchiladas one-eighty, so that the back of the tray is front and vice versa. Her oven is a little temperamental and tends to burn that which is nearest to the door. She removes her oven glove and rests her back against the worktop. As she does this she hears Pete's BMW reversing into the driveway. She hears the extra rev he likes to do just before cutting the engine. She hates this extra rev.

In the time it takes for Pete to climb out of his car and let himself in through the front door Carrie thinks of the other things she currently hates. There are too many to list but sometimes she makes a game out of starting at the top of Pete's head and working all the way down to the tips of his toes. Each time she does this the list grows longer. Yesterday, she added a new thing, a new habit: Pete was trimming his toenails in front of the TV and when he thought she wasn't looking he took the large, curved sliver of nail from his big toe and surreptitiously slid it inside his mouth. He then proceeded to clean between his back teeth with it. A substitute toothpick, so to speak.

He walks in. Glances at her. Takes a second look. 'I see you've got a face on you again,' he says. 'What a nice fucking change that makes.' He begins sorting through the mail she has left out for him on the kitchen table.

The swearing washes right off her. It used to snag. Catch her in the area right around her sternum, but not any more.

'I had lunch with Helen Carter today,' she says and Pete lifts his head. Gives her a look as if to say, *And?* 'And she said you were seeing someone. Someone new.'

Pete doesn't reply.

'Well, are you?' she asks.

'Helen Carter's an idiot.'

'I thought you liked her.'

'I like *Rob*. I tolerate Helen for his sake . . . What are we eating?'

'Enchiladas.'

He frowns. They're not his favourite. Which is why they feature on the menu at least once a fortnight. 'Is there anything else?'

'There's not.'

Carrie used to look at Pete and like who he was. They met in '96 and Pete was the first boy from Morecambe she knew who didn't switch off subtitled films and had ambitions beyond owning a red Toyota Celica. He was close to six feet tall, with dark hair, dark eyes and a thick, dense, pleasing musculature that was the result of good genes rather than steroid use and the occasional gym session.

Carrie opens the oven door and removes the enchiladas. She sets the baking tray down on the extra piece of granite she had cut specifically for this purpose – to protect the work surface from hot pans, plates, etc. – and she slides a spatula around the edges of the tray to loosen each breaded envelope.

'I might go out,' Pete says.

She collects the plates from the cupboard and puts them into the oven to warm through. 'I'm sure Mia would appreciate it if you stayed,' she replies casually. She has her back to him and she suppresses a small smile. She hears him sigh, long and hard. She can picture him running his hand through his hair, conflicted. She hears footsteps as he crosses the floor. He is walking to the fridge, grabbing himself a can. Then she hears the clunk–hiss sound of him opening his beer and she smiles to herself again.

Tonight, she has won. It's a small victory. But she collects her small victories, nurtures them.

Some days they're all she needs to keep her going.

Now

Tess and Avril stand side by side in Greggs bakery behind at least nine of Morecambe's unhealthiest citizens. Avril is peering around the queue in front to get a glimpse of the produce. There is only one person serving behind the counter: a slow-moving millennial who's made a poor attempt at Kardashian hair and make-up, and now there is a woman at the front of the queue who is putting in an inordinately large order for herself and, one must assume, her co-workers. Avril is beginning to get twitchy.

'There'd better be something left for the rest of us,' she whisper-shouts, glaring at the back of the woman's head.

Behind Tess, a man is on his phone. He is mid-sixties, nattily dressed, and must be some sort of property developer as his conversation is about the removal of storage heaters from a block of flats near to Happy Mount Park. Tess turns and sees he has the phone plugged to his ear but is unaware he has it set to speaker-phone, so the entire shop can hear the other side of the conversation. A few customers turn to look at him too but he continues, oblivious, and Tess is grateful for small mercies: he could be talking to a mistress who is telling him what colour knickers she is wearing. Tess is thinking this just as her *own* phone begins to vibrate inside her pocket and she withdraws it, looks at the screen, before pressing 'decline'.

Tess weighs up her options. She can either continue to wait here, the odours of the warm pastry and Avril's sickly floral scent

41

combining to provoke an olfactory catastrophe inside her nostrils, or she can deal with her caller. 'Listen,' she says, turning to Avril and rummaging in her handbag for the keys, 'can we meet back at the car? Say, twenty minutes? There's something I could do with taking care of while I'm here. Two birds and so forth,' and Avril tells her no worries.

As she's handing the keys over, Avril asks, 'What should I get for you?'

Tess takes a couple of pound coins from her purse. 'You choose. Winter vegetable soup or something.'

Tess leaves the shop and makes her way through town. She keeps her head down, mostly avoiding eye contact with those that she passes. Every so often she checks her reflection in shop windows, makes like she's fixing her hair, whereas really she's on the lookout. She's checking she's not being followed. Not being watched. She does all this without thinking, of course. It's part of who she is. Part of what makes Tess *Tess*.

When she sees the dry cleaner's her heart stutters inside her chest, and she's not altogether sure she has the resolve to go through with her plan after all. Next to the dry cleaner's is a red door and next to that door is a seafood shop. The seafood shop advertises fresh, 'the freshest', cockles, mussels, whelks and, naturally, Morecambe Bay potted shrimps. The flavours of Tess's childhood come back to her in a rush when she sees the sign for the shrimps: butter, mace, a hint of cayenne. The small pinky-brown crustaceans had to be pulled from the ramekin with a long-handled spoon and eaten with thinly sliced brown bread, according to Tess's mother. To serve them any other way was considered sacrilegious.

Tess heads for the red door. On the adjacent brickwork is a small steel plaque with the words 'William Menzies Solicitor' engraved on it.

She opens the door and mounts the stairs. At the top, she hears voices and almost turns on her heel before recollecting that he likes to have the radio on in the background. Radio 4, if she remembers correctly. She sees his receptionist is not at her desk – perhaps she's out to lunch? – and then she catches sight of Bill Menzies. He's in the adjoining office, standing at the open window, surveying the street below, eating fish and chips from the paper wrapping with a plastic fork.

'Hello, Bill,' she says.

It takes him a moment.

He stares at Tess and she knows it's not that he can't place her straight away, not that he doesn't recognize her after all these years, but rather he simply never expected to see her again. Not here, anyway.

'Jesus Christ,' he says. 'I just called you.'

'Sorry to turn up unannounced.' He is dumping his fish and chips in the bin, wiping his hands on his trousers. 'No, Bill,' she says, 'finish your lunch . . .'

But Bill is shaking his head. 'My cholesterol's through the roof. Maggie'd kill me if she knew. Sit. Sit down, for God's sake. How are you? I've been calling you. I just called you. Well, I've been calling *a* number. Not sure if it's still yours?'

Tess sits in one of the chairs meant for clients. 'I got the calls.'

'I've sent a couple of letters too,' he adds, but Tess doesn't tell him she got the letters. 'Are you still moving around a lot?' Tess tells him that she is. And it's then that Bill stops blustering for a second and looks at her. He really looks at her and smiles sadly.

'Ants in my pants,' she says, brushing it away. 'Can't seem to stay in one place.'

'Or maybe you don't like the thought of any unexpected visitors?'

'Something like that . . . Anyway, Morecambe's looking *good*, Bill,' she says, avoiding his question. 'What the hell happened? The town used to be so ugly.'

'They ploughed money in. Cleaned it up. It's nice, isn't it? Don't tell anyone, though, will you? We're trying to keep it a secret. We don't want people moving here and enjoying it for themselves . . . What brings you back?'

'I'm working on a case.'

'Carrie Kamara?'

Tess shrugs as if to say she's not at liberty to divulge, and Bill says, 'You know she's innocent.'

'Aren't they all?'

'No, I knew Carrie. We all did. She's not capable of doing something like that.'

'Nobody is until they do it the first time.'

Bill laughs. He hasn't changed. Not really. Sure, he's greying at the temples, and he's lost a bit of height, lost some of that young man's vitality that she could have found attractive if they'd met under differing circumstances. But other than that, he's the same. Still the same kind-eyed gentleman. Still the same decent human being who tried his best for her even though she wasn't his client.

'What is it that you wanted, Bill? You seem pretty determined to get hold of me.'

'Ah, yes,' he says, standing and heading towards a filing cabinet. He pulls open the second drawer and flicks through the suspension files until he comes across what he needs. He pulls an envelope from the file. 'I promised I'd hand this to you face to face.' He pauses, choosing his next words carefully. 'Wanted to make doubly sure you got it . . . There've been some developments. Things have changed. It's important you've been informed.'

He hands the envelope over and she puts it in her handbag without looking at it. Tess doesn't ask 'What developments?' and Bill knows her well enough of old not to push.

He smiles awkwardly. 'It's so good to see you. I often wonder how you're doing. Are you OK?'

'I'm OK. You?'

'Yeah,' he says. 'Life's been good, all things considered.'

'That's good to hear, Bill.'

'Yeah.'

'Well, I should be going,' Tess says, and she stands. There's a moment of awkwardness when she thinks Bill might go to hug her, but he doesn't. He holds out his hand instead.

'You take care.' He squeezes her palm and she tells him she will. Then they break off and she heads towards the door. She's glad she came. She needed to. If only to stop Bill trying to track her down.

'Tess?' he calls out just as she's about to descend the stairs. 'Do you think you might read it?'

And she says, 'Sure, Bill.'

But they both know she won't.

Now

WITH A LARGE glass of wine in her hand, and dressed in her pyjamas, Tess stares at the whiteboard which runs almost the entire length of the exterior wall of her home office. Boxes of case files are stacked from floor to eye level and Tess can feel the muscles in the middle of her back – around the site of her bra strap – starting to complain. It seems as though every case takes some new toll on her body, and carrying the boxes up the stairs, stacking them, then restacking them every time she needs access to a different set of notes, is not the way to be kind to your body. Or maybe Tess is just getting old. Or *maybe* the visit to solicitor Bill Menzies' office today has left her feeling tense and uneasy, and it's showing up in the musculature of her back. It certainly wouldn't be the first time her body's taken the brunt of her emotional state.

There is very little space left on the whiteboard. This is how Tess likes to work; she likes to have the information all laid out in front of her, so she can stand back and make sense of it. The crime scene photographs of thirty-year-old Ella Muir don't make for pleasant viewing. Neither do the ones from the post-mortem. The nature of the attack – frenzied, violent – left Ella's neck and upper torso covered in an array of two-inch, vivid gashes. To Tess, each of these wounds looks like a tiny open mouth, or the inside of a fig.

Tess is relieved she lives alone because she can plaster the walls of her spare bedroom with evidence and photographs, but this life is not for everyone and she wonders how Avril will deal with this aspect of the job. She wonders how the 'wonderful, brilliant, fantastic' William will deal with Avril bringing her work home each evening, and whether he'll have an issue if Avril decides to redecorate *their* spare bedroom with pictures of prisoners, bloodied corpses, CCTV stills, route maps.

Tess takes a gulp of wine and sits at her desk. Her laptop is open, the screen frozen on news footage taken on the night Ella's body was found. She presses 'play' and sits back in her seat, ready to watch it all over again. She sees Ella's street, a number of police vehicles, crime scene tape, and then a young reporter fills the screen: 'Police say Ella Muir was found by a neighbour. The bubbly thirty-year-old is said to have died from multiple stab wounds to the neck and chest. Specially trained officers are with Ella's family and—'

Tess closes the window. She takes another gulp of wine and clicks on a new tab. She mutes the audio, so she can concentrate. This news footage is from sixteen months later. Carrie Kamara is arriving at court and is dressed demurely. Carrie is an attractive woman. She has pretty blonde highlights running through her short, Sharon Stone-style hair, and she has a smooth, blemish-free complexion. Tess thinks this is the result of clean living, rather than from any cosmetic procedure, but she can't be sure. Carrie is slim, but not gaunt, which Tess thinks has to be some kind of miracle, since the build-up to this trial will have been the single most terrifying thing to ever have happened to a woman like Carrie. Newsreels of most of Tess's clients show them arriving at court looking haggard and twitchy, like addicts. But Carrie has an assured air as she mounts the steps, as if she's fully expecting justice to be done. Tess plays the clip again, and again, and again, and she finds Carrie's body language difficult to read. Is she assured because she's innocent, and certain the court will find her so? Or is it because she really did murder Ella Muir, and a woman capable of such a cold-blooded crime has no trouble presenting a mask of deceit to the world?

Impossible to tell. The very nature of Tess's work means she must start from a position of doubt. It's very easy for a prisoner to proclaim their innocence, to write letter upon letter to the likes of Innocence UK, asking them to hear their story, to recount the errors committed at their trial. What have they got to lose? Very little. With time on their hands, prisoners will go to the greatest lengths to try to persuade those on the outside that they've been betrayed by the criminal justice system. That the real murderer is walking around free – 'Free to kill again!' – if nobody does anything about it.

Tess unmutes the audio and watches the clip once more. The newscaster is speaking over the images. 'Carrie Kamara, accused of stabbing Miss Muir, who the court heard today was in a relationship with Mrs Kamara's husband.' Tess pauses the clip on a close-up of Carrie's face.

'Are you a killer, Carrie?' she whispers.

The following morning, Tess and Avril arrive at Styal Women's Prison, south of Manchester. Behind the chain-link fence are a number of red-brick buildings. These were built at the end of the nineteenth century for Styal's original purpose: an orphanage.

The site was converted into a women's prison in 1962 when the female prisoners from Strangeways were transferred. It has a village feel to it, or perhaps that's making it sound nicer than it actually is, but it is quite unlike many of the category A men's prisons Tess has been inside, in that behind the perimeter fence and the barbed wire, you can imagine civilians living here. Should there be a sudden decline in women offenders, Tess can imagine this place being bought by property developers and converted into a well-to-do gated community. Just as they did with many of the psychiatric hospitals when deinstitutionalization took place in the eighties.

Tess has never been to Styal in her current capacity. As Tom rightly pointed out at the last case meeting, Innocence UK has, to date, only investigated alleged miscarriages of justice involving men. So it was in Tess's previous life, as a probation officer, that she was required to visit Styal Prison regularly. And it was in that role that she developed her skills as a listener, a reader of people, and where she came to the understanding that the person a prisoner presents to the world is often very different to the one inside.

The place is busy with bodies when Tess and Avril walk through the doors. There are two lines, each with two prison officers in charge of validating visiting orders, as well as checking property and allocating lockers for the visitors to place their belongings into. Tess is authorized to take in the case notes, as well as the materials needed to record any statements made by Carrie, so when she and Avril reach the head of the queue, their briefcases are checked by the officers rather than placed inside the lockers. One officer is wearing a pink sash with 'YVONNE'S HEN PARTY – AMSTERDAM' written across it which she appears to be trying on for size; she's unhappy with the way it's falling across her midriff. The officers chatter amongst themselves as they work, searching Avril's briefcase first.

'I've told her,' says one prison officer to the other, 'I said, "I'm not sharin' a room with Teresa again. She's an absolute disgrace."'

Avril appears nervous. She has appeared nervous since Tess collected her this morning and chattered non-stop in the car about nothing that Tess can recall right now. Avril tells the prison officer that she's never been inside a prison before, but if the prison officer is at all interested in Avril's announcement, she doesn't show it. She chooses to ignore Avril and instead continues her conversation with her colleague, telling her that 'Yvonne said she's not switching the rooms round again on account of me' before looking back at Avril and handing her a box of antacids, saying, 'You can't take these in with you, love.'

Their bags are returned, and they're instructed to move along the hallway, following the signs for the visitors' area – which is on the right. As they walk, Tess is about to ask Avril more about her previous job as a legal secretary, when out of nowhere Avril stops dead in her tracks, as if she's received a bullet to the small of her back.

'I'm afraid,' declares Avril.

'Of what?'

'Of going in there. I tried to tell you . . . I've never *done* this before.' She pauses. Takes a breath. She's unsteady.

'What are you afraid of?'

Avril drops her head. This admission, whatever it is, is not easy for her and it takes a moment for her to answer. Tess wonders if there is an element of PTSD going on here. Something she failed to divulge in her interview with Tom.

'I'm scared of being attacked,' she admits, and Tess can't help it but she laughs. She doesn't mean to but she laughs out loud right in Avril's face.

'You're laughing at me?' Avril says. 'You're *laughing*? This is not some joke. I am *not* some joke for you to poke fun at. I didn't come here – I didn't take this job so that someone could—'

'Avril,' Tess says levelly, and she looks her right in the eye. 'I don't know what's going on inside your head right now, but I promise you, scared is the last emotion you are going to feel in there. Now come on. Let's go. We're going.'

Now

THE VISITORS' AREA has been renovated since Tess was last here. She looks around, impressed. Real effort has been made to make this a non-threatening place for visiting children: the chairs are soft, there are prints on the walls, and the whole place has been painted in a sunny shade of yellow. On the floor, in boxes, there are toys and drawing materials; Tess even sees two trikes.

They stand next to the doors and wait. Avril is trying to appear relaxed but she shifts from one foot to the other, intermittently wiping her brow with the sleeve of her coat, and so far she has sighed twice. Tess ignores her and surveys the room, looking for Carrie. There are several young women prisoners, children on their laps, sitting opposite older women – their mothers, Tess supposes. The atmosphere is jovial, gossipy even, but to Tess, and she imagines to Avril too, the scene is just very, very sad.

They wait for five minutes and there is still no sign of Carrie.

Avril says, 'Should I go and ask someone?'

Tess tells her they'll hang on. 'There must be a problem. If she's not here by quarter past,' she says, 'I'll go and check.' But then Tess's eyes alight on a woman shuffling towards them from the far corner of the room. She's four dress sizes bigger than the Carrie Kamara of old, and her short, serious hair has grown out. This woman looks as though she belongs on *The Jeremy Kyle Show*: her skin is acned and her eyes are sunken. She is a woman beaten down by her situation and Tess lets out a quiet, emphatic '*Fuck*' under her breath.

Gathering herself, Tess strides towards Carrie, her hand outstretched. 'Carrie,' she says, briskly, as they shake. 'How very nice to meet you. I'm Tess Gilroy. Where would you be most comfortable talking?'

Carrie gestures to the far corner of the room, whence she came, and they head over there, Avril following closely behind. 'You didn't recognize me from my photographs, then?' Carrie asks. Her tone is challenging but she's half-smiling and Tess sees a flash of mischief in her eyes.

Tess can only assume Carrie knows she looks terrible. Tess does think about lying, pretending Carrie doesn't look quite as changed as she does, but decides it would be insulting. 'You do look a little different.'

'I've given up on my appearance,' Carrie explains. 'It can take a month just to get deodorant in here.'

They sit.

'This is my colleague, Avril Hughes,' Tess says, and Carrie offers Avril a wan smile. Tess gets her case notes out. 'So, we don't have a ton of time, Carrie, and there's a lot to get through, so it's probably best if we get straight to it . . .' She smiles as she organizes herself. 'That OK with you?' and Carrie intimates that it is. 'Excellent . . . So, you understand the role of Innocence UK? That's already been explained?'

'You try and get my case before the Court of Appeal.'

'That's right,' replies Tess, 'but as I explained to Mia yesterday—'

At the mention of her daughter's name, Carrie's whole bearing changes. She sits up, and her eyes, previously sunken, kind of glassy-looking, are now alert and focused. 'How is she?' she asks. 'Did she say if the baby's turned yet? I was on the list to call her last night but the girl ahead of me overran and I didn't get to speak to her. Is she OK? I didn't realize you were visiting her first. Did she tell you anything about the baby?'

Tess is a little embarrassed that in the whole hour she spent with Mia the day before she didn't once think to enquire about the health of either mother or child. 'She seemed fine,' she says weakly, and tries not to watch as Carrie's face falls. 'She said to tell you not to worry,' she adds, avoiding Avril's gaze. 'Anyway, as I said, lots to get through, so . . .' Tess pauses and looks at Carrie, making sure she's got her full attention. When she's certain Carrie's back with her, she continues. 'Now, I'm sure it's already been explained to you too that if we're to take on this case, we'll follow the evidence wherever it leads . . . even if it reinforces your guilt. But I think it's important to reiterate that point.'

'I understand.'

'And if I ever believe you're lying to me, or if you ever provide me with false information, your case will be dropped immediately.'

Carrie nods.

'There are no second chances here, Carrie. Is that clear?'

'Crystal.'

'And you still want to proceed?'

Carrie nods again.

'I'd prefer to hear you say it.'

'I would like to proceed.'

A baby girl starts crying at a nearby table and a young, skinny inmate – broken teeth, skin of a user – stands, cradling her daughter against her shoulder. She begins to sway her baby, walking around the room, singing to her softly. As she passes, Tess hears her words and remembers her own mother singing the same nursery rhyme, 'Miss Polly Had a Dolly', to Tess when she was a little girl:

> He looked at the dolly and he shook his head,
> And he said, 'Miss Polly, put her straight to bed!'

Tess is momentarily taken out of her surroundings and is back on her mother's knee. She is four years old. She is happy.

Tess leans forward. 'OK, Carrie,' she says, 'tell me why a jury wrongly convicted you of Ella Muir's murder.'

Avril pauses from taking notes and looks up. Again, she appears rattled by Tess's straight-to-the-point talk, but Tess takes no notice. It's Carrie she's interested in, and if *she's* rattled, she doesn't show it. Carrie begins the process of repeating her narrative, her tone uniform, her delivery colourless, as if she's done this a million times over.

'The police made me fit the story they'd concocted. I was a woman scorned. I had a massive grudge, they said. It didn't matter that there was no murder weapon, that they didn't find blood on my clothes or in my car or in my house. It didn't matter that I didn't care Pete was screwing that girl.'

Tess pauses. 'But you *did* care, Carrie,' she says. 'I read in the case notes that you went around to Ella Muir's house just a few weeks before she died. Why did you do that if you didn't care?'

'Because they were embarrassing me. It's no secret that me and Pete had not had what you'd call a traditional marriage,' she says. 'He saw other women, Ella Muir certainly wasn't the first, and if I turned a blind eye to what he got up to then things tended to run smoothly. But with Ella it was obvious pretty quickly it was different. He was really taken with her, and he'd got sloppy. Friends were seeing them out together, flaunting their relationship, and even though they were aware Pete liked to play around sometimes, they weren't used to seeing him out with someone. Like a proper couple. They started asking if me and Pete had split up. It was humiliating. And it was bad for Mia.'

'So you went around there and – what? You told Ella to stay away?'

'I asked her to be more discreet. I told her Pete could be a bit of a balloon sometimes and would she mind toning it down for Mia's sake. We had a cordial conversation.'

'It says here that you knew her?'

'In passing.'

'As in how exactly?'

'She was married to one of Pete's friends – before they divorced, that is. So I'd see her at the odd get-together, parties, that kind of thing.'

'And when you went around to her house to talk to her you never stepped inside?' At this Carrie sighs and shakes her head sadly. 'You're quite sure you *never* stepped inside?' repeats Tess. 'Because, I'll be honest with you, the presence of your blood inside that house is a real stumbling block for me.'

'I didn't get past the front step. I wasn't with her longer than two or three minutes at the most.'

Tess considers this. Carrie has stuck to this story right from the start. Tess has been over the police interviews, the criminal solicitor's notes, and every time Carrie was asked, she said the same thing: she did not go inside Ella Muir's house. This interests Tess for two reasons. Firstly, if she didn't go in, how did the blood get there? Sure, Tess can debate lab cross-contamination, shoddy forensic work – either in the collection of the sample or the storage of it, she can even discuss whether the blood was somehow *planted* at the scene intentionally, but each of these ideas is unlikely. When Tess looks at the facts coldly, she comes to the same assumption as the jurors: Carrie Kamara *was* inside that house. That's how her blood got there. Which begs the question, and the second thing Tess can't get her head around: why didn't Carrie just *admit* she was in there?

Carrie has never hidden the fact that she went there to talk to Ella. When her blood was found inside, why not simply say, 'Yes, I went in.' Why not say that she spoke with Ella, went inside, and then she left? She could have had a nosebleed, a nail bitten down to the quick that happened to ooze? 'Why, yes, that's certainly possible,' she could have said.

But Carrie didn't say that. She stuck to her story and refused point-blank to admit she'd ever entered the property at all.

'OK,' Tess says. She was hoping for something new here, a clarification of a point, something missed from trial records, but it's clear Carrie has nothing to add and so, disappointed, Tess decides to move on. 'OK, what I need to know now, Carrie, is: why *did* you stay with Pete? This is the part that doesn't make sense to me. Why stay in a marriage like that? Why not throw him out if he was screwing around?'

'I did,' she replies. 'I did throw him out once.'

'But he came back . . .'

'He came back a few months later,' Carrie says. 'Pete began seeing someone else, and I made him leave. And we were OK without him, or at least I *thought* we were OK. I was certainly OK – I was relieved. But Mia,' and this is when she sighs, saddened by the memory, 'Mia has always felt things more deeply than other people, certainly more deeply than girls her own age anyway. She didn't always cope well with just the day-to-day stuff of being a teenager before this, and so when this new arrangement happened, it began to make her unwell. Her emotional state deteriorated, she didn't want to go to school, I couldn't get her out of her bedroom, couldn't get her to engage, and then she stopped eating. It seemed to come out of nowhere but her weight began to plummet – fast – and it was such an awful time, so stressful and so fraught, that I was scared every single minute. I thought we might actually lose her at one point if it went on. We saw a number of different professionals and though none seemed to be able to actually help Mia with what she was going through, they all agreed on the same thing: the trigger for this deterioration in her health was Pete's departure. So he came back.'

'Simple as that?'

'None of this was simple. But he moved back in and we forged a relationship, an arrangement is probably a more accurate description, and we agreed to try our best and see how it went . . . for Mia's sake.'

'And how *did* it go?'

'It went fine. We made it work. Pete was discreet in his liaisons, we got along as a family very well, all things considered, and he agreed to stay in the family home until Mia was nineteen.'

'So all was OK in the world until Ella, then?'

'Until Ella.'

'Why didn't this come out at the trial?' Tess asks.

'Because Pete refused to acknowledge that he had ever agreed to stay with us until Mia was nineteen. He said it was fabricated nonsense, and my lawyer didn't pursue it and so . . .' She lets the words hang.

Is she lying? Tess wonders.

Hard to say for sure. Tess will need to speak to Pete Kamara to find out his side of things, see what he's got to say on the matter, but right now her gut tells her that Carrie Kamara's claims are genuine.

Tess makes a couple of short notes on this but when she looks up Carrie is staring at her intently. Out of nowhere, it seems, Carrie appears quietly stricken. And Tess wonders if she's missed a beat. Has a section of time vanished without her being aware?

'Is there something else, Carrie?' she asks, and Carrie tells her yes, yes there is.

'Mia is alone,' she says urgently.

And Tess nods.

'Mia's having this baby and she's *completely* alone.'

Carrie's words are rushed and desperate and Tess is not quite sure what to make of this rapid change of state.

'Mia has no one at all . . . and she thinks the child will make things better. She thinks her anger and her grief at my being wrongly accused will get better when the baby arrives. But it won't. She *won't* cope. She has no idea of what's ahead of her and how hard it's going to be and I'm scared. I'm scared her anxiety will overcome her and there's nothing I can do to stop it. I'm scared no one will see how much she's struggling. She'll tell them she's OK. She'll hide it. She'll try to hide it until it's too late.' Carrie drops her head. Her hands are laced together in her lap. Her knuckles are white. 'You have to help me,' she says. 'You have to try to get me out of here.'

Heading away from the prison, Tess tries to organize her thoughts. She is expected to present her findings to the Innocence UK panel meeting the following morning and she's still not sure what she's going to say. Usually, even at this early stage, she's leaning towards either guilt or innocence; usually it's easy to make a judgement call, easy to determine whether she will advise the panel if they should pursue or abandon a case.

But this? This is tricky. Carrie is not Tess's usual type of customer. She's more intelligent for one thing. More articulate too. But she does *seem* genuine. Her recollection of events and the love she feels for her daughter certainly seem genuine too. And yet, Tess reflects, Carrie can love her daughter and still be a murderer.

Tess thinks about Mia. So far, there has been no mention of a father, and Tess wonders why Mia is alone with her unborn child. Tess wonders what happened there. Did he not stick around? Did he flee when she was pregnant? Could he have fled when he discovered Mia's mother is serving life for murder? Or is it something else entirely?

Is it possible that Mia became pregnant on purpose, neglecting to tell whoever was responsible, keeping the entire thing to herself?

Tess is very aware this is not an uncommon occurrence among girls with fractured home lives. Girls wanting to create their own perfect family, a little unit, when their own families have turned out to be a bit of a shit-show, will often have babies young. These girls make the mistake of thinking that their attempts at mother-hood will make everything that's wrong in their lives suddenly right. They have no idea of the emotional cost they will pay for having children when they are still really children themselves. They have no idea of the effect it will have on them for the rest of their—

Avril interrupts Tess's thoughts from the passenger seat. 'Carrie didn't look too good in there, did she?' she says.

'How so?'

'Well, to start with she looked a lot older than I was expecting.'

Tess agrees that prison life is not exactly doing much for Carrie's complexion.

'D'you think they hurt her?' Avril asks.

Tess frowns. 'Hurt her? Who?'

'The other women.'

And Tess shakes her head. 'They hurt themselves, Avril,' she replies. 'Not each other.'

'Why?'

'Because', Tess says wearily, 'nearly every woman in there is there on account of some idiot man. And they'll usually end up losing their kids on account of him too. That makes them feel the kind of anguish they don't know what to do with, anguish they tend to take out on themselves. They self-harm.'

Avril goes quiet, digesting this, just as Tess takes a left and loops around the northern perimeter of Manchester Airport. On Ringway Road, a plane thunders over the top of the car, coming in to land. Avril turns her head to watch as it hits the tarmac, the sound of the reverse thrust deafening them. At the T-junction they take a right and it's when they've travelled a few hundred metres further that Avril declares: 'Anyway, Carrie is definitely innocent.'

'You think?'

Tess is tempted, of course, to shut Avril down. She's tempted to list the many prisoners whom Tess believed in totally and utterly because of their sob stories, their devotion to their families, their broken spirits, only to discover after a painstaking and lengthy investigation that they were lying. Just as they had been all along.

But it's the faith in the innate goodness of human beings, the faith that the British justice system sometimes gets it spectacularly wrong, that gave Tess staying power in the early days. It gave her the necessary energy to pursue justice when it seemed as though everyone else had given up. And Avril will need this faith if she's to make a go of the job. So Tess says nothing. She lets Avril believe that it can be that simple. That Carrie Kamara is innocent because she appears innocent. And she drives on to the slip road, ready to join the thick traffic on the M56.

Now

CARRIE KAMARA SITS on her bed and looks at the wall. Her cell-mate is in the shower. Carrie has been assessed, reassessed, and is not deemed a risk either to herself or to anyone else, which is kind of amusing when she thinks about it, because she's in here for stabbing a young woman eleven times in the throat and chest. But Carrie's considered a benign inmate. Not someone they need to keep an eye on.

Carrie gets up and looks in the mirror. She pulls a comb from her washbag and runs it through her hair. Her hair has been coming out in handfuls since she became perimenopausal and as much as she pretends she doesn't care about her appearance any more, the hair loss distresses her deeply. 'Your crowning glory,' Pete used to say, back in the beginning.

Perhaps magnesium could help, she thinks as she removes the tangles of hair from between the teeth of the comb. Not that she'd be able to source any in here, but it appears to be the current cure-all. An article she read recently claimed that middle-aged women experiencing fatigue, muscle cramps and mental decline could be suffering from reduced magnesium levels, and Carrie thought, well, if that's the case, every woman she knows must be deficient.

After Tess Gilroy and Avril Hughes left, Carrie returned to her cell, opting to miss lunch, and lay on her bed for a while. Had they believed her? It was hard to say. She finds it difficult to assess her effect on people nowadays. Before this, back when she was living what she now considers her other life, Carrie barely gave other people a second thought. She didn't go out of her way to be rude to anyone, she had no reason to, so she didn't lie in bed wondering what the world made of her. For all intents and purposes she was invisible. Now, everything she says is analysed, scrutinized, gone over again and again for hidden meaning, and it has made Carrie become extraordinarily careful in her choice of words. There are no off-the-cuff remarks, she has tempered her personality accordingly, and the Carrie Kamara of old, the essence of her anyway, she keeps locked away in a small box beneath her bunk.

Carrie was described as a high-functioning psychopath by an expert witness, a psychiatrist, called to the witness box by the prosecution. Which she thought at the time was a bit of a stretch. She had to look it up to verify what the difference was between a high-functioning psychopath and a low-functioning one. The distinction wasn't completely clear but, as Carrie understands it, it's to do with intelligence. She's supposed to have superior intelligence and the ability to delay gratification in a way that the low-functioning set can't do. Which was mildly flattering for a time, considering Carrie only achieved one O level in home economics, and a CSE in art. But when she began her sentence here at Styal, she met a number of women who described themselves as high-functioning psychopaths, and it became immediately clear to Carrie that this label is slapped on willy-nilly. These women were *not* intelligent. They were actually rather stupid. But they had managed to return to education, schooling themselves to a higher level than the average person, and every time their stories were challenged, every time they were out of their depth, they would declare how intelligent they were, listing degrees and so forth, and they were believed without question. Ridiculous.

Carrie thinks most high-functioning psychopaths in Styal Prison should be rediagnosed simply as liars. Or perhaps as people who believe their *own* lies. That would be more accurate.

And therein lies the distinction.

Carrie *is* a liar. But at least she knows she is.

Now

THE ROOM IS in semi-darkness. The panel, not really visible, sits around the conference table as Tess stands by an enlarged illuminated image of a map on the projector screen. A route has been highlighted in pink and Tess directs the laser pointer to the beginning of the route and then to the end. She is talking them through timings, witness statements, CCTV, and the group gathered at the table takes notes, listening to Tess as she interprets the evidence for them, using language each can understand. This is where she shines. Give Tess a thousand pages of courtroom jargon and she can pluck out the necessary, turning idiom into key fact.

Tess hits the lights and the image fades. 'So, what do we think?' she asks the panel. 'Do we continue with the case?'

Clive clears his throat. 'Ella Muir was stabbed . . . ten . . . ?'

'Eleven times,' says Tess.

'Eleven times. OK, so how does Carrie get home with no blood on her whatsoever? You say forensics found no weapon? And there were no traces of Ella's blood on Carrie and no blood inside Carrie's house?'

'None at all.'

'And nothing in her car?'

'None there either.'

Clive shakes his head. 'Well, that alone would make me want to pursue this.'

This is how the investigation works: Tess goes out and speaks to those involved – the prisoner, their family – and she gets a general feel for things. She reads the trial notes, considers the evidence, and she then returns to Innocence UK to present her findings and the case is re-evaluated. The panel gets to vote on whether the case has merit, whether they think they're likely to attain a positive result, and each case may be re-evaluated as many as five or six times throughout the investigative process, because, if they think they're getting nowhere, it makes more sense to cut their losses and move on.

Tess has a quote printed out and Sellotaped to the inside cover of her diary: 'Don't cling to a mistake just because you spent a lot of time making it.'

'Anyone else?' Tess asks. 'Thoughts? Anyone else got anything jumping out at them?'

'The fact that she continues to protest her innocence is interesting,' Tom says. 'I mean, it's really drummed into them when they begin their sentences, very early on in the rehabilitation process, that if they own up to their crimes, show sufficient remorse, et cetera, then they'll serve a lot less time. The fact that she's still sticking to her story, when she knows it'll result in her serving the full life sentence, is rather telling, don't you think? Not everyone does that.'

Tess is nodding. She hadn't considered this, and Tom is right. It *is* unusual. Even prisoners who Tess was certain were victims of a wrongful conviction, and who were later released after a trial at the Court of Appeal, agreed to confess their guilt in return for lighter sentences. How this is supposed to help people, God only knows. You're guilty? Confess your sins and you get to go home early. You're innocent? Protest your innocence and you get to stay in jail . . . for years. Who came up with such a farcical system?

'OK,' says Tess, 'so that leaves us with the blood smear. Carrie's blood found on the inside handle of Ella's front door. What are we thinking?' Tom tells her that this is what the entire prosecution's case was built on and Tess agrees. 'I do wonder if we're going to be able to get past this,' she says. 'The presence of the blood said to every single jury member that Carrie was there in that house and I'm not sure the appellate court will ever be able to overlook it.'

'Even after all the cross-contamination fuck-ups in the labs?' suggests Clive.

'It's a big ask.'

Tess looks around the table. The face of each member is unreadable. She knows there is reasonable doubt in this case. Things are not clear-cut; they do not add up neatly. But is there enough doubt to warrant all the time and resources they are about to plough into getting Carrie Kamara's case overturned? Tess isn't sure. 'Let's vote,' she says decidedly. 'Do we proceed? Show of hands please.'

And all hands are raised.

'Then thank you very much for your time.'

As they walk to the bar their heads are dipped. A fine drizzle fills the air, rain which seems to stay suspended rather than hitting the ground, rain which typifies Manchester. The climate is wet and mild. Perfect conditions for the manufacture of cotton and the reason so many mills sprang up across the north of England during the Industrial Revolution. Tess remembers learning about the properties of cotton in school in Morecambe. It is hygroscopic – meaning it absorbs or releases moisture depending on the relative humidity of the surrounding air. So if the surrounding air is dry, the cotton will relinquish its water content and become thinner, weaker, less elastic and more brittle, and if the air is moist, then the cotton is workable. Workable by the many thousands of millworkers, their lungs filled with cotton dust, workers who would head by steam train *from* the industrial towns surrounding Manchester *to* Morecambe. They came for one week's respite, hoping that by some miracle a few days by the seaside would stave off the tuberculosis and brown lung disease, diseases that were killing their comrades in droves.

They enter the bar and take off their coats. Tess grabs some napkins from a waiter's station near the door and dries off her hair, handing a couple to Avril too, before finding an empty table. Clive makes a big show of going for his wallet before Tom stops him. 'My round, Clive. You got them last time, remember?' and Clive pretends as though he can't recollect. 'Ladies,' Tom says, 'two white wines? And what about you, Clive? A pint of John Smith's?'

'Oh, I think I'll join you in a glass of Peroni this time, Tom, if you don't mind.'

'One Peroni.'

Tess watches as Tom heads to the bar. He wears an expression of mild confusion, as if he's been had in some way, but he's not sure how.

'So, Avril,' Clive says, clapping his hands together. 'What's your gut feeling on this? Carrie Kamara, innocent or not?'

'Oh, she's innocent,' Avril replies, delighted to have been asked her opinion. She's blushing under Clive's gaze, absently touching her hair, moistening her lips, and Tess wonders how Clive does it. He's certainly no Clooney. And there is an age gap of around twenty-five years between Clive and Avril. And yet here is Avril, ready to offer it to him on a plate, if she weren't so besotted with William. 'Carrie's definitely innocent,' Avril reiterates to Clive. 'You only have to look at her to know she's telling the truth.'

Clive is amused. 'You seem quite certain . . . Tess?'

'Jury's still out,' she says.

Clive is naked beneath the sheets. He is sitting up in bed, propped up by pillows, watching as Tess re-dresses after sex. He always watches her put her clothes back on, and this makes her feel self-conscious and awkward. 'Which is exactly why I do it,' he says. Clive insists this is Tess at her most appealing. When she's not wearing her authoritative hat, when she's not in control of the room, but when she's aware she's being looked at, like *really* looked at, and she can't handle it. 'You're so bloody beautiful,' he tells her now, and he laughs. Of course, Tess could avoid being on show like this by remaining in bed until after Clive leaves, but therein lies the problem: Clive *won't* leave. He'll stay in bed all day. He will call his wife and make an excuse, and though Tess knows what she's doing with Clive is wrong, wrong on a lot of levels, she draws the line at depriving two young children of their father – particularly because he is the chief cook and bottle-washer, and she thinks they all deserve a decent hot meal in the evening at the very least.

She has told Clive to go home. 'Go home and tidy the house for your wife. She's been at work all day, Clive, she'll be tired.'

'I want to stay with you.'

'If you keep staying here all the time, she'll begin to suspect.'

'I keep *telling* you, Rebecca has no idea.'

Tess is struggling to fix her left earring in place. She pauses and turns. 'This is exactly why men get caught, because they think they're too clever to get caught.'

'I was a detective for twenty-two years,' he says, pulling a face. 'I think I know a thing or two about stealth. Anyway, you said we were going to do this at your place from now on. Why am I always here in this godawful room?'

Tess turns her back on him, buttoning up her shirt. She said no such thing to Clive, but it does strike her again that perhaps she is being unfair to him by continuing this when she has no intention of letting it go further.

But then, she thinks, they *did* discuss all of this right at the start. And Clive assured her he wanted a no-strings coupling. He told her he wasn't in the market for a full-blown relationship, that he had neither the time nor the inclination. Which was exactly why she agreed to it.

Except now Clive has changed his mind. He wants more. He wants to leave Rebecca and to be with Tess. And if Tess were capable of giving Clive what he wanted then she would. Because she is so very fond of him. But she cannot.

'I don't even know where you live,' she hears him say quietly. 'We've been doing this for close on two years now and I don't even get to know that?'

She regards him in the mirror, then looks away. 'I don't understand why it's so important.'

'It's important because what if you need me? What if you need *someone*? No one knows where you are, Tess. No one knows how to reach you.'

'Clive, this is all I have. This is all I'm *able* to give right now. You know that. You said you understood. Don't make it difficult. Please.'

Clive wants more. But she can't give him more. He wants to save her from something. Herself? She doesn't want saving. And what Clive fails to grasp is that the reason she agreed to this in the first place is because Clive *is* unavailable. He has commitments. Places he needs to be. People who rely on him. She agreed to this affair precisely for these reasons.

'Don't you ever feel alone?' he asks her.

And Tess doesn't answer. She dampens a tissue, running it beneath her lower eyelashes to remove the mascara that's bled into the lines there. She probably needs to buy a new tube. Like replacing toothbrushes regularly, it's something Tess forgets to do. She tucks in her shirt and smooths down her skirt, before turning to Clive and smiling as brightly as she is able.

Clive's expression is one of deep sadness. 'Who are you running from, love?' he says.

Now

A̲VRIL IS IN the passenger seat with Tess's folder – a summary of the pertinent points of the case – open and resting on her lap. They have returned to Morecambe and unusually for November the sun is out. Hurray! Tess looks up and the sky seems bigger here. More expansive. Tess is feeling buoyed after weeks of foul weather and she's ready and eager to begin. It's one of Tess's favourite aspects of the job: revisiting the prosecution's facts and theories, retesting them for herself to see if they hold up against further scrutiny. She's looking to find inconsistencies, she's looking to challenge assumptions made, and, if she's really lucky, she's looking to expose shoddy and substandard policing.

'So, Ella Muir was murdered some time between five and six thirty p.m.,' Avril reads. 'But it says here that the phone records show Carrie's mobile was in the general area of her home during that time. That's good, isn't it? That there's no record of her phone being near Ella's house? Surely that means—'

Tess cuts her off. 'The prosecution argued she left it there on purpose – this being a premeditated attack and all. They said Carrie would have been aware her phone would've been traced to Ella's so she didn't take it along with her. For now, forget the phone. Start with the CCTV.' Tess follows the instructions given by the satnav and within a couple of minutes she is outside Pete Kamara's house. Well, what was once Pete and *Carrie* Kamara's house. It's an oversized, mock-Tudor detached, crammed on to a small plot. There is barely any room between Pete's house and the one next door, probably just enough to drag a wheelie bin through. Tess leans across and flicks through the notes on Avril's lap until she finds a copy of the highlighted map she printed out last night. 'We're here,' she says, pointing, 'and this is Ella's house, here.' Avril follows her finger and begins to nod. 'And the first CCTV camera that picked up Carrie's car was here, at the Eagle and Child pub.' Tess flicks to the following page. It's a side-on still of Carrie's white Honda SUV. 'This image was taken at seventeen forty-seven from the camera outside the pub.'

'No registration plates?'

'Not visible from this angle,' says Tess. 'But the driver's a woman. Blonde too, they reckoned.'

Avril pauses, and Tess keeps quiet while the cogs in Avril's brain begin to turn.

At the beginning of her career, Tess would find these initial stages almost unbearably thrilling. The whole puzzle would lie ahead of her and she couldn't wait to take a piece of evidence and play with it. Everything looks very different outside of the court-room. Each 'fact' can be read so many ways when you've not got a pompous barrister in a black gown and a horsehair wig instructing you what to think.

'Do we know how many white Hondas there are in Morecambe driven by women?' asks Avril.

'Not yet. But let's assume for now that this *is* Carrie driving. Let's assume she's lying, and she *did* go out that evening.' Tess flicks over the page to show the next CCTV image. 'Is this her at eighteen oh six coming back in the opposite direction? And . . .' Tess pauses while she adds up the time difference on her fingers. 'And is nineteen minutes enough time to get from this camera here, to Ella's house here, stab her eleven times, and get back to this camera again?'

Tess puts the car into gear. And Avril looks at her expectantly. 'Get your iPhone on to stopwatch,' Tess tells her, 'and I'll tell you when to press start.'

She sets off towards the pub and after a short time she glances in her mirror. There's a car. A dark-green car. A Subaru perhaps? Tess has a feeling of déjà vu wash over her – she's sure she saw this same car as she drove towards home the previous evening. She looks again in her mirror and the driver pulls back a little, creating some distance between them. When she checks her mirror once more, he drops his sun visor so that the top half of his face is hidden.

Tess frowns. How odd.

'William's taking me out tonight,' Avril says.

'That's nice,' replies Tess, distracted.

'It's a surprise.'

'How is it a surprise if you're telling me about it?'

'It's a surprise *where* we're going,' explains Avril, unoffended. 'I'm hoping we're going to that new place in the Trough of Bowland. It's had really good reviews and I want to try the cuttle-fish ravioli . . . William'll have the steak. He *always* has the steak. I try to persuade him to go for something different what with the cancer risk from red meat but he can really be quite stubborn when he wants t—'

'Stop talking.'

'Sorry?'

'Stop talking, Avril. We're nearly at the first camera.'

Avril's thumb hovers over the start button as she awaits Tess's instruction.

'OK, go.'

They follow the route on the map. The route Carrie Kamara took the evening she allegedly murdered Ella. As she drives, Tess tries to put herself in the mindset of a killer. There's a temptation to come at these cases from the opposite direction. To think through all the reasons why the murder could *not* have been committed by their client. But in Tess's experience, focusing solely on this aspect is short-sighted. Far better (and more fun) to play at being the murderer for a time. Better to imagine she's inside Carrie's mind, better to try to get beneath her skin and experience what she's feeling on her way to execute her husband's lover. In the past this approach has produced some surprising results.

She pulls into Ella's road and she feels a shiver of excitement. She stops at the kerb outside Ella's house and she thinks: *Is this how the killer felt that day? Excited? Is this how Carrie felt that day?*

'Stop the clock,' she says to Avril, feeling very Anneka Rice.

'Eight minutes and four seconds.'

Tess blows out her breath. 'Eight plus eight is sixteen. That leaves . . . three or four minutes to kill Ella.' And Tess's heart sinks. 'That means it can be done,' she says to Avril. 'Carrie could have killed Ella in that time. Four minutes is adequate.'

'Yes, but it's not a very big time frame.'

'It's big enough,' Tess says. 'Which means we need to drive the route again. As the killer would have done. At rush hour.'

When she checks her rear-view mirror, the Subaru is gone.

Five Years Ago

FAMILY THERAPIST: Are you all warm enough? This room never gets any sun. You are? Good. Yes, it doesn't matter which chair you sit in. Wherever you're most comfortable . . . I usually pick this one because it's nearest the radiator. All OK? Great. So, Mia, your assessment has been discussed with the wider team and they feel you could benefit from some sessions of family therapy. My job is primarily to listen to the concerns you and your parents have – I believe you've been facing some challenges of late – and then we'll work out a programme that suits you, hopefully give you some tools to help you overcome these challenges. That all sound OK? Excellent. Let's—

PETE: She doesn't come out of her bedroom.

FT: It can be very worrying for parents when they see their child disengage from the world. Mia, are you able to explain to your dad why you'd rather spend time alone right now?

MIA:

PETE: She won't go to school. She won't see her friends. She won't get dressed.

CARRIE: Pete, give her a chance to answer.

PETE: I'm trying to explain what the problem is. What's the point in coming here if she's not going to speak? We're wasting everyone's time.

FT: Try not to be too concerned about time. I know you're very worried and anxious about Mia right now but we've got plenty of time. The important thing in these sessions is that everyone feels heard. Mia? Are you able to vocalize the reason you don't want to go to school at the moment?

MIA:

PETE: This is what she's like. She won't speak, she won't go out, she won't eat. We're being held hostage.

FT: Carrie, do you feel as though Mia is holding you hostage too?

CARRIE: I just want her to feel better.

PETE: So you really don't mind when you have to leave work early because you've got another call from school telling you to come and get her? You *do* mind. You *told* me you mind. And that's the other issue we're dealing with: school. They don't know what to do with her. She's missed, on average, three days a week since the start of term. How can they educate her if she won't go?

FT: Let's put the issue of exams to one side just for now. Mia? Can you help us understand what you're feeling? I know it's hard. The first time you speak it out loud is the hardest.

MIA: I feel scared.

FT: When do you feel scared?

MIA: All the time. That's why I don't want to leave the house.

PETE: Well, we're all bloody scared. Life is scary.

FT: Can you remember when this feeling of being scared first started, Mia?

MIA: Not really. I don't remember feeling like this when I was little.

FT: So, you were generally happy to go to school, play with friends, when you were in primary school?

MIA: Yeah.

FT: You can't remember being scared at all?

MIA: I'd get nervous about swimming lessons. Sports day. But I can't remember feeling dizzy like I was going to pass out. Like I just wasn't brave enough to face the world. I can't remember being too afraid to go out of the house.

FT: That's what it feels like to you? That you're not brave enough to face the world?

MIA: Pretty much.

FT: That must be difficult. I can see how you'd prefer to stay at home. I think I would too.

When you were assessed there was also an issue raised about your relationship with food. Do you think you would be able to think about this and perhaps talk about it a little? It would be great if you could talk about why you find it difficult to eat sometimes.

MIA:

FT: Try to describe for me how you feel when you don't eat. Do you feel better about yourself? Is it a good feeling?

MIA: No.

FT: It's not a good feeling?

MIA: It's not that I don't eat on purpose.

FT: Do you feel the need to purge after eating? Does that ever happen to you?

MIA: I'm not anorexic.

PETE: Oh, what would you call not eating, then?

FT: Pete, if you could just give Mia some time to answer it would really help.

MIA: My tummy feels in knots all the time. It hurts. I get pain when I walk. It hurts when I sit in class. Sometimes I need to lie down because the pain is so bad.

PETE: She's been checked out by numerous doctors.

CARRIE: They don't know everything, Pete. Just because they can't find anything doesn't mean there's nothing wrong with her.

FT: So do you think it's the pain in your tummy that stops you feeling hungry, Mia? Is that it?

MIA: Yeah. I think so. When the pain goes away, I want to eat again. I like food. Normally, I enjoy eating.

FT: OK, that's useful to know. I know you've tried some medication previously and I'm wondering if—

MIA: It made me sleepy. I didn't want to get out of bed.

FT: That can be a side effect, but I'm wondering if we tried another approach, there are a range of medications we can try that—

MIA: I didn't feel like myself. I felt strange. But not in a good way. I didn't feel better.

CARRIE: Mia felt like she didn't have control over her life when she was on the medication. It was not a good fit for us.

FT: OK, then let's come back to that. Is there anything you do for yourself, Mia, that does make you feel better? Sometimes it's good to hear how you've tried to solve the problems of anxiety yourself.

MIA: I just like to stay at home. When I'm out I feel like something bad might happen.

CARRIE: She's happier at home.

FT: I understand, Mia, you feel vulnerable when you're out. I understand that. If you can, I'd like you to tell me when you feel really *unsafe*? Is that possible? In what situation do you feel really unsettled?

MIA:

FT: It's OK. Take your time. This stuff is very hard to talk about. Sometimes you don't even know the answer.

MIA:

FT: Is it on your way to school? No. OK. How about when you're with friends from school, is there anyone in particular that makes you feel worried, stressed, bad about yourself? OK. Not really that either. How about the teachers?

CARRIE: She feels very uncomfortable when she's at Pete's house.

PETE: Oh, for fuck's sake. This? Again?

CARRIE: She does. You know she does. Why don't you step up and take responsibility for making her feel this way?

PETE: She doesn't feel this way. *You* feel this way.

FT: Mia? Is Mum right? Do you feel unsettled at your dad's house?

MIA: Sometimes.

FT: Are you able to explain exactly why that is, Mia?

MIA: Not really. I just feel on edge. And Mum's not there, I suppose, so that's kind of weird. And even though I like Nina . . .

FT: Nina is . . .?

PETE: My girlfriend. And she's done nothing wrong. She's *nice* to you, Mia. She tries really hard. She's not some wicked—

CARRIE: Pete, can't you understand she doesn't feel comfortable around Nina?

PETE: It's *you* who doesn't—

MIA: Nina *is* nice. I like Nina. I'm not saying Nina is a bad person. I just feel really strange going around there and I can't explain properly why I feel that way. I don't know if it's that that's making me the way I am right now, but you asked when I feel most scared, and it's when I go to my dad's house.

PETE: You've made her like this.

CARRIE: No, I've not.

PETE: You've poisoned her mind against me.

CARRIE: You've done that yourself.

PETE: You sulk when she comes to my house. You make her feel like she's betraying you. If she has a nice time she's frightened to tell you in case it pisses you off and you ignore her all night. It's no wonder she's the way she is. She's starving herself so I'll come back! You want her to be like this!

CARRIE: Well, maybe if you didn't have to screw every single woman who walked past you in the street, then—

FT: Please. You have to calm down. This is not the best way to help your daughter. Mia, try not to cry. This isn't your fault. Sometimes adults have a difficult time expressing themselves and—

CARRIE: Oh, yeah, Pete. Walk out. That'll solve everything.

Now

THEY WAIT ON the promenade just south-west of the Midland Hotel as dusk falls. There's no sunset to speak of, not even a suggestion of amber light over to the west, where the Irish Sea meets the sky. The cloud has come in now and it's too dense. Too thick. It looks like rain.

They'll wait until around 17.45, just before the time the first camera captured the white Honda SUV – 'Carrie's' car – when rush hour is properly underway, and then they'll make the journey to Ella Muir's house once again. Morecambe is not a big town. The current population stands at around 35,000, but the population is condensed into a tight area, clinging as Morecambe does to the Lancashire coastline, so this time Tess is expecting a line of slow-moving traffic on the way to Ella's house, as Morecambe's working residents make their way home.

A man passes by on foot. He's wearing a football shirt over the top of his hoodie. His shirt triggers a thought: Tess should get hold of the fixture list from four years ago because if Morecambe FC – 'the Shrimps' – were playing at home that evening, it would further complicate the journey Carrie supposedly took, again reducing the time available for her to murder Ella. Tess touches the microphone icon on her mobile and dictates a reminder: 'Check fixture list', and then she swipes though her emails to pass the time.

'I feel like I'm on a stake-out,' Avril says.

'Except the suspect's already in prison,' replies Tess.

'Yeah. But it is pretty exciting though, isn't it? It's a ton more exciting than family law, anyway. Two years of that and you want to run into the nearest church on a Saturday afternoon and yell at people not to get married. "Do you know of any lawful impediment . . . ?" Yeah. You're gonna end up really hating each other.'

Tess smiles. 'You don't want to get married?'

'Oh, I want a life partner and all that. But I think something about the marriage contract makes couples really detest each other when the love starts to fade. More than, say, if they'd just decided to share their lives without the ceremony. It's like they're trapped, and they blame each other for *getting* trapped . . . Dealing with that day after day gets depressing.'

'Is that why you left?'

Avril nods. 'Some mornings I'd wake up filled with dread to the point I was throwing up before work. I had to make a decision: do I spend the rest of my life dealing with these people? Or do I get out before I become laden with responsibilities and I've got no choice but to stay?'

'Brave . . . What did William think?'

'Oh, he supported it. He could see how unhappy I was. I've had to take a cut in wages, but he said he was prepared to ditch the takeaways, et cetera, if it meant I was happy.'

'Sounds like a keeper,' says Tess.

'He is,' replies Avril happily.

The clock on the dashboard shows 17.40, and the traffic on the promenade has increased to the extent that Tess is satisfied they can now drive the route again. She sets off, and as she catches sight of the Winter Gardens her left leg begins to shake. She's not driven along this exact stretch of road since the day her mother was killed here and she's making herself do it now to get it out of her system. To lessen her response. She's doing it so that the next time she travels along the promenade, her leg *won't* shake, and her throat *won't* feel as if someone has both their hands around it, slowly, slowly tightening their grip. Exposure therapy, she believes it's called.

Tess didn't learn to drive for eight years after the accident. She didn't even try. When, finally, she did get behind the wheel, she was living in Oldham, and the steep gradient of the streets meant that the town was enough unlike Morecambe for her to drive without suffering from the PTSD-like symptoms she's experiencing now. *Breathe*, she tells herself. *Just breathe.*

She puts her hand on her left leg to steady it and feels Avril's eyes drift downwards. 'You OK?'

'Lactic acid,' lies Tess. 'I went for a run last night and I must've overdone it.'

They approach the pub and this time Avril has her thumb poised, ready. 'Say when.'

Tess puts both hands on the wheel. 'When.'

The temptation of course is to dawdle. To hang back and try to make the journey to Ella's last as long as possible so that Carrie's statement stands up and the prosecution's time frame is proven to be false. This is all about proving Carrie couldn't have done it after all. But dawdling won't help Tess. Far better for Tess to be aware of what she's up against from the off, far better to know the stakes are high, that Carrie *could indeed be lying*, because then she knows what she's working with. Then she can adjust her approach accordingly.

She pulls on to Ella's street. Another fifty yards and Tess indicates left, before lining the car up neatly against the kerb. 'Stop the clock.'

And Avril tells her the journey has taken 'Eleven minutes and forty-three seconds exactly'. Tess can hear the smile already forming in Avril's voice. 'In total,' Avril says, 'that works out at twenty-three minutes, and that doesn't even include time for Carrie to go inside. The time frame put forward by the prosecution was nineteen minutes. It means it can't be done.'

Point to Carrie, thinks Tess.

Four Years Ago

Opposite the Midland Hotel is Morecambe's stone jetty, extending 250 metres into the Irish Sea. Close to the end of the jetty is a small lighthouse and a squat building of stone construction that was once an early railway station. In the mid to late nineteenth century, the rail line extended along the length of the jetty, and the station served as a terminal for both cargo and passengers destined for the steamers going to the Isle of Man and to Ireland. The steamers ceased operating from Morecambe with the opening of Heysham Port in 1904, and the small station is now a café.

'Why are we doing this again?' asks Mia.

'Because you've not left your room in three days, because fresh air and exercise are natural elevators of mood, and because,' Carrie says, pulling her daughter in close, 'I'd like to treat you to a milkshake.'

Carrie and Mia walk south along the promenade, arms linked, their heads dipped against the prevailing wind. When they reach the jetty, they take a right and make their way along the walkway towards the café at the end. The deck is covered with a red sandstone-coloured concrete and grey granite cobbles. It's pretty. Nice to walk on. There are places to sit and enjoy the view, and Carrie and Mia pass a number of couples sitting on the benches, bundled up, like them, against the cold, watching as the waves roll in. The jetty has been made safe by a set of sky-blue railings running around the perimeter. And on the railings is this warning: 'Dogs must be kept on leads'. Which Carrie thinks is a sensible approach because any dog slipping into this rough sea won't be coming out.

'I'd prefer a Radford's cheese and onion pie to a milkshake,' Mia is saying as they push open the doors to the café. Mia has become hooked on these artisan pies, produced by Britain's largest family, the Radfords (twenty kids? twenty-one? – Carrie forgets how many there are of them now). She's found herself traipsing along to the shop in Heysham more often than she would like to of late. Occasionally, Carrie sees Sue Radford in the supermarket, matriarch and mother to all those babies, and Carrie is filled with the urge to stop Sue and tell her what a remarkable human being she is. But she doesn't, she backs out at the last second, because shyness overcomes her. Carrie has found raising one child challenging enough. Bringing up Mia has required everything she has and so she looks at Sue Radford with something close to awe.

'It's too cold for a milkshake,' Mia is saying. 'Why don't we—'

'It'll make a nice *change*.'

Carrie must sound rather shrill because Mia turns her head to her mother and regards her, arched brows knitted together to form a frown. 'It was only a suggestion,' she says sulkily.

Mia makes her way to a table, removes her coat, looks at the menu, and it's as she's removing her own coat and gloves that Carrie looks along the length of the café and spies Ella.

Ella Muir, Pete's new girlfriend.

Ella doesn't notice Carrie. She is pouring coffee beans into the espresso maker and so Carrie can study her, unobserved.

Carrie met Ella for the first time at a barbeque the previous summer. Friends of Carrie and Pete's, Damian and Michelle, had spent a small fortune on landscaping their garden, and wanted everyone to enjoy (admire) it. Michelle invited Ella along as the only singleton as Ella was in a bad relationship and Michelle wanted to give her some time to breathe away from Stuart – whom Carrie had only heard negative things about. When Carrie and Pete arrived, Ella was already pretty addled by drink, and was doing a headstand over by the gazebo. Carrie could immediately see where this was headed and so wasn't surprised to find Ella an hour later slumped by the side of the toilet, crying into a pint glass of water someone had thoughtfully supplied her with. And so Carrie decided to sit with Ella, consoling her as Ella sobbed about what a fuck-up her life was, while encouraging her to take small sips of water and holding her hair back for her while she puked.

Carrie wonders now if Ella remembers that night. She wonders if she remembers pouring her heart out to Carrie, and if she remembers Carrie, in return, sharing some truths about her own relationship to make the girl feel better. It's always been in Carrie's nature to try to make a person who is suffering feel a little less alone, a little less of a disaster, by giving away some of the not-so-appealing details about her own life. In between Ella's retches, as the toilet bowl filled with sour-smelling regurgitated red wine, Carrie confided to Ella that her life was less than perfect. She told of Pete's many peccadilloes. And when Ella raised her face, her hair plastered with sweat to her forehead, and asked, 'Why would he cheat on someone as lovely as you?' Carrie replied truthfully that she didn't know why.

Carrie hangs her coat over the back of her chair and sits down. She is facing away from the small area used for food preparation at the other end of the café. Mia continues to peruse the menu and decides she would like to have a toasted teacake and a hot chocolate. 'What are you having?' she asks her mother.

'A pot of tea.'

Carrie clasps her hands together and places them on the table. She observes a slight tremor. She thinks about removing them, settling them in her lap instead, but Mia hasn't noticed so she leaves them where they are. Mia, for all her claims of sensitivity and tender-heartedness, can be remarkably blind to the plight of others. It's Mia's world, and she is only interested in her place in it. Typical teenage traits, Carrie supposes.

Carrie senses a presence to her right and so she raises her head. 'Are you ready to order?' asks Ella Muir, and for a brief moment there's a disconnect. Some kind of stutter in Ella's brain. She looks at Carrie and smiles but there is no recognition. Until, suddenly, there is. And then Ella's expression shifts, contorts, and now her smile is that of a lunatic.

'Please can I have a hot chocolate with chocolate sprinkles,' says Mia, happily unaware, 'and . . . well, I know it doesn't say this is an option on the menu, but would it be OK if I had some extra mini marshmallows on the top as well? I have a total weakness for them. Don't I, Mum?'

Carrie is nodding. 'She does.'

Mia's request to Ella goes unanswered. Ella is glancing behind, looking over her shoulder, checking out the other tables in the café. Carrie thinks that this would probably be *her* first instinct too, if she were presented with an equivalent set of circumstances. *Who else is in here? What will they witness? What . . . is about to go down?*

Ella turns back around to face Carrie but still she doesn't speak. She stares at Carrie, a look of real fear in her eyes, wondering perhaps what Carrie's next move will be. 'I'd like a pot of decaffeinated tea, please, if I may?' Carrie says politely.

Ella swallows. She bites her lip. 'I'm afraid we don't do regular tea in decaf . . . We have peppermint, camomile and fennel.'

'I'll try the fennel.'

Ella nods and leaves in a hurry.

'Well, *she* was weird,' whispers Mia. 'She didn't even take my food order.'

'Go and tell her,' suggests Carrie. 'She's probably having a bad day, so be sure to be nice. Go and tell her what you want.'

Mia gets up, saying, 'I'm always nice. When am I not nice?' and Carrie resists the urge to swivel in her seat and witness Ella being put under further pressure.

She hears Mia courteously putting in her request for attention and almost instantly there is a loud crash. It's the sound of pots falling to the floor, the sound of broken crockery. The other patrons of the café crane their necks to see and begin sending sympathetic glances Ella's way and so don't see the small smile playing at the corners of Carrie's mouth.

This is turning out to be so much more enjoyable than she first thought.

Mia returns, eyes wide. 'That woman is *so* jumpy.'

'What happened?'

'I don't know. I said excuse me, she turned around, and then everything just slipped from her fingers.'

'How odd,' says Carrie.

A few minutes later, their order is delivered by another member of staff, a pleasant young woman whom Carrie observed busying herself in the kitchen area when they first arrived. She leaves and as Carrie sips her tea, she can hear the young woman asking Ella if she's sure she's OK now, and Ella must whisper her response because it's inaudible.

Carrie imagines Ella jerking her head repeatedly in Carrie's direction. 'That's *her* . . . that's Pete's *wife*.' And she imagines Ella's co-worker whispering, 'Oh my God,' her hand flying to her mouth in response.

Has she given them something to titter about today?

She really does hope not.

It was not her intention to be an object of ridicule.

Without thinking, Carrie rises from her seat. Mia is studying her phone so Carrie's movement barely registers. Mia lifts her gaze, lowers it again, goes back to scrolling. Carrie wends her way between the tables and finds Ella standing with her back against the tiled wall of the kitchen area. It's immediately evident she has not shared Carrie's identity with her co-worker. The co-worker is happily dealing with a large cabbage; she's slicing it into thin strips – for coleslaw, Carrie supposes – and she does not look at all perturbed by the sight of Carrie approaching.

Ella, however, looks as though she's ready to break into two. Her head is dipped and she is shielding her face with her hands. Her skin is a deathly white. It's as if she's aged ten years in the space of a few minutes.

'Ella, would you mind serving this lady, while I finish off here?' says the young co-worker with the cabbage, and Ella drops her hands, closing her eyes for an extended moment when she sees Carrie.

Ella approaches. 'What can I get you?' she asks in a quiet voice. She appears vulnerable and weak. She appears . . . sorry.

But Carrie has been *nice* to this girl. When their paths have crossed, she's even tried to help her. And what has Ella done in return? She's fucked Carrie's husband.

'I'd like you to know that I can come here at any time,' Carrie says to Ella. Her voice is low and steady. There's a calmness to her manner that she knows must be unnerving.

Ella's big eyes are fixed upon Carrie. She does not blink once.

'I can come here every day if I want to,' Carrie says, and Ella nods as though she understands. 'I can come in here – Every. Single. Day.' Carrie reaches out her hand and brushes her fingertips across Ella's cheek. Ella remains perfectly still. The only movement is the pulse in her neck.

Carrie drops her hand and smiles. It's a warm smile. Genuine. And Ella is terrified. 'Just wanted you to know that . . . Now, take care of yourself, Ella, won't you?'

Now

TESS STARES THROUGH the windscreen at the rain that's begun to fall. Her beige woollen coat will smell like a wet Labrador if she goes out in this, but there's not a lot of choice. 'Look lively,' she says to Avril. Avril, who is not much better prepared herself, wearing as she is a summery mac in pale blue, with large indigo flowers dotted all over it. Tess really should invest in some Gore-Tex. Something waterproof and breathable. But she supposes it's a bit late for all that now.

She tells Avril to grab the folder with the case notes inside and hands her a carrier bag in which to keep it dry. She has an emergency stock of plastic bags in the pocket behind her seat, because she never knows when someone is going to hand her another thing to cart around.

Avril places the case notes inside and balances the lot on top of her head to keep her hair dry. 'Don't you have an umbrella?' she asks, and Tess doesn't bother answering because, evidently, if she had one she would be using it.

'Always visit the site of the murder,' she tells Avril. 'It's rare you're going to get to see the actual scene, but always visit the property. Visit the street at the very least. Things look different on the ground.'

Tess looks along the street, first one way and then the other. They're in Torrisholme, which is a small suburb of Morecambe. Ella Muir's house, or what *was* Ella Muir's house, is a neat-looking

1930s semi-detached; Ella lived in the left-hand side of the dwelling. Dividing the front garden is a tall privet hedge, which Tess knows from the crime scene photographs was here, and largely unkept, at the time of Ella's death. There is also a street lamp outside the house next door, but the front of Ella's house is largely in darkness.

Tess wipes the rain from her face. 'Come on,' she says to Avril, and she sets off, walking diagonally across the road at a brisk pace, Avril trotting behind to keep up.

'Where are we heading?' asks Avril.

'There,' she says, pointing.

A moment later, Tess stops outside number 53. She turns and looks left towards Ella's house. 'Yes,' she says to herself, 'this is the one.'

The door is answered by a doddery old gentleman, well into his seventies. He wears a brushed-cotton shirt and a maroon acrylic cardigan, buttoned all the way. His nose hair is almost plaitable, which Tess thinks is a sure sign that he lives alone, and he wears thick-lensed spectacles, behind which his eyes appear to be twice their natural size.

'Mr Hurst?'

'Yes.'

'I'm Tess Gilroy. We're from Innocence UK and we're looking into the murder of Ella Muir. I believe you were a witness for the prosecution?'

'I was indeed,' he answers proudly, and doddery old Mr Hurst comes alive at the mention of the murder.

'I wonder if we could ask you a few questions, if it's not a bad time?'

'Come in,' he says enthusiastically. 'Come in.'

Mr Hurst is clearly starved of company and purpose as he's beaming at the two women now standing in his living room, excited by the prospect of what they have to say. He didn't ask

Tess for any identification, and not for the first time Tess is astonished by the unguarded trust exhibited by the elderly. Tess and Avril could tie him up and scarper with his valuables if they were that way inclined.

Tess opens up the case file. She doesn't need to do this. She knows exactly what the file says, but she senses Mr Hurst will respond favourably to a degree of page-flapping – indicating official business – so she makes quite a meal of it. 'As I understand it, Mr Hurst, you told the police you saw Carrie Kamara leaving Ella Muir's house on the evening of the murder?'

'That's correct. I saw her. It was definitely her. No doubt in my mind about it.'

'Would it be a lot of trouble to take me through exactly what you were doing at that moment? It's not completely clear in these notes and I'd like to get it straight in my head.'

Hurst is way less unsteady on his feet now. He smiles and takes Tess to the front bay window, parts the curtains and gestures in the direction of Ella's house. 'She came out there, right by that van, got in her car and drove off in that direction.'

Tess notes he has mistaken her saloon car for a van. How far can he see? she wonders. 'You're talking about Carrie Kamara?' she asks.

'Aye. It was definitely her. The *murderer*. I was relieved when they found her guilty. You don't want a woman like that loose on the streets. Morecambe used to be a safe place.'

'But you'd never seen Mrs Kamara prior to that, had you? You weren't familiar with her? You weren't familiar with how she looked?'

'No, but I know it was her. Who else could it be?'

Who else indeed.

Tess closes the file as if to suggest she's all done and dusted. She watches the disappointment register on Mr Hurst's face. Just as she hoped, he's desperate to be involved.

Could it have been desperation, Tess thinks, that led Mr Hurst to make his witness statement in the first place? Is he one of those lonely individuals who'll do anything to be included?

Tess waits for a moment, making sure he's watching, before signalling to Avril with a flick of the head that she's ready to leave. She says, 'Right, I think we have everything we need now.'

And again, Mr Hurst's face drops.

So she smiles.

It's Tess's best, most beatific smile. 'Mr Hurst,' she says warmly, 'I have a bit of a crazy idea. How would you feel about helping us with something?'

Tess and Avril are outside what was Ella's front door. They are hidden from view by the privet hedge, which runs between the neighbouring properties. There's no one at home, which is just as well because then she'd have to introduce herself, ask the householder if they'd mind them using their front pathway for a time, and there would be questions, lots of questions. *A miscarriage of justice! How exciting.*

Tess has her phone clamped to her ear. 'Can you still hear me there, Mr Hurst?'

'Loud and clear.'

'OK, I'm going to set off walking along the pathway in a few seconds and I want you to tell me the *exact* moment I come into view. OK?'

'I'm ready,' he says, quite giddy.

Tess nudges Avril and gives her a thumbs up. And Avril, as instructed by Tess, sets off walking at a slow pace along the path towards the road, while Tess remains hidden.

Tess can hear Mr Hurst's outward breath in her ear. 'Righto, I can see you now,' he says. Avril continues towards the car and takes the keys from her pocket. 'Yep. I've got you. I can see you next to the van.'

'Excellent. And can you make out my beige coat from where you are, Mr Hurst?' she says loudly.

Avril smiles at Tess and she does a sort of shimmy before turning on the spot as if she's a runway model, showing off her coat which is of course nothing like Tess's.

'Clear as day,' he says. 'And I can see your blonde hair.'

'My blonde hair? Excellent.'

Avril is, of course, brunette.

'Excellent, Mr Hurst,' Tess says again. 'You've been such a marvellous help to us.'

'Not at all,' he says.

And Tess thinks: *Another point to Carrie.*

Four Years Ago

THE DAY OF her arrest, Carrie can feel the gusset of her swimsuit riding up as she marches on the spot. 'Knees nice and high!' She'd bought the curve-enhancing, body-shaping, essential plunge in size ten, and is now realizing this was a mistake. She should've gone for the twelve. She keeps her knees *nice and high* as she reaches behind and extricates the material from between her buttocks, only for it to slip straight back up there again. She glances around. No one else here seems to be having swimsuit issues. They are all marching, their arms thrust straight out, their eyes fixed on Gavin at the poolside.

Gavin comes highly recommended. He is the *best in the area*, according to her friend, Helen Carter, whom she lunches with, and Carrie wonders just how many aqua-aerobics instructors there can be competing for that title. Helen insisted Carrie try one of Gavin's classes when Carrie made a point in passing that her upper arms were beginning to lose their tone. Carrie can see Helen at the front of the class. Her head is bobbing, the muscles between her shoulder blades standing proud as she begins circling her arms enthusiastically. Helen had wanted Carrie to take a place at the front, alongside her, but Carrie made an excuse. 'Maybe next time,' she'd mumbled.

Carrie's arms are beginning to ache. She's just out of condition, she tells herself, and she grits her teeth and digs deep, as Gavin is telling them to do. He's in Lycra, of course, and now, as he spreads his feet wide, and he steps from one foot to the other, arms still circling, Carrie has a hard time knowing where to look as his penis bounces jauntily from side to side along with him.

Perhaps she should've opted for horse riding instead. She used to enjoy it. As a pre-teen, Carrie would canter along Morecambe's shore, hair blowing out wildly behind her, jodhpurs soaked in the spray, and she would think that life was pretty wonderful. The horse's name was Fernando. He was a palomino with a white-blond mane and tail that Carrie would lovingly comb for hours, before plaiting it for his owner in readiness for a show. Fernando had two white socks and a white blaze down his face and if Carrie could've married that horse she would have. In fact, thinking about it now, as they punch the air high above them before turning on the spot and clapping twice, Carrie remembers wishing as a twelve-year-old girl that she could actually *be* a horse.

'And splash!' Gavin shouts. 'Splash those troubles away!'

They are supposed to smack the water in time to Pharrell Williams's 'Happy', but Carrie senses the women on either side of her are not keen to get their hair wet, so she goes easy.

Gavin instructs them to turn a full three-sixty, only this time they are to crouch in the water, using their arms to beat themselves around. 'Like fins!' Carrie is late in starting this, concentrating as she is on the swimsuit again, and so when the woman in front of her manoeuvres herself round using an odd sidestroke action, Carrie is still facing front. She recognizes the woman instantly and so her first instinct is to smile – Carrie was brought up to be a friendly sort – but the woman does not return the gesture, and Carrie feels foolish. She drops her smile and is left wearing a kind of dopey expression that she doesn't quite know how to get rid of. It lingers as she completes her turn.

The woman is Nicki Entwistle. She is short in the leg, with thick arms, no breasts to speak of, and has a pad of fat sitting beneath her lower jaw that she inherited from her mother (her mother used to work as an ice-cream seller on the prom and the children would gobble like turkeys when they cycled past the van). Carrie could describe Nicki's less alluring features, even if she wasn't in front of her right now, because, for the last few years, Carrie's focused on these points whenever she sees her.

Nicki's daughter, Paige, accused Carrie's daughter, Mia, of bullying, back in Year Seven. Which was completely hysterical since everyone knew Paige Entwistle had been an atrocious bully all the way through primary school. But Morecambe High wasn't aware of this, and so Paige's claims that Mia was bullying her psychologically and emotionally were treated seriously. Carrie and Pete were asked to attend a meeting with the head of year, as well as the deputy head, where they were informed that bullying of any sort would be stamped out before it had a chance to take root, and 'Paige Entwistle is entitled to a worry-free education', they were told. Carrie and Pete listened, their mouths gaping, knowing Mia had been set up somehow, but were powerless to argue against it since Paige had got the first word in.

The sense of injustice Carrie felt was all-consuming. Mia had always been so sensitive, a worrier; she got headaches when she had a test looming, she became dizzy if she had an altercation with another girl. But she went ahead and questioned Mia and Mia was also aghast; 'I've never bullied anyone,' she told Carrie, and even though Carrie hadn't believed it for one second, she was relieved to hear her say it. 'I don't even dare speak to her,' Mia said. And when Carrie asked why that was, Mia replied, 'Because she's *Paige*.'

She went on to tell Carrie that the only thing she could think of that could have prompted such a lie was an incident that happened during drama class the previous week. A popular boy had mocked Paige's attempt at an American accent, and 'I smiled, Mum,' Mia said, 'that's it. I didn't even think she saw me.'

Carrie didn't need to hear more. She understood what she needed to do. These powerful girls had made her own high-school experience a living hell, with their mind games and their constant humiliation, and Carrie would not allow Mia to suffer the same fate. So she waited for Paige. She lingered outside school; she knew Nicki had younger children to collect first and so there would be a window of opportunity, fifteen minutes perhaps, when Paige would be alone. She followed Paige to her pick-up point and, once there, she stood beside her.

Carrie didn't speak. She didn't demand answers from the girl. She didn't even warn her away from repeating the trick she'd pulled which had landed Mia in isolation for two days and put a black mark against her academic record. She merely waited along with her and when Paige became unnerved, when she became flushed and awkward – sorting through her rucksack repeatedly, draining the last of her drinks container, arranging her hair in a scrunchy and taking it out again – Carrie kept a level gaze on her.

Naturally Carrie expected repercussions. She expected the school to get in touch. In her more paranoid moments, she expected the *police* to get in touch. She knew she'd overstepped the mark. You weren't supposed to take matters into your own hands; it was prohibited to approach a student. She knew that. So she marvelled when nothing happened. And again, when nothing happened to Mia either. If anything, Mia reported back, Paige had begun going out of her way to be accommodating – which was unexpected to say the least; and the only real consequence of Carrie's action was the furious death stare she received from Nicki Entwistle every time their paths crossed.

Did Nicki know Carrie had approached her daughter? Carrie thought not. Nicki was a real bulldog of a woman and had undoubtedly made school hell for many when she was there herself, so Carrie had to assume from Nicki's lack of retaliation that Paige kept their encounter from her mother, and that the reason for Nicki's glowering lay entirely in her assumption that Mia really had bullied her precious girl.

'And march!' shouts Gavin now, and Carrie lifts her knees up high and swings her arms backwards and forwards, the resistance of the water against her limbs a pleasant distraction from the worry that Nicki Entwistle might turn on the spot again and choose this moment to finally exact retribution.

Then they are sidestepping across the width of the shallow end, arms out at their sides, faster, faster still, as some of the older ladies struggle to keep their balance, and there are honks of laughter and trills of 'Oops! I've lost my footin'', and Carrie is just thinking that this class is definitely not for her when the music stops. Gavin apologizes for the halt in the proceedings, and adjusts his mic, before saying, 'Do we have a Carrie Kamara with us today?'

Carrie stands stock-still. Her first thought of course is Mia. Because there are two people standing at the side of the pool who, even though in plain clothes, look very much like police officers. She racks her brain, trying to think of Mia's movements. Where should she be? Has Carrie heard an ambulance this morning?

She raises her hand. 'If you wouldn't mind making your way to the side of the pool please, my love,' Gavin says, a faux smile slapped on his face, and as she wades across, doing a kind of half-walk, half-swim, she can see by the expression on the faces of the officers that this has nothing to do with Mia.

She stands at the base of the ladder steps, ready to haul herself out, and watches as the woman officer takes a set of handcuffs from her jacket pocket. 'You are under arrest on suspicion of the murder of Ella Muir . . .' the officer is saying very quietly, aware, Carrie presumes, of the many eyes upon them.

The urge to flee is overwhelming. She looks over her shoulder. Thirty sets of eyes are upon her. The faces are a blur. All except for those of Helen Carter and Nicki Entwistle, which have come into clear, sharp focus. She turns around. Pulls her swimsuit out from between her buttocks and mounts the steps. 'I didn't do anything.'

And the woman officer tells her, 'This will all go smoothly if you don't make a fuss.' So Carrie holds out her hands numbly, ready to receive the cuffs, but the woman officer says, 'We'll let you get dried off first,' and Carrie is led silently towards the changing rooms.

Four Years Ago

THE OFFICER'S VOICE seems to come from far away. 'How are you getting on in there?' Carrie murmurs something in reply but she's not exactly sure what comes out. She sits on the wooden bench inside the cubicle with her towel wrapped around her shoulders. Her swimsuit clings to her body and her skin is cold and clammy beneath. She needs to take it off, but she's not sure she can move.

Carrie closes her eyes. She pinches the bridge of her nose and tries to bring her mind into focus. Outside, she becomes aware of the officer sending a text message, clearing her throat.

What just happened?

Has she been arrested? She isn't sure.

Carrie's mind feels as if it's operating via a third party. She pictures the Wizard of Oz, frantically pulling his levers from behind the closed curtain, and this is the nearest she can get to making sense of what she's feeling. Someone has invaded her body and she's no longer in charge of her faculties.

'Carrie, you need to get a move on.'

The officer's name is Gillian Frain. Carrie remembers that now. As she was being led away from the pool, she said, 'My name is Gillian Frain and I'm the senior investigating officer on this case.'

Bewildered by what she was hearing, Carrie had replied, 'Case?' But whatever Gillian had said after that had been lost for now.

'Do you need some help?' Gillian asks.

And Carrie looks down at her hands, sees they're trembling, and she hears herself say, weakly, 'I think so.' She leans forward and manages to reach the latch. She slides it across and the door drops open outwards.

Gillian Frain stands with her arms crossed, an expression on her face that Carrie can't read. 'You're sitting on your dry clothes.'

Carrie looks at the bench and realizes she's right. So she lifts the left cheek of her bottom and pushes her T-shirt and leggings away. She keeps pushing until they're lodged in the corner of the cubicle. 'I don't know where my shoes are.'

'Did you put them in a locker?'

'I can't remember.'

'We can deal with the shoes later,' Gillian says, and it's only now that the fog starts to lift and Carrie becomes aware of her surroundings. 'You need to get dry,' Gillian tells her impatiently. 'You need to get dry now before . . .' She lets the sentence hang and Carrie thinks, *Before what?*

Carrie tries to pull the strap away from her left shoulder but her fingers can't seem to get beneath it. She tries again and still she can't get the thing off. She looks at Gillian Frain helplessly and the detective seems undecided as to what to do. Does she step in and get this sorted out? Get the woman into some dry clothes? Carrie can feel her mulling it over.

Carrie takes a few steadying breaths. She is now lucid enough to think through the repercussions of remaining like this: she'll be stuck inside this cubicle while they wait for someone with the right authority to witness her nakedness. And she'll be forced to listen to the aqua-aerobics ladies, re-dressing, speculating quietly on what this is all about. Except they *know* what this is about: Ella Muir. Carrie imagines Nicki Entwistle's pugnacious face looming over the top of the cubicle door. She visualizes her offering Carrie her first smile in years, satisfied that justice is finally being done, and Carrie knows she couldn't stand that. Frantically, she tries the strap again, but it's as if her fingers are made of putty; they've become useless to her and she can't see a way out. She starts to panic. Terror fills her. She's never felt like this so she has no idea what to do. She feels her chest tightening. She's going to vomit. She looks at Gillian Frain, stricken. 'I need you to help me.'

The detective steps forward. 'How about you hold the towel loosely around yourself and I'll ease the costume down? My daughter has me do it that way at the beach. I'm kind of an expert.'

And Carrie says, 'I'd really appreciate that,' and then she starts to cry.

Now

Tess is ferreting around in her fridge for something to chuck in the NutriBullet. She eyes some week-old Brussels sprouts and half a yellow pepper and wonders if she's up for such a level of self-punishment at this hour. Regardless of what she puts in the blender, it all comes out an unappetizing grey-brown, but, she concedes, she's not getting any younger, and she's unlikely to eat a single vegetable for the rest of the day, so she sets to work.

Sipping her smoothie, which is not as bad as she feared, she leans her weight against the kitchen work surface and watches the bird station though the kitchen window. The fat balls she purchased yesterday were a mistake. Her back yard is now a frenzy of jackdaws, all shouting at one another, all crapping on her rotary washing line as they compete for a turn at the feeder. Her little birds – the bullfinches, greenfinches, goldfinches, chaffinches; the blue tits, great tits, coal tits, long-tailed tits; the nuthatches; the sparrows – have all left the yard in fear of their lives. Even the blackbirds, who can be monstrous bullies at times, have taken cover in next door's sycamore, and are watching over the proceedings, quietly vexed.

Tess bought forty fat balls from Home Bargains in Accrington and is now regretting her impulse purchase. She'll have to bin them, which is a terrible waste, but with the jackdaws taking over, her little songbirds will go hungry unless she does something radical. For some reason the jackdaws were never interested in the sunflower-seed hearts or the millet and mealworms she puts out daily, and she's just deciding whether to go out now in her pyjamas and remove the fat balls altogether, when the office phone goes.

She checks her watch: 8.52 a.m. The caller is early.

Tess mounts the stairs and picks up. 'Tess Gilroy,' she says, but no one responds. Instead, she hears a series of clicks, before an automated voice announces, 'You have a call from Her Majesty's Prison Styal. Prisoner number 46453. Press hash to receive.'

As she waits for the call to connect, Tess examines the noticeboard. She looks at the picture of Ella Muir covered in stab wounds, and then at the new photograph she printed out last night. It's of Carrie arriving at court. Carrie as she was then, though, not the Carrie she knows now. Tess lets her eyes move between the two pictures and quietens her mind. She tries to survey the prints with an uncritical eye. *Let whatever thoughts you have come to the surface and simply observe them.* Tess has a mindfulness app that she uses sometimes to help her drop her preconceived ideas about a case. She's pretty sure the authors of the app did not intend for it to be used for this purpose: they talk about looking at a bottle of water, other inanimate objects, as if seeing the objects for the first time. Tess substitutes crime scene photos for such objects. And since she believes in using every tool she can get her hands on to achieve a result, she's not above a bit of meditation (even though in her everyday life she's come to the assumption that living in the moment is really *not* for her. She's far happier dreaming about the future and has come to accept that this is OK, regardless of what Eckhart Tolle and his disciples have to say on the subject).

'Hello?'

'Hi, Carrie. You got my message.'

'Yeah, they told me last night that you wanted to speak to me.'

'Excellent. How are you?'

'Pretty good,' Carrie replies, but it's evident that she's not. Carrie's voice is reedy and weak. 'I don't have long, we have cell inspections this morning.'

'OK, I'll be brief. I just wanted to update you really. Let you know how it's all progressing . . .' Tess is careful not to sound too upbeat during these conversations. It's all very well for her to feel heartened and cheered by her findings so far, but this is a long road for the prisoner. An astonishingly long road, with no guarantees. Tess has had cases reach the Court of Appeal only to be dismissed without any real reason and the only option available to the prisoner is to start the very lengthy process all over again. 'I want to talk about the CCTV if that's OK,' she says. 'We have the images of your car – well, what the prosecution claims was your car, and when we revisited the route they said you took on the evening of Ella's murder, we found the time frame they'd allowed was not enough. Meaning there was not enough time for you to murder Ella.'

Carrie is silent.

'Are you still there?' Tess asks.

'Just a bit overcome.'

'That's understandable. There's more, if you're OK for me to go on . . . ?'

'I'm OK.'

'There was a witness – Mr Hurst – I'm sure you remember him, he's an elderly gentleman who—'

'I remember him.'

'Well, me and Avril spoke with Mr Hurst yesterday evening. We did what you might call a reconstruction, and it was immediately evident that Mr Hurst's sight is severely compromised. He had trouble making out what was happening outside Ella's house and I feel certain that if we were to call him for an eye test, his witness statement would be classed as unreliable. We're going to get hold of his medical records and see what state his vision was in at the time of the murder but we're assuming for now it wasn't good.'

'He was really adamant in court it was me he saw.'

She's right. Tess has reread the transcript and Hurst really wouldn't be budged. He staked his life on Carrie being in the street that night.

'People can get things wrong for all sorts of reasons, Carrie,' Tess says. 'The problem is they have no idea that they're wrong.'

'Oh, he knew he was wrong,' replies Carrie angrily. 'He knew it and he said it anyway. The fucker.'

'That's the spirit,' replies Tess. She decides Carrie could do with a bit of anger. Anger is sometimes what's needed to sustain you through the appeal process. Resignation to your fate is not always helpful.

She tells Carrie the next thing on the list is to get the CCTV images of her car checked by an independent forensic photography analyst. 'He's a good guy. He's done some excellent work for us in the past. He can see things other experts can't seem to see.'

'Well, I really need a miracle right now,' says Carrie.

'I'll see what I can do.'

Four Years Ago

CARRIE MUST WAIT whilst a drunken man is booked in first. He's *gone a bit mental* – his words – and smashed up the front of his ex-girlfriend's house. His ex called the police and the arresting officer caught the man trying to get through the front window, which he'd shattered, to steal his own dog, and the man got away with only a minor laceration to his palm. He is sitting on the floor of the station, his head in his hands, saying, 'I've really fucked it up.' By the weary look on the custody sergeant's face, Carrie gets the impression that they've all been here before.

'Come on, Craig, stand up.'

'I need a doctor!'

'You've seen a doctor. Stand up so I can get you booked in.'

Gillian Frain leans over to Carrie and whispers in her ear, 'Shouldn't be too much longer,' and Carrie nods as if all this is very normal. In fairness to the officers, they're trying to make it all *feel* very normal. No one has yet looked at her and pointed. No one has said, 'You're being arrested for *what*?' If anything, they've gone out of their way to avoid the subject, save for Gillian who, during the journey over here, gave Carrie tidbits of what she might expect. 'You'll get something to eat . . . it's not great, but it's edible. Are you a vegetarian?' And Carrie told her she wasn't, even though in truth she rarely eats meat these days. She isn't sure it agrees with her. Her bowels tend to complain.

She looks down at the red depressions on her wrist from where the cuffs were and rubs at them with her thumb. They've left the skin itchy rather than sore. Pete wanted to cuff her to the bed back when they were first married, when he was still interested. She refused, of course. Because Pete is the kind of stupid bastard who would get sidetracked by a full bladder, or a ringing telephone, and forget all about her.

She wonders if Ella Muir liked being tied up. She wonders: Is that one of the things that made Pete so crazy about her? Is that what made him lose his head and act like a lovestruck teenager, made him fawn over her in public, have sex with her in his car on the promenade, made him make her the centre of his entire world?

'Carrie Kamara?'

She feels Gillian rise to her left. 'Ready?' she asks Carrie.

They walk towards the desk and the custody sergeant says to Gillian, 'OK, what have we got?'

'Carrie has been arrested on suspicion of the murder of Ella Muir.'

The custody sergeant nods, doing his best to keep his expression neutral, before beginning to type at the desktop computer in front of him. He wears a short-sleeved black shirt, with black epaulettes on the shoulders, which display his sergeant's chevrons. His white hair is cropped neatly to his head. He glances at Carrie. 'Do you understand why you're here?'

'Yes,' she replies.

He then asks her for some basic information: full name, address, date of birth, and as she answers she feels as if she's watching all this play out from a vantage point at the top corner of the room. She's out of her body, observing herself dispassionately, standing there, supported at the elbow by Detective Frain – which she assumes is to prevent her from falling over rather than running away. Carrie wears a T-shirt, leggings and trainers with the laces removed, and her hair, stiff with chlorine, has dried in clumps which are sticking up from her head at wild angles. Her face is make-up-free and her features are being pulled downwards. She looks sad, scared, tired and old.

'Are you taking any medication?' the custody sergeant asks.

'Just birth control.'

'And you feel all right at the moment, in full control of your faculties?'

'Yes,' she hears herself say, even though she isn't sure she could use the toilet independently right now.

The custody sergeant hits a key with his right index finger and the printer next to him springs into life. He pulls a sheet of paper from the machine and places it in front of Carrie. 'You need to have a quick read of this and then sign here, and here.'

'I don't have my glasses.'

'What strength do you use?'

'Two point five.'

He reaches beneath the desk and hands her a pair with tortoiseshell frames. 'These are two point two five,' he says. 'My spare set.' Even with the glasses, though, the words swim around on the page. She manages to make out her name and that's about it, so she signs where he indicated and slides the form back towards him. 'Lovely,' he says, before addressing Gillian: 'Pop her in number six.' And then he looks at Carrie. 'We'll keep you nice and far away from Craig. He gets quite weepy when the alcohol starts to wear off.'

'Thank you.'

Gillian now links her elbow and shepherds her towards the cells. The woodwork is newly painted in a bright cerulean blue, and the walls are an off-white. The floor is spotlessly clean. 'Eat your dinner off it,' her mother would say. Funny the things you think, Carrie marvels as she passes cells one to five. She can hear

Craig in number one booting the base of the door in a half-hearted way.

They arrive at number six and Carrie's breathing stutters. She stares at the open door and imagines it closed. She can't go in there, she realizes. If she enters she'll never get out.

She stops in her tracks and instantly she feels Gillian's body react next to her. Gillian goes from gently guiding Carrie to gripping hold of her tightly.

'This is a mistake,' Carrie whispers.

'Carrie, you—'

'No, you don't understand, I didn't do it. I didn't do what you're accusing me of. I can't go in there.'

'It's going to be OK. I promise it's going to be OK. I know this is scary but—'

'I can't go in there!'

Carrie starts to breathe heavily and her eyes bulge.

'I need help down here!' Gillian calls out.

'I can't go in there! I didn't do it! Get off me. I need to get out. My chest is burning. I don't think I can breathe.'

She shakes herself loose of Gillian's grip and backs away. Her trainers are loose on her feet and she trips a little, the right one coming completely off.

'I didn't kill her. I didn't do it.'

Gillian is holding her hands up in front of her protectively. 'Carrie, just calm down. You have nothing to be frightened of. Nothing bad will happen to you.' She turns her head in the direction they have come from. 'Terry! Terry, I need you down here!'

Nobody comes. And Gillian is simultaneously trying to protect herself from Carrie and blocking Carrie's path.

'I can't go in there.' Carrie's breath is coming out in raggedy gasps. She looks at the open doorway to cell number six and again a surge of deep panic runs through her. 'Mia,' she says to herself. 'Mia . . . I can't leave Mia.'

'TERRY!' Gillian screams. 'Where the hell are you?'

Carrie hears footsteps. She looks to her right. A uniformed officer is running towards her with the custody sergeant close behind.

The blood rushes in Carrie's ears. 'Don't touch me! Don't you dare touch me!'

'Where were you?' Gillian is saying but her question goes unanswered. 'She got to the cell and panicked. Careful with her. Careful.'

Carrie is now being dragged, her feet scrabbling beneath her, by the two male officers. 'I didn't do this!' she's shouting and she starts to vomit. She vomits down the front of her T-shirt and down the trouser leg of the custody sergeant.

'Jesus,' she hears someone say.

'I didn't do this,' she's whimpering, but she's gagging and heaving and still bringing up the contents of her stomach. They put her on the floor and step backwards away from her.

Carrie wipes at her mouth with her hand and dips her head. She's aware of the sounds of disgust, aware of the officers' heavy breathing.

'I'll be back with a towel for you,' Gillian Frain says, and then the door closes. There's a metallic thud as the bolt is thrown across.

Now

TESS AND AVRIL are travelling to Edinburgh by train. It's faster than going by car. Under normal circumstances, Tess wouldn't make this journey at all; she would get the information she required over the telephone. But Tom has instructed Tess to take Avril along to meet their various advisors in the flesh; he thinks it's important she gets a flavour of what they do, and he believes any real working relationship should begin in this way.

'I've never been to Scotland,' Avril says wistfully.

Tess raises her eyebrows. 'You only live two hours from the border.'

'I know, but I've never had call to go. Do they really drink a lot of Irn-Bru?'

'They really do.'

The train stops at Oxenholme Station – 'The Gateway to the Lake District', the sign says – and a number of Chinese tourists get on. They stand in a huddle by the doors, chattering quietly. They are looking at their tickets and Tess thinks it can't be easy: trying to navigate the rail network when neither signage nor tickets carry one familiar symbol. Really, she should help. She should point them in the right direction for their seats, but just as she's about to shift across to the aisle, they decide to move, en masse, into the adjoining carriage.

Tess goes back to examining the CCTV stills of what the prosecution claims is Carrie's car again. She could easily enlarge the digital images on her laptop, but enlarging a low-quality blurry CCTV image simply gives a larger low-quality blurry image. You can almost see less than if you were to hold it at arm's length. Tess won't find anything that hasn't already been found on these images, she knows that, but it doesn't stop her from having a go. It's all part of the fun. All part of the puzzle.

Avril unpacks her lunch and lays it out carefully on the table between them. She has two boiled eggs, a homemade salad (which she's housed in an old Flora margarine container), a sachet of salad cream, an orange Club biscuit and a carton of Ribena. With the exception of the Ribena – which Tess's mother refused to buy, claiming every single one of her teeth would fall out – this could be Tess's packed lunch from a school trip in 1983. Avril catches Tess eyeing her haul and says, quietly, 'I wasn't sure what the food would be like in Scotland,' and calls to mind those stories of Ringo Starr going to India with a suitcase full of Heinz baked beans, and the actor Sean Bean travelling with box upon box of Fray Bentos pies.

'Would you like an egg?' Avril asks as she begins peeling away the shell.

'No thanks.'

Tess glances behind her and sees the compartment is now full. The passengers won't thank Avril for the hit of hydrogen sulphide they're about to experience, particularly if the tilting action of the Pendolino carriage has already got them feeling queasy. It's not as if they can open a window. 'Are you sure?' Avril asks, and Tess nods. 'Suit yourself,' she says, just as the Chinese tourists return and begin making their way in the opposite direction. The carriage they'd gone into was first class.

Ninety minutes later they pull into Edinburgh. They pour out of Waverley Station with the rest of the passengers and head south. The trees are clinging on to the very last of their leaves and the sky is a pewter grey, but the air is mild. Jed Acton's lab is a fifteen-minute walk, on the edge of the university campus, and Tess told Avril to wear comfortable flats. Tess likes to stretch her legs after being cooped up rather than take a cab, but as they set off down the street, after only a few steps it's evident that Avril is not much of a walker. She looks at Tess, horrified by her pace, and Tess has to slow considerably to accommodate her. 'What's the great rush?' Avril says breathlessly, intimating Tess is some kind of uptight woman on a mission. Which Tess supposes she probably is.

They reach Jed's without getting wet – a small miracle in Edinburgh in mid-November – and wait outside as he finishes up with a student. Avril keeps shifting in her seat. She's excited. Tess now knows Avril well enough to tell the difference between nervousness and excitement. Avril's also still a little out of breath, even though they've been here for at least five minutes, something which Tess is trying not to judge her for.

The door opens and a young woman in her late teens wearing a white lab coat walks out. Her whole life ahead of her, Tess thinks idly, and then she finds she's thinking of herself at that age. Would she make the same choices, given her time again? Same professional, same personal decisions? If she got to the fork in the road would she still choose left instead of right? Considering this makes Tess finger the letter that's deep inside her handbag, still unopened. If she hadn't run away from that life, what would her life look like now? She probably wouldn't *be* alive, she supposes, and she tries to shake the thought. Still, she had no choice. She had no choice and yet—

'Tess!' Jed Acton has a big, booming Brian Blessed-type voice, except there's a faint trace of a Highland lilt. He's not unlike Brian in stature too. He stands in the doorway of the lab, his arms thrown wide, waiting for Tess to approach so he can pull her in and hug her fiercely. Never has Tess known a man so overtly tactile and yet so utterly benign. 'How are you, my dear?' he says into her hair, not letting her go.

'Good to see you, Jed.' Tess tries to pull away. 'Meet Avril, my colleague. I'm training Avril to do my job, so we can cover more ground.'

Jed releases Tess and steps forward, hand extended. 'Avril,' he says warmly. 'Learning from the best, are you?' and Tess can see Avril is utterly charmed.

'Very pleased to meet you,' she says.

He ushers them into the lab, which is in semi-darkness, and asks the technician, Yun – a small, neat Korean lady, whom Tess has tried to engage in conversation many times before and failed – if she'll bring them all some tea. 'I keep trying to get her to bring me alcohol but she's very much against it,' he says.

This is clearly untrue as Tess has not once visited Jed without him sipping whisky from a tumbler. He's one of those functioning alcoholics that seemed to populate Tess's youth but that you don't see so much of any more.

They settle in front of a screen. Yun brings the tea. Jed moves the mouse around until he has the stills of the CCTV that Tess was looking at on the train. 'So pleased you didn't want to do this over the phone,' Jed says. 'You know me. Never can resist a visit from such pretty girls. Don't tell Yun though,' he says as Yun pours from the teapot, 'she gets terribly jealous.' Yun pauses, looks at him pointedly, before continuing. 'See,' he mouths silently to Avril.

Tess knows Jed won't talk about the CCTV until Yun is in her technician's room, safely out of earshot, so she fills the air with some small talk. 'Been busy, Jed?'

'Aye. Either that or I'm getting slower. Can't tell which.'

'How's Veronica? It's Newcastle she's at . . .?'

'Durham . . . She reckons she's learned all she needs to know now and we're wasting our hard-earned money paying for university.'

Tess smiles. Yun adds milk to each cup without asking their preferences, and then disappears. Tess gestures to the screen. 'What d'you reckon?'

Jed sighs. 'What are you hoping for here, Tess?'

'I'm hoping you'll go against what the expert for the prosecution said and tell me that these are two different cars. One Honda going towards Ella's house and another Honda coming back. We have a time frame now that's workable, a time frame which would make it hard for Carrie Kamara to carry out murder within it, but it would be a real coup if you could tell me these are two different cars altogether, Jed. It would be a huge step towards exonerating Carrie.'

'No can do, I'm afraid,' Jed says and points to the screen. 'You see the way this spoiler here is reflecting the light? It's chrome. Which means the vehicle's a limited edition.'

Tess leans in. 'OK.'

'They're a lot less common than the average Honda CR-V,' he says, 'and in a town the size of Morecambe, chances are there's maybe one, perhaps two at the most. I'd say it's almost certain that this is the same car. And' – he pauses and looks at Tess sadly – 'the car Carrie Kamara drove wasn't an ordinary CR-V, Tess. It was a limited edition.'

'Oh.'

'I'm sorry.'

'I wasn't aware of that.'

'Wish I had better news for you, my dear.'

Tess nods. *A point for the prosecution.*

Now

B RIGHT AND EARLY the following day, Tess and Avril are outside 'P. J. Kamara Estate Agents, Sales & Lettings'. It's a single-storey, flat-roofed, felt-topped oddity of a building. Tess vaguely remembers it being a hairdresser's when she was a kid, and then, later on, an Indian takeaway.

'So, you're still thinking it's definitely Carrie's car in both those CCTV stills?' Avril asks.

On the train on the way home yesterday, they'd mulled over Jed's verdict. And yes, until they had the actual number of limited-edition white Honda CR-Vs in the Morecambe Bay area at the time of Ella's death, they couldn't say for certain whether it was Carrie's car or not. But if she had to call it, Tess thinks it's unlikely they're going to find more than one. Which is a blow. A real blow. Because up until now, she's found no reason to doubt Carrie's version of events. Everything she's said adds up and is provable.

So now there is uncertainty. And Tess doesn't like uncertainty. Even though she reminds herself that every case she's ever worked on was uncertain. The truth is never clear-cut. Stuff happens. An innocent man is in the wrong place at the wrong time and suddenly his life is turned upside down and he finds himself in prison.

But Carrie is adamant she never left her house that evening. And she's also adamant no one broke *into* her house and took her car. Carrie said she knows this for a fact because she liked to read in the small second lounge at the front of the house in the evening, the lounge without a TV, the lounge that Pete never frequented because there *was no TV*, so it was considered Carrie's space, a space away from blaring football matches, the depressing local news, the stupid survival programmes that Pete liked to watch, a space that looked out over the front garden, and over her car. And she says it never moved.

'I think it's possible that the Honda in those pictures *is* Carrie's car,' Tess says in answer to Avril's question.

'But what about the time frame?' Avril asks. 'We measured the time it took to get from the camera to Ella's, and it was impossible.'

'Not totally impossible. We showed there could be an alternate version of events to what the prosecution claimed was fact, that's all.'

Avril is put out. 'So, now you think she *did* do it? You think she went around there that night and killed Ella?'

'I didn't say that. But I think she could be lying to us about using her car. People lie, Avril. And prisoners lie *a lot*.'

'But she seems so genuine.'

'She does,' replies Tess.

'So I really don't see how she *could* be lying.'

Tess cuts the radio. She turns in her seat to face Avril. 'OK, here's something you need to know about people who commit premeditated murder . . . They're cold-blooded individuals who do not operate like the rest of us. Except you already know that. Of course you know that. But . . . do you think those individuals are capable of elaborate lies to cover up their crimes? Do you think they're willing to pretend to be devastated about what's happened to them? Do you think they're able to hoodwink well-meaning individuals such as yourself?'

Avril doesn't answer.

'Really think about it,' continues Tess. 'Consider what it would take for you to go around to Ella Muir's house and plunge a knife into her. Consider the state of mind you'd have to be in to do that. Could you do it?'

'You know I couldn't.'

'But someone did. And is that person capable of delivering a slew of lies to try to prove their innocence?'

Avril closes her eyes. 'OK, I get your point.'

'Prisoners are, by and large, liars,' says Tess. 'And it's our job to figure out which ones are the exception.'

Avril takes a boiled sweet from her handbag. She offers one to Tess. Tess declines. They make her teeth itch. Avril's going to have to become a lot more sceptical if she's going to make a go of this job; she'll have to take what she thinks of as facts and pull them apart until she's sure they're not facts at all.

'We've really no idea what's going through Carrie Kamara's head,' Tess says. 'She could have done it . . .' She pauses, takes a breath. '. . . but then again, she could be telling the truth, and it could simply be that the CCTV camera *itself* is inaccurate.' Avril looks at her wide-eyed. 'Those things are hardly high-tech,' Tess continues. 'People purchase them cheaply, and it could very well be that Carrie's car was recorded on that camera the night before the murder or even the night after.'

'But how do you even prove something like that?'

'You don't. You move on and take apart the next piece of evidence until you find something that—' Tess glances in her rear-view mirror. Did a green Subaru Forester just drive past? She snatches her head to the left.

She's imagining it, she thinks.

Conjuring up images.

She does this when her brain is working overtime. She needs to get more sleep.

Just before 9 a.m., a Kia Picanto pulls up at the side of Tess and a woman with stiff hair and exceptionally thin legs gets out. She marches towards the entrance, holding a key out in front of her, ready to put it into the lock. They give her a moment and then follow her inside. The woman introduces herself as June. 'The assistant to Peter Kamara,' she says officiously. She is a sour-faced woman whose make-up comes to an abrupt halt halfway down her neck, giving the impression of her having swapped heads with another person. She is immediately suspicious of Tess and Avril.

'You can wait there,' she tells them, pointing to some chairs over in the corner of the room. In front of the chairs is a low table and on it is a stack of well-thumbed *House Beautiful* magazines. Tess picks one up and flicks through it idly. She is admiring a kitchen extension in Gloucestershire which the owner of the house declares to have been 'a labour of love, but so absolutely worth it', while surreptitiously watching Pete Kamara's assistant set up her workspace. This is the woman who provided Pete's alibi. 'Never left the office until six fifteen,' she said in her statement, which Pete's phone records supported as he made a phone call to a client just before that. Tess flicks over the page and lingers on some images of homemade Christmas wreaths, wondering if she'll ever have the kind of life in which making one was a possibility, when she hears an engine revving loudly outside.

The door opens and in steps Pete Kamara. Two minutes after that and assistant June is closing the door on Pete's office, so Tess and Avril can talk to him without prospective house buyers listening in. Pete is in his late forties. His hair is dyed two shades too dark and his shirt's straining slightly across his middle. But he's still got it. Or at least he thinks he has anyway. He sits at his desk with his hands behind his head, enjoying Tess and Avril's full attention.

'How is the old witch, anyway?' he asks, referring to Carrie. 'I heard she'd got someone to fight her case for her. Well, I can tell you right now you're wasting your time.'

Tess takes out a notepad. 'I'm curious, Mr Kamara,' she says, 'what is it that attracted you to Carrie in the first place? Because it's clear there's no love lost between the two of you now.'

Pete looks up to the ceiling, as if casting his mind back. 'Do you know what I mean by the phrase: *Je ne sais quoi*?' he asks.

'"I do not know what",' translates Tess.

'Ah, well, let me define it for you . . . It means "a certain something",' Pete says, mansplaining magnificently. 'It's something you can't put your finger on. Carrie, at least when she was younger, anyway, had that.'

Tess glances at Avril and sees Avril is smiling broadly at Pete's gaffe. Pete is unaware.

'You didn't support her when she was arrested, as I understand it?' Tess says.

'Because she murdered Ella.'

'Yes, but you didn't know that right away.'

'Who else would it be?'

'But this is your wife we're talking about. You really never once thought to question that Carrie might be innocent? You didn't question it, not even for the sake of your daughter?'

At this Pete sighs wearily. He drops his arms down and seems to drop weaponry at the same time. 'That's the one thing I would change in all of this if I could.'

'Mia?' asks Tess.

He nods.

'I'm told you're not in touch with her.'

'She won't speak to me,' he says. 'I keep trying to be in her life but . . .' He makes a helpless gesture. 'She's completely shut me out.'

'That must be very hard.'

'She's my only child and it's not like I'm going to have any more. Obviously, it's all down to Carrie,' he says resignedly. 'If she wasn't so intent on poisoning Mia against me, I might have a chance. As it stands, Mia won't have anything to do with me. I'll keep trying, because that's what you do, isn't it, when you're a parent? You never give up.'

Pete looks out of the window, his brow furrowed, before pulling down the lower lid of his right eye and making as though he's removing a lash caught next to the jelly of the eye. Is this a show? Tess wonders fleetingly. A demonstration of his heartache?

Not having the measure of the man yet, she can't tell.

She decides to move things along. 'When we spoke to Carrie recently she seemed quite adamant that she had no problem at all with your relationship with Ella.'

'She would say that.'

'Would she?'

'Wouldn't you say that, if you were in her position?'

'Are you saying she absolutely *did* have a problem with Ella? Because Carrie states that she was used to you seeing other women. She states Ella was no different.'

'Well, she went round there, didn't she?'

'To ask Ella to be more discreet. She felt the two of you were being too open with your relationship.'

Pete doesn't answer straight away. He just looks at Tess as if to say she's being a bit of an idiot by believing all of Carrie's lies. When he does finally speak he says this: 'Carrie had two issues with Ella. One, she thought Ella was too lower class, a bit rough. Not that I cared, but Ella was brought up in a council house, and for some reason – you'll have to ask her why – it irked Carrie that I was running around with a girl like that. Her other issue was that she couldn't stand to see me happy. So Carrie went around to Ella's house and she threatened her. She told her if she didn't stay away from me, she'd kill her. You don't believe me? Go and ask Carrie.'

As they drive away, Avril is shaking her head. 'Bloody hell,' she says, 'it's as if he's making out like those women were fighting over him.'

'That's the way he sees it.'

'He seems like a bit of a dick,' says Avril.

'He *is* a bit of a dick,' replies Tess. 'But that doesn't mean he's lying.'

Avril thinks about this. After a moment, she says, 'Can I ask *you* a question?'

'Sure.'

'It's something personal.'

'OK.'

'You don't have to answer, not if you don't want to.'

'Well, how about you give me the question?'

'OK,' Avril says, 'why is it that you don't have a proper relationship with Clive?'

This throws Tess for a second. 'I don't have a proper relationship with Clive, as you put it, because Clive is married.'

'Yeah, I know that, but how come you're OK with that? I mean, most women would want more. I think *Ella* probably wanted more, don't you? She didn't want to be the other woman for ever.'

Tess nods, seeing her point.

'I'd say most women would want what I've got,' continues Avril. 'They want to wake up with a partner. They want to feel supported. They want to share their lives with the person they love. Why don't you want that?'

'Is that your question?'

'Yes. If it's not too personal a thing for you to talk about. Because you seem like a really nice person. And you seem like you have your head screwed on, and your life together. And, you know, you're great at your job and stuff, and you're clever. And I actually think you're still really pretty, so I don't get it.'

'It's just not my thing.'

'Really?' asks Avril.

Tess shrugs.

'You really don't want to be loved?'

And Tess laughs. 'Maybe I don't *deserve* to be loved.'

At this, Avril looks at Tess as though she may have lost her head entirely. 'That's ridiculous,' Avril says dismissively. 'Everyone deserves to be loved.'

'Do they?'

Now

TESS IS ASLEEP.

She's dreaming. It's the same dream she has every night. Always the same – whereby she relives a pivotal moment of her life over and over.

She's learning to drive and the day is hot. Tess can feel the heat pressing down on her, feel the humidity in the air making it hard to breathe. Tess's mother is in the passenger seat and she is beautiful. Still only in her thirty-eighth year, Angela is wearing cut-offs, a clingy vest top without a bra, and thong sandals with leather ankle straps that make her legs look long and lean. Tess's mother's hair is streaked blonde from the sun and she has pretty laughter lines around her eyes. She has her feet up on the dashboard and a cigarette in her hand and Tess knows, knows without a doubt, that she'll never be as beautiful as her mother.

Tess drives along the promenade. She has her eyes fixed front and her hands glued to the wheel. If she were to take her eyes away from the road for just one second, if she were to glance north-west, Tess would see that the Lake District fells are looking particularly splendid this afternoon, appearing pink in the midday sun. But Tess does not do this. She does not glance north-westwards. Instead, Tess grips the wheel even more tightly as she checks her rear-view mirror, where she sees a long line of cars is beginning to form behind her.

Tess is already a nervous driver and this makes things worse. She doesn't want to hold the drivers up but she is frightened to increase her speed. Really, she should have the courage to let go, she should press on the accelerator and allow the people behind to get on with their day. She's been learning to drive for three weeks already and this resistance to speed is getting embarrassing.

So, she goes for it. She *makes* herself do it. She presses on the gas a little, a little more even, and just as she's starting to pull away, astonishingly, she hears the clunk-click of her mother's seatbelt, and, seemingly out of nowhere, her mother is clambering between the seats, trying to reach something in the back of the car.

'What are you doing? What the hell's wrong with you?' yells Tess.

Angela is laughing. 'I need a mint. Do you want one?'

'No, I don't *want* one. Of course I don't *want* one. Can't you see I can't drive and eat at the same time?'

Tess is rattled by her mother's brazen disregard for basic safety as Angela continues to laugh and so she focuses more intently on the road. And it's a good job really because up ahead a toddler has broken free from his mother's grasp and is running. He is running and running. His chubby legs carry him across the promenade towards the Winter Gardens and his expression is set. He's a determined little fucker, Tess is thinking, as his arms pump hard, and his legs carry him faster, faster, towards the road, and Tess realizes that if she hadn't seen him he would most likely be pulled beneath her wheels, and she would be destroyed by this incident and would never drive again.

But she does see him. And whatever it is, instinct, or some deeply buried aptitude that makes Tess a preserver of life, forces her right foot across on to the brake, whilst fractions of a second later she depresses the clutch, and the car stops dead. Without her seatbelt on though, her mother is thrown hard against the dashboard, but is, astonishingly, left unharmed.

In the split seconds afterwards, Tess and Angela share a look of stupefied relief. The child is OK. *They're* OK. Tess did it. She stopped the car. How the hell did that happen? Her mother even gives out another small laugh. 'My girl,' she says, and goes to squeeze Tess's arm. 'You are a bloody *great* driver!' she declares, just as they are slammed from behind.

This time Angela will not bounce back from the dashboard and smile at her daughter. She will not say, 'My girl.' Instead, she will stare at Tess, no life at all behind her eyes. And Tess will hear, not her mother's voice, but a high-pitched keening sound. A sound that will remain even when they pull her mother's body from the car. Even when, a week later, they lay her in the ground.

Tess wakes from the dream and shoots upright in bed. She's aware she's been dreaming. The same dream. Unusually for her though, this time she wakes and she is covered in sweat. Her bed-clothes are soaked right the way through and her heart is pounding as if it might break free from her chest. Tess tries to calm herself. She inhales deeply and as she does her mother's lovely face fills her vision. 'My girl,' she says to Tess. 'I love you. I miss you.'

This is *not* what happens.

This is not what happens when Tess wakes. Ordinarily, when the dream is over, her mother's face disappears and Tess will not be able to conjure it without looking at a photograph. Ordinarily she only sees her mother in her dreams.

Tess scrambles from the bed. She flicks on the light and imme-diately she's blinded and has to feel her way around the room until her eyes adjust. She's filled with an urgency. An urgency to find her handbag. She needs it; she must have it.

Tess squints, allowing a small amount of light to enter between her eyelids, while at the same time using the toe of her right foot to poke and prod the floor, exploring as she goes.

She discovers the bag wedged partially between the bedside table and a potted plant and she empties the entire contents on the floor. There's a year's worth of crap inside. Squatting down, she opens her eyes just as much as she can bear while scavenging through the rubbish until she finds the letter.

The letter.

Why must she read the letter now? She isn't entirely sure, and yet, after many years, after many *letters*, she is compelled to do so. Could it have been Avril's words, spoken to Tess today: *You really don't want to be loved?* Could Avril's words have triggered something?

Sitting on the edge of the bed, Tess holds the letter with both hands. She cradles it. It seems too beautiful to open. But she does open it. And she begins to read:

I wish I knew your name.

Whenever I write to you, I toy with the idea of writing 'Dear Mum'. But I wonder if that might scare you off for ever?

Tess winces. Forces herself to read on:

Do you read these letters? I don't think you do. I expect you've never read one. Sometimes I fantasize about putting in a code word, and I'll be – I don't know – standing at the checkout, in the queue at the bank, and you'll whisper it from behind. And I won't even turn around, but I'll know you're there and that you've been looking out for me. That you love me.

Stupid, I know. Stupid, because I know you don't read what I write or you'd have made contact already, and it's clear to me you don't want to do that. And stupid, because you've no idea what I look like.

I've enclosed a picture of myself this time. Just in case you feel differently. But I know I'm wasting my time. You don't want me. Can you imagine what that feels like? Can you?

Anyway, the picture – do I look like you? I've always wondered . . .

Tess picks up the envelope and takes out the photograph. The girl is fresh-faced with clear skin and bright, bright eyes. Her hair is fashioned into a distinctive Heidi braid: two plaits pinned across the top of her head, and she looks a lot like Tess. Her own daughter looks a lot like her and for some reason this comes as a complete surprise.

I need to tell you something. It's sad. I'm still very sad.

My beautiful mother, Marianne, who I know you never met, lost her battle with cancer in September and

Tess folds the letter in half abruptly.

This must have been what Bill Menzies meant when he told her there had been *some developments*. Things had *changed*. Why the hell didn't he tell Tess her daughter's adoptive mother had died?

Tess slides the letter back inside the envelope along with the picture. She cannot read on.

She turns off the light and crawls back between the sheets.

They're damp and cold and feel like punishment.

Now

APART FROM THE caravan park, it is perhaps Morecambe's most depressed residential area. Windows are boarded up. Cars are on bricks. Children too young to be unaccompanied play alone in the street. Tess spots a lone toddler waddling along the pavement, wearing a nappy that's long needed changing. It's hanging low between his knees, the weight of the urine pulling it down.

As they drive, Tess is checking house numbers, but they don't seem to follow any logical order. Most, in fact, don't display a number at all, so she's making slow progress.

'And then William finally tells me that he prefers it if I *don't* shave my legs in the bath,' Avril says. 'And I'm like, how long have you been keeping that piece of information to yourself?' If Avril is aware Tess is trying to concentrate, she's not showing it. She's prattling on, relentless as always. She's supposed to be taking more of a lead. That's what they've discussed. Avril is here to learn how to do the job, so she needs to start *doing the job*.

Tess decides she's going the wrong way so she executes not a particularly good three-point turn in the road. She touches the kerb twice. Is that an automatic fail? she ponders. She'd never pass her driving test today.

'But I do think sometimes we're just *too* compatible,' Avril continues on, unabated. 'Does that make sense? Like it's one thing finishing each other's sentences, but I wonder if when you know what the other person's thinking most of the time, I wonder, is that actually a good thing?'

Tess has no idea if she's even on the right road now and she wishes Avril would just shut up or else talk about someone other than William as she tries to figure out where she is. Eventually, she loses her temper and snaps, 'Does it always have to be about William? Don't you have any *friends*?'

And Avril glares back at her. 'Don't *you*?'

Another ten minutes of toing and froing and Tess eventually finds number 35 Coronation Drive. She finds a parking space a little further along where a man is working beneath the bonnet of his car. As they climb out, he raises his can of Tennent's Extra at Avril and eyes her legs. 'I like fat girls,' he tells Avril appreciatively, and Tess tells him to fuck off.

'You're sure you're still OK to take the lead?' she asks Avril as they approach the pathway to the house. The front garden is mostly weeds with some white plastic furniture, blackened with mildew, upended and scattered about.

'I'm sure,' replies Avril brightly.

But Tess can hear the quaver in her voice. 'Do you want me to run through the introduction one more time?'

'No, I've got it.' Then Avril swallows and smooths down her skirt in readiness.

Tess knocks on the door and steps back a little behind Avril so they don't look like a pair of Jehovah's Witnesses. The door is opened by a stringy-looking guy in his late twenties. He doesn't say hello, just eyes them suspiciously from beneath his baseball cap. Avril clears her throat. 'Good afternoon. Is Mrs Muir at home?'

The man turns; he yells, 'Mam!' over his shoulder, before disappearing inside. A dog barks from within. A small toy thing, Tess supposes, from the pitch of its yaps. Avril smooths down her skirt again and Tess has the urge to step forward and take over, before reminding herself that Avril is more than capable of doing this. And she has to start some time.

A fierce, pit bull-like woman in her fifties appears. She's around four feet ten inches, and is almost as round as she is tall. She wears a cleaning overall and is lighting a king-size cigarette. This is Ella Muir's mother: Tess recognizes her from the TV footage of Carrie's trial. Ella must have got her looks from her father.

'Mrs Muir?' Avril asks.

'What?'

'Mrs Muir, I'm Avril Hughes. We're from the charity Innocence UK, and we're looking into an alleged miscarriage of justice that involves your daughter's case.'

This seems to pique Ella's mum's interest. Her name is Sandra. Tess knows this from the case files. 'Our Ella?' she asks.

'That's right,' replies Avril.

Sandra frowns. She takes a drag on her cigarette and waves it around in a gesture of *go on*.

'Well,' says Avril, gaining in confidence, 'it's possible that evidence presented by the prosecution in court against Carrie Kamara—'

'Who?'

'Carrie Kamara.'

'Hang on. You're working for the woman who killed Ella?'

Avril hesitates. 'Yes,' she says quietly. 'But I'd really like to explain wh—'

Sandra switches her cigarette to her left hand before drawing back her right arm. Her face is without emotion as she throws a hard punch. A punch straight at Avril's face.

Avril is knocked to the ground.

And Tess rushes to her side.

The front door is slammed shut.

*

The Royal Lancaster Infirmary is four miles from Morecambe. Morecambe itself is too small to warrant an A & E department so Tess drives, with Avril whimpering quietly, holding against her nose a wad of tissues which Tess keeps in the car specifically for hay fever season. Tess does her best to avoid potholes and drives carefully, as someone might with a newborn in the car.

'You get checked in and I'll find somewhere to park,' she tells Avril when they arrive. Tess should've talked to Ella's mother herself. She has a sixth sense for impending violence and she knows when to duck. Stupid of her to allow Avril to make the introduction. What had she been thinking? But Avril had insisted she wanted to take the lead, had persuaded Tess when Tess had aired doubts, and so now here they are.

She finds Avril in a cubicle. She's already been booked in, her nose has been packed by a nurse and now she is waiting to see a doctor. 'Fast service,' remarks Tess, and Avril answers by blinking her eyes twice. She's having difficulty talking, Tess presumes, so she sits beside Avril and waits in silence for the doctor to arrive. This takes close to an hour and during this time Avril does not say one word.

'Are you OK?' Tess asks her every fifteen minutes or so and Avril blinks her response. Eventually a young medic pops his head around the curtain and upon seeing Avril's bloodied nose, as well as her eyes – which are already starting to blacken – he asks if Avril's been offered pain relief.

'Yes,' she manages bravely.

He smiles and comes closer. He angles the lamp towards Avril's face and says, 'I'll need to take a proper look if that's OK?' And then he pulls on some surgical gloves before gently beginning to extract the packing from inside Avril's nose.

Avril's eyes widen in fear. She makes a primitive sound, a sound almost bovine in nature, as the packing begins to come loose, and Tess winces and has to look away. She's not a natural when it comes to ministering to the infirm. In fact, Clive reckons she would've made a 'bloody godawful nurse', but she thinks that's unfair.

Twenty minutes later and Avril is freshly packed, a large dressing across her nose, and for some reason she is now being remarkably stubborn. Tess has been arguing with her for some time and cannot fathom what on earth is wrong with the girl.

'He'll *want* to know,' repeats Tess sternly.

'I don't *want* him to know,' replies Avril.

'But he's your boyfriend.'

'So?'

'So he needs to know.'

'I don't want him to know! I don't want him to see me like this!'

Tess exhales. They'd left Avril's car in a layby this morning rather than make the journey to Morecambe in two vehicles and Tess is not happy to leave it there overnight. But after the amount of pain medication Avril has received, she's not happy about Avril driving it home independently either. She could really do with speaking to William about this, arranging to collect him and dropping him at Avril's car, but Avril is flat out refusing.

'Look,' Tess tries now, a softer approach, 'he really cares about you. He'll want to help and he won't want you to go through this without him knowing. Let me call him and stop being so silly.'

Avril shakes her head.

And Tess has no choice but to press her further.

'Pass me your bag,' she tells Avril. 'I'll call William and explain what's happened. I'll tell him you're pretty banged up so he'll know what to expect. He's not going to dump you, Avril, just because you got your nose broken. I can't believe you're worrying about this.' Tess reaches across the bed and grabs Avril's handbag. She'll just have to overrule her in this instance for safety purposes and if Avril has a problem with that then—

'Don't,' Avril says and she seizes Tess's hand.

Tess pulls her hand away, crossly. 'What d'you mean: *Don't?* You're always going on about what a caring guy he is. Well, let's see him in action, because he's really not going to—'

'Don't call him.'

'Why not? C'mon, Avril. This is getting—'

'Because he doesn't exist!' Avril cries out.

Tess stops.

Her mouth drops open and she looks at Avril as if to say, *You have got to be kidding me.*

'I made him up,' whimpers Avril. 'I'm sorry, but I made him up.'

Tess closes her eyes. 'Jesus Christ.'

Now

'YOU THINK I'M ridiculous,' says Avril.

Tess does. A little bit. But she's trying not to show it. They are in the hospital canteen, both nursing cups of coffee, and Avril's battered face is drawing questioning looks from both nursing staff on their breaks and visiting relatives. 'I don't think you're ridiculous,' says Tess.

'You think I'm pathetic for inventing a boyfriend.'

'No, I don't.'

'You must.'

Tess puts down her cup. 'Why are you telling me what I'm thinking? You don't know what I'm thinking.'

'You think I'm stupid.'

'I don't,' Tess tells her. 'I'm not judging you.'

Tess picks her cup up again and sips her coffee. The coffee is neither good nor bad and she's trying to remember a time when she was last served a really lousy cup. Everyone has upped their game. She kind of misses the old days. Everyone's such a bloody connoisseur now; it can all be rather wearing.

'I do it so people won't ask,' Avril says quietly.

'Do what?'

'I do it so they won't be all, *Do you have a boyfriend?* and when I tell them that I don't, they feel they have to comment on my weight.'

Tess raises her eyebrows. 'People do that?'

'Not directly. But they tell me what diet their mother's on, or what diet's working for their sister.'

'How helpful,' remarks Tess.

'I did have a boyfriend,' Avril continues, as if Tess hasn't spoken, 'in the summer. I had this guy I was kind of into. But he was sleeping with someone else.' Avril rolls her eyes. 'I found out she was a big girl too . . . so it was like a fetish thing.' Avril adds more sugar to her cup and stirs.

'You'll meet someone.'

'To be honest, I'm not even that bothered. I'm pretty happy by myself, but I get sick of all the questions, you know? People asking why I've not settled down. Acting like there's something wrong with me.'

'I think I know how *that* is,' replies Tess, half-smiling, referring to Avril's interrogation of her own love life the day before.

'Oh, yeah, sorry about that.'

A guy in a shirt and tie with a stethoscope slung around his shoulders sits at the table next to them. He has two cheeseburgers on his tray and two cans of orange Fanta. Systematically, he eats around the outside edge of each burger until he has two perfect mini burgers left in the centre of his plate.

'So,' Tess says, dragging her attention away. 'William?'

'Oh, he was completely made up,' replies Avril. 'He's not even *based* on a real person.'

'You were very . . .' Tess pauses. 'You were very thorough in your description of your life together.'

'Too much?'

'A little. Maybe. You might want to tone it down a bit in future. It'd be kinder to the person listening.'

Avril smiles. 'Gotcha. Maybe it's time to be done with all that now. I reckon I'm going to take a leaf out of your book. You live your life the way you want to. You're single; you're independent.

You don't care what people think of the way you do things. You're not afraid of their questions. I admire that.'

'I certainly don't have it all figured out.'

'From where I'm sitting, you do.'

Avril lifts her coffee to her mouth and winces when the rim of the cup touches her nose.

Tess watches as a lone tear escapes Avril's left eye and trickles down her face, absorbed into the dressing running across her nose.

'It's nothing,' Avril says when she sees Tess has noticed. 'My eye's weeping from the punch. I'm fine. Honestly.'

Tess can see that Avril has a sensible reason for making up a boyfriend, she can see how that could work for her, but whatever she is saying now, however brave she's attempting to be, Tess knows there's a loneliness underneath regardless.

'Don't go thinking I have all the answers,' Tess says quietly.

'I don't.'

'We're all fuck-ups. Everyone is just walking around doing the best they can.'

Avril is looking at Tess as if to say, *Thank you for being nice. Thanks for trying to make me feel better.* She smiles at Tess gratefully and Tess feels like a complete fraud.

'We've all done things we're not proud of,' she tells Avril.

And Avril nods her head repeatedly, while taking a tissue from her pocket and dabbing at her eyes.

'Everyone has secrets. Everyone wishes they were better than they are.'

'I know. It's all right. You don't have to—'

Tess closes her eyes. And against her better judgement, says, 'OK. OK, listen, this is not something I like to talk about but . . .' She pauses. Sighs heavily before continuing, 'I had a baby. I had a baby girl when I had just turned eighteen.'

Avril opens her mouth to say something, before closing it again quickly.

'My mother died in a car accident,' Tess explains. 'I was driving. Not my fault but . . . well, maybe I thought it was my fault. Anyway, that's not why I got pregnant. My dad had shacked up with another woman overnight, and I suppose I couldn't cope with it. I hated her for being there. She was *always* there, cooking in my mum's kitchen, lying in her bath, lying in her bed. She was there all the time and the worst thing was that my dad acted like a completely different person around her. He was like a stranger and it was weird, uncomfortable. Unbearable, actually. So I . . . well, I'm not exactly sure what I was thinking, I was very young, but I started going out a lot. I didn't want to be in the same house as them and I found a friend who also had a shitty home life and she wanted to be out as much as possible too. So out we went and needless to say we got attention from the wrong type of men. Older men. Men who should have known better but didn't. They saw these scrappy, angry, skinny girls and they gave us attention. And alcohol. And we had sex with them because it made us feel powerful and, I don't know, the attention made us feel a little less angry for a while, I suppose.'

'And you got pregnant.'

Tess nods. 'Yeah, and my dad kicked me out. But I didn't get pregnant in the way you might think. I got pregnant because I *wanted* to get pregnant. I did it on purpose. I think I must have been desperately lonely, craving love, missing my mother, all of those things, and I thought, stupidly, I could create my own family. I thought I could get all the love I needed from a child.'

'What happened to her?' Avril asks carefully.

'Ultimately, I couldn't look after her. I tried really hard, but, you know, babies cry, she actually wouldn't *stop* crying, and even though I knew all of that before I got pregnant, when you're on your own, and it's endless, and there's no one to help, and you're broke, and scared, and you begin to not trust yourself around your own baby because of something you might do, well . . .'

Avril is quiet. Taking it in.

'I'm sorry that happened to you,' she says after a moment.

'Yeah.' Tess shrugs. 'It was my own fault though. I could tell you I tried my best, but I know in my heart that I didn't. I could've tried harder. I could've done more to keep her. I gave up on the whole thing. I gave up too soon.'

'I'm sure you did everything you could, you were so young, you were only eighteen—'

'No, Avril. I gave up.'

Four Years Ago

CARRIE DOESN'T KNOW how long she's been locked inside the police cell as she isn't wearing a watch. She can smell vomit on her clothes and her throat is dry and sore. She has been offered a microwavable lasagne but declined. She cannot eat. She wonders if she'll ever be able to eat.

They won't answer her questions. She's asked about Mia. Asked if anyone has told Pete that he needs to collect Mia from school. But all they'll tell her is that she needs to keep calm and someone will deal with her shortly.

What if Mia is waiting? What if she's panicking because Carrie isn't there to pick her up?

Carrie bangs on the door again. 'Please!' she shouts. 'Please, someone help me in here.'

But no one does.

They think she's murdered Pete's girlfriend. They think she's capable of murdering another living, breathing human being. She looks down at her hands. She examines them, turns them over so that the palms face up. What is it that's led them to think this way? What has she done to make them jump to this wild conclusion?

There's a noise: the sound of a bar striking metal. Carrie looks at the door and sees the service hatch is open. The top of Gillian Frain's face fills the rectangular space and she surveys Carrie coldly before speaking. 'You can make a phone call.'

'What about Mia?'

'You can make one phone call. Are you calm, Carrie? I don't want a repeat of what happened earlier.'

'What about Mia?'

'Can we trust you to remain calm?'

Carrie hesitates. There's so much she needs to tell them. So much they need to know before they keep her here like this. 'I'm calm.'

The detective closes the hatch and Carrie hears the bolt being thrown back. The door opens slowly and of course Gillian Frain is there, as well as another officer who is new to Carrie. 'There's nowhere to run,' Detective Frain says. 'Can we trust you to walk slowly and sensibly to the custody officer without making a scene?'

Slowly and sensibly.

Inside her head she's screaming *no*. The noise is deafening. It's so loud she can barely think. 'Yes,' she says. 'No scene.'

Carrie's eyes dart from side to side. She knows there is no way out, but this doesn't stop her from frantically trying to find an escape route. She feels Gillian Frain's hand on her elbow, guiding her, and she wants to shake her off. 'Just to the right,' Gillian says, and Carrie lets herself be guided like a docile farm animal. *No scene,* she's saying over and over inside her head. *No scene.*

She approaches the desk and she's aware of the custody sergeant's eyes landing on the vomit crusted on the front of her T-shirt. She dips her head so she doesn't have to meet his gaze and when he tells her she's free to use the phone on the desk she merely nods her response. She had thought this part would be done in private. In the movies, the prisoner makes his call away from the prying eyes of those who've incarcerated him. But that doesn't seem to be the case here so she picks up the phone and she dials Pete's mobile.

It goes to voicemail.

She presses redial, without asking if this is allowed.

Voicemail again.

Her hand is shaking.

On the third attempt, he picks up.

He doesn't speak though, he doesn't say hello, but she can hear him breathing. His breathing is laboured and she can hear the anger in it, hear the hatred as it goes in and out of him.

'Pete,' she says, the word half-dying in her throat.

'Carrie.'

'I'm at the police station. They arrested me.'

'I know where you are.'

Relief washes over her. Even though she's aware of the hostility in Pete, he knows what's happened at least.

'Mia's home,' he says. 'I told her you'd had to go for some tests.'

'Tests?'

'Yeah, like cancer tests or something.'

'Pete, can't you tell her something else?'

'I didn't know what to tell her! How was I supposed to know what to tell her? Don't go lecturing me on what to say to my own daughter when you've done this to yourself.'

Suddenly Carrie's mind is perfectly clear. The dissociated feeling she's had since the police escorted her from the swimming pool is gone and she's back inside her own body again. Finally, she can think. 'I need a lawyer, Pete.'

'I can't help you.'

'Can't?'

Carrie looks at the custody sergeant. He's reading the screen in front of him but he's listening. Of course, he's listening. They're all listening.

She lowers her voice to a whisper, turning her back on the sergeant. 'If we don't find a lawyer, they'll provide one. You do know they're talking about murder? If I don't find decent representation . . .' She doesn't finish the sentence. He knows how this works. She doesn't have to spell it out to him.

'I can't help you, Carrie.'

'I didn't do this!' she flares. 'You know I didn't.'

'I don't know anything any more.'

'Pete. Don't leave me here. Don't do that! Don't leave me when you know I had nothing to do with this. You know I couldn't. Christ, I didn't even care what you were doing. You know that!'

Pete is not speaking.

But she knows he's there. She can hear his breath sounds again. She can feel his loathing coming at her down the phone line.

She makes her voice barely audible. 'Don't you dare leave me here after what you've put me through, you fucker.'

And the line goes dead.

Now

NIGHT HAS FALLEN by the time they leave the hospital and there is a noticeable pinch in the air. The temperature is dropping fast and already the paving stones outside the main entrance are becoming glassy with frost. Avril is a little unsteady on her feet after the blow to her face, so Tess stays close, ready to catch her.

There is still the problem of Avril's car, of course. Now that there's no William to speak of, Tess decides it will have to remain in the layby for the night and Avril is compliant with this. She's sure her dad will collect it with her in the morning, explaining he won't want to come out now, as 'He doesn't like to drive in the dark.'

They make their way towards the car park. 'Don't take this the wrong way,' Tess says, 'but I'm kind of glad I don't have to spend any more time listening to how great William is.'

Avril smiles. 'Yeah, he was beginning to get on my nerves as well.'

They make slow progress. Tess has Avril's handbag, along with her own, slung over her shoulder, and she's taking care to pick out the best route as Avril says the dressing across her nose is compromising her vision somewhat. They cross behind an ambulance and Tess is just thinking how poorly lit the car park is when a figure steps out, seemingly from nowhere, blocking their path. Instinctively, she grabs Avril's arm, and she feels the tension in Avril's body escalate when Avril lifts her eyes from the floor and sees the figure before them.

It's a man. A young man. He's dressed completely in black and as Tess goes to step around him, trying to give him a wide berth, he holds up his hand. 'Wait,' he says. He has an edgy energy and the two women are immediately on guard. Tess glances behind her. She's looking for help should this turn nasty but sees there is no one. 'You came to my house,' the man says, and he gestures to Avril's nose. 'My mam gave you that. I'm Kyle Muir.'

Tess now realizes who the man is. He is Ella Muir's brother. Earlier, his stringy black hair had been covered with a baseball cap.

'We really don't want any trouble,' Tess murmurs. 'It was a misjudgement on my part to come to your home. I should have telephoned first. I apologize.'

Kyle frowns. 'You said there's been a miscarriage of justice. That's what you came to tell us, right?'

Tess hesitates. Kyle is standing with his hands in his pockets and is avoiding eye contact. He is completely unreadable and she's not sure how to play it. 'An *alleged* miscarriage of justice,' she replies carefully, 'that's what we're looking into. Is there something we can help you with?'

Kyle is now nodding. He has something to say but it's as if he's finding it hard to come straight out with it. He looks over his shoulder to make sure he's not being watched. Finally he says, 'Look, she was my sister an' everythin', but I don't think it's as cut and dried as they made out. That woman they said killed her mightn't've killed her.'

Tess lets Avril's arm fall from her grasp and steps towards him. 'What makes you say that?' she asks, her unease vanishing in an instant.

'You can't tell anyone I'm talking to you.'

'I won't.'

'No, like, they *can't* know. No one can know I'm talking to you. Especially my family. Especially my mother.'

'We are very discreet. Why don't you think she killed her, Kyle?'

Kyle shifts his weight on to his other foot. He swallows. 'I heard rumours. You need to talk to Ella's friend. She knows stuff about Ella that no one else knows. You need to talk to her.'

'Why didn't you come forward with this before?'

Kyle looks taken aback.

'If you had your doubts,' presses Tess, 'why not say something earlier?'

''Cause everyone seemed so sure it was her.'

'OK,' says Tess, taking a notepad from her handbag, 'what's the friend's name?'

'Steph.'

'Surname?'

'Reynolds,' he says. 'Don't say I sent you.'

'I won't. Any idea how we can contact her?'

'She used to work with Ella at the café on the stone jetty. She might still be there.'

Tess jots this down. 'OK, but what else can you tell us? Why do you think they got the wrong person? Did you—'

Kyle is gone.

Later, they drive towards home, lost in their own thoughts. Tess is trying not to get too carried away. *The wrong person?* This never happens. Things never fall into her lap like this. For Tess, investigating cases can at times be so boring and laborious she wonders why she ever agreed to take the role in the first place. But the thought that somebody knows something – the thought that someone potentially knows who really did murder Ella Muir – has her twitching in her seat.

'How do you feel about the CCTV footage of Carrie's car *now*?' asks Avril, substantially perkier than an hour ago.

'Better,' replies Tess.

'Is this how it is? One minute you're thinking they're guilty, the next they're innocent?'

'Not always. But it's exciting when it happens.'

She drops Avril at her home and is almost disappointed to see the place in darkness. Up until now, she'd envisioned Avril arriving back to a cosy stone cottage: fire blazing in the hearth, a mug of strong tea and two buttery crumpets waiting for her on a tray, courtesy of William. 'Will you be OK?' Tess asks. 'Do you want me to come in with you?'

Avril climbs out. 'No, I'm good. Hot bath and a frozen pizza and I'll be back to myself. Thanks for looking after me,' she says, and she slams the door shut.

As Avril ambles along her pathway towards the house, Tess pretends she's checking her phone as she furtively watches Avril until she's safely locked inside.

Then she knocks the car into reverse, and she heads towards home.

The green Subaru is there already, of course, waiting for her. Watching. Hiding in the darkness.

Now he knows where she lives, he's there almost every night.

Now

CARRIE HAS BEEN tasked with spending time with a vulnerable prisoner today. The officers do this: pair them up for a time, and Carrie's not criticizing the programme, she can see how beneficial it is for the younger girls, the girls who come in here without hope and will most likely return to a hopeless situation. What Carrie has to offer other than a sympathetic ear, though, she's not sure. But apparently it's enough. Certainly, the girls seem to act as though it's enough, often thanking Carrie profusely after they've aired their life stories, when really all she does is sit in a chair and refrain from speaking for a couple of hours. If she's allowed to, she prefers to get the girls busy. She likes to get them working in the gardens or helping out with food preparation. They seem to talk more easily when their hands are busy. It's as if the very act of purposeful movement allows them to forget themselves for a while and they're able to get out of their own way. Able to talk freely without overthinking things.

Carrie sometimes wishes there'd been a Carrie to listen to her when she first arrived at Styal. Someone to help her see her life wasn't over. Someone to help find a way through the despair.

Today Carrie's working with Abi. Abi is a 23-year-old chronic self-harmer, who's in Styal for the second time on drugs charges. She was brought up in foster care – 'Nice people, they were very good to me,' she's always quick to point out to Carrie, or to anyone else for that matter – and she has five months left to serve of her sentence. In Carrie's previous life she'd have been eager to know how the disconnect happened: how did Abi go from a loving home, with decent parents, to long-term substance abuse? But after three years of listening to girls like Abi, she doesn't ask. What does it matter? They're here because they're here.

Carrie is waiting for Abi in the television room of C wing. C wing is where the vulnerable girls are housed and where there are systems in place to keep them 'healthy'. Read healthy as: not dead.

They are all suicide risks and so are required to be in groups a lot of the time so they can be observed. But this comes with its own set of stresses: girls with mental health issues can find their mental health compromised by being in the constant company of girls with mental health issues. This is where the mentoring programme comes in. Pair up a vulnerable girl with an experienced prisoner like Carrie and it's a win-win. Abi benefits from Carrie's sympathetic ear, her understanding, her calmness; and Carrie's day is broken up nicely by ministering to a girl in need. Because, as everyone knows, if you want to feel better about your own shitty situation, help someone out with their shitty situation. *Yes*, thinks Carrie, *a win-win*.

Carrie wishes she knew what she knows now back when Mia was struggling with anxiety, during her mid-teens. The vulnerable prisoners she deals with today have taught her she could have done things differently. She certainly wouldn't be as tit for tat with Pete if she had her time again, as she can see how that only screwed things up further for Mia. She shouldn't have used Mia to get at Pete in the way that she did. Pete said she used Mia as a pawn, and she's had to admit that she did. She's since apologized to Mia for this.

Abi arrives looking washed out and forlorn. She's taken to dragging a blanket from her bed around with her – as a toddler might do for comfort – insisting she's always cold. Carrie doesn't comment on the blanket as the other women have. She can see the appeal as Abi sits and wraps the thing around her, cocooning herself from her environment. 'Is there anything you want to do today?' asks Carrie. 'D'you fancy going outside for a walk?'

Abi shakes her head. 'I don't feel well.'

'Your tummy bothering you again?'

Abi nods.

'Are you up to talking just for a little bit?' asks Carrie.

'Can I sit next to you?'

'Sure.'

Carrie shifts across the small two-seater to make room for Abi. And Abi climbs on next to Carrie, folding her feet beneath herself and laying her head on Carrie's shoulder. The tactility doesn't bother Carrie so much any more. She's used to it. She would even go so far as to say she needs it. She barely gets to touch her own daughter, will barely get to touch her own grand-child when it arrives, and so she must get her fix from these sad, broken girls.

After a few minutes, Abi's breathing slows and her head starts to become heavy. It's pressing into a tender spot halfway along Carrie's upper arm and the arm is beginning to throb. Gently, Carrie shrugs Abi away from her, before putting her arm around Abi's shoulders and letting the girl cosy in. Abi starts to weep. This is not unusual and so Carrie doesn't comment. She lets the girl cry, while stroking her hair.

Mia used to do this, Carrie remembers. When life became too difficult: when she'd been shunned by her friendship group for a reason she couldn't fathom; when a boy called her ugly (a boy undoubtedly uglier than her); when she'd bled right through to the chair in the lunch hall and no one had told her. When these crises hit, Mia would fold herself next to Carrie's body on the sofa, and Carrie would stroke her hair until the traumas began to melt away.

Sometimes, Carrie pretends girls such as Abi *are* Mia, and she's surprised at the comfort she can gain.

'Can we just stay here for a while?' Abi whispers.

And Carrie tells her they can.

Now

THE FOLLOWING MORNING Tess wakes late. She is ravenously hungry with a thumping headache behind her right eye. She lies in bed feeling both outrageously angry at the world and unbearably sad. Sad to the extent that she could burst into tears. So, before doing anything else, she heads to the kitchen and takes two Nurofen. She then makes a large coffee, along with a toasted English muffin, dripping with butter, and finally, she collects the large box of Lindor chocolates from the back of the cupboard, chocolates she'd been hiding from herself until today, the start of this month's bout of PMS.

Tess eats the lot. She knows the signs. No point in fighting it. Best to just give in and let it happen.

An hour later, fortified, Tess feels able to face the day. She has a second coffee on the go and is in her home office, dialling the number she's found for the café on the stone jetty in Morecambe. As the call connects, she looks at the crime scene photograph of Ella Muir. She makes a point of looking at Ella at least once a day. Even if she doesn't want to. Even if, like this morning, the sight of poor Ella makes her sick to her stomach. It stops Tess getting ahead of herself, keeps her cognizant of the fact that no matter how hard she pushes to clear her client's name, someone has died. Also, Ella has a way of talking to Tess from the photograph. Her wounds, the angle of her head, the expression on her face are the only things she has left to communicate what happened to her, so the least Tess can do is look.

There's a click on the line and a voice says, 'Stone Jetty Café.'

Tess stops chewing. 'Hi, is that Steph Reynolds?'

'Yes.'

'Oh, great . . . I hope I'm not disturbing you. You don't know me, my name's Tess Gilroy, and I'm looking into a case that involves your friend Ella Muir?'

Silence from Steph's end.

'I appreciate it's probably a bit of a shock to hear her name after all this time but I was wondering if we could meet? Maybe talk about Ella and what you know about her death?'

'What do you want to know?'

'I work for a charity called Innocence UK, and we help people who may have been wrongly imprisoned. We believe that the person serving the prison sentence for Ella's murder may have been the victim of a miscarriage of justice, and we're investigating if—'

'I don't want to be part of any investigation.'

And Tess hears three staccato beeps.

Steph has ended the call.

Tess frowns. 'Well, what are *you* hiding?' she says aloud.

Later that morning, at Styal Prison, the prison officer searching through Avril's bag looks at her beaten-up face and refrains from commenting. She hands the bag back to Avril and tells her she can proceed through to the visitors' area.

'Why d'you think Ella's friend doesn't want to talk to you?' Avril asks Tess as they walk.

'Some people just don't.'

'*Do* you think she's hiding something?'

'Maybe. But also, you've got to think that as far as Steph Reynolds is concerned, justice has already been done. The person who killed her friend is in prison, where she belongs, so from her point of view that's the end of it . . . How do you think you would feel if someone called you up saying they believed the person who'd killed your loved one was innocent?'

'Not great. Or I'd think it was a crank call.'

Tess agrees. 'Yeah. The general public has no idea that such a thing as Innocence UK exists, so you can hardly blame them for wanting nothing to do with us. I'll give Steph another try later. Use my powers of persuasion to change her mind.'

'And if she won't?'

Tess shrugs. 'Move on to something else for now, try our next lead.'

They file into the visitors' area and Carrie's at the far end of the room again. She tries to smile when she sees Tess approach, but it's as if she can't quite make her face work in that way today.

When Carrie catches sight of Avril, following on behind Tess, her black eyes shining, she averts her gaze just as the prison officer did, and this is interesting to Tess. It's something Tess has done herself in the past upon seeing a woman's bruised face. The instinct of blurting out: *What happened to you?* overridden at the last second in case the woman is the victim of domestic violence and is embarrassed. No wonder that shit stays hidden, thinks Tess.

'Good to see you, Carrie,' Tess says. 'How are you holding up?'

'OK,' she replies, but she's clearly not. 'Mia's in labour . . . I should be with her. She's on her own.'

Carrie is obviously stricken and instinctively Avril puts her arm around her shoulder to comfort her. 'Will you be Nanna or Grandma?' Avril asks gently, and Carrie says she thinks Nanna.

'She won't get through it,' Carrie goes on, panicked. 'Her head's not in a good place. She's not prepared and she really can't tolerate pain.'

'Can any of us?' replies Avril.

And Carrie tries to smile a little. 'I'd just really like to know how she is.'

Tess removes a folder from her bag and sits down. The tension in the air around Carrie is palpable and Tess can see she's struggling to hold it together. Tess almost says something inane like *people have babies every day*, but she catches herself at the last second. She decides the best option here is to wait. She'll go against type and will refrain from advising that speculating about Mia's labour won't get Carrie out of prison any faster, and she will wait for Carrie until she herself is willing to proceed with today's meeting.

This takes less time than she thinks and when all involved appear ready, Tess picks up her pen and says to Carrie, 'So, we visited your ex-husband.'

'Did he call me a witch?'

Tess smiles. 'He might have done.'

'I thought as much.'

'I don't understand why he was never investigated for the murder.'

'Oh, he didn't do it,' replies Carrie matter-of-factly. And when Tess raises her eyebrows, she adds, 'You met him, didn't you?'

Tess nods.

'Did he strike you as someone clever enough to do something like that and get away with it?'

Tess considers this. It was a bit of a stretch.

'And his alibi,' Carrie says, 'his secretary – June? Did you meet her?'

'Yes.'

'She vouched for the fact he never left the office and the phone records show he placed a call. He made one phone call from his office when Ella was already dead. And besides,' Carrie says, almost sadly now, 'whatever else there is to say about Pete, he did love that girl. He was besotted with Ella. I don't see how he could've hurt her.'

Tess makes a note of Carrie's logic. She can see her reasoning. Carrie knows Pete better than anyone so is probably in the best position to speculate on what he's capable of. Tess decides to cut her losses and move on. 'OK, let's go back to what we have.' She pauses. A prison officer is making her way between the rows of chairs, checking on her flock. Tess waits for her to pass. 'Look, Carrie,' Tess says, when she's out of earshot, 'I'll be totally honest with you. So far, yes, we have found a couple of promising bits of evidence to substantiate your claim, but they're not enough. And we need more. Can you think again for us? Really think this time. Is there anything else you can tell me? Anything at all that will help your case?'

'I've been over it again and again,' Carrie says.

'One last time?'

'I've been over it more times than you can imagine, and everything I know I've already told to the police.'

'All right,' replies Tess, 'all right. I understand. I know it must be frustrating, it's just that before we go back to the Innocence UK panel, I could really do with another lead, something else to—'

'Why did you even go to Ella's house in the first place, Carrie?' cuts in Avril unexpectedly. She has removed her arm from around Carrie's shoulder and there is now some space between the two women. 'You say that you didn't care about Pete's affairs, and yet you visit the woman he's involved with. Why do that? You could have phoned to tell her to be more discreet. You didn't need to turn up at her door.'

Carrie is a little startled by Avril's sudden interrogation, as indeed is Tess. They have discussed Avril taking more of a lead – becoming less of the good cop to Tess's bad cop, but after Avril's punch in the face, and subsequent admission about the fantastical element of her relationship status, Tess did not expect Avril to jump in quite so readily.

'And how did you know where Ella lived?' Avril continues, ploughing on.

Carrie has lowered her head as if she doesn't want to answer.

'You say she was an acquaintance of yours,' presses Avril, 'but had you been to her home in the past?'

Carrie says she hadn't.

'So how did you know where Ella lived, Carrie?'

Reluctantly, Carrie replies, 'I followed Pete.'

'OK, so you followed him.'

Carrie nods.

'Just once?' asks Avril.

'A couple of times.'

Avril leans in. 'How many times are we talking about here, Carrie? Twice? More than twice? How many times was it?'

'Four times,' she tells them.

Back in the car, exiting the prison grounds, Tess is issuing instructions to Avril. 'Grab my phone out of my bag and dial the last number I called.' Avril pulls Tess's bag on to her knee. 'You were great in there by the way,' she tells Avril. 'You caught Carrie off guard. I liked how you handled her. It was a good time to step up and take the lead . . . But why the hell does Carrie tell us *now* she stalked him?' she says, dumbfounded. 'Why wait until now?'

'Well, she wasn't exactly stalking him,' replies Avril. 'She *was* married to him.'

'You know what I mean.'

'OK, then she doesn't tell us because it doesn't look good,' says Avril. 'She follows her husband multiple times when he's having an affair and is then charged with his lover's murder. Would you confess to stalking him?'

'She's supposed to tell us everything. She knows that.'

'Yeah, but would you? I don't think I would.'

Tess doesn't answer. Avril finds the phone and holds it out for Tess to apply her thumbprint to disable the lock, just as they are driving past the airport runway. A plane is taking off, heading towards them, and Tess thinks she could just do with a holiday right now. Somewhere hot. An all-inclusive, so she could pour cocktails down her throat without worrying about the price.

'Is this the number?' Avril asks. '01524 73—'

'That's it.'

'OK, I'm dialling.'

The call automatically connects to the car's Bluetooth and Tess clears her throat in readiness.

'Stone Jetty Café. Steph speaking. How can I help you?'

'Steph, hi, it's Tess Gilroy calling again from Innocence UK.'

There's a moment of silence, before they hear, 'I said I didn't want to be part of any—'

'Yes, yes, I know what you said,' replies Tess flatly. 'And I appreciate that. But what I don't think *you're* appreciating is that Carrie Kamara's going to spend fifteen years of her life in prison for something she might not have done. Just think about that for a moment. How do you think you would cope, day in day out, being separated from your family? How would you cope, Steph, knowing the truth was out there, but no one cared enough to take a second look at the evidence?'

Silence.

Avril gives Tess a worried look.

Tess presses on. 'I'm not saying that you have to *want* to do this. I get it. I understand. You miss your friend. Something truly horrible happened to her and you don't want to have to think about that again. So I understand that you don't want to meet me. But that doesn't mean you shouldn't. Not if you're a compassionate human being who could put herself in someone else's shoes, not if—'

'Tomorrow,' says Steph.

'Tomorrow?' replies Tess, surprised her admonishment has had some effect.

'Yeah, I've got a day off.'

Four Years Ago

THE BLANKET IS tangled between Carrie's legs and her hair is plastered to the side of her face. The room is silent and for a brief moment, a wonderful moment, in fact, she's not sure where she is. And then it hits her. She swallows, trying her best to be brave. She is in a police cell. She has been arrested and she's in a cell.

She can't believe she slept. She really tried not to fall asleep, even though her body was crying out for it, even though her head seemed as though it was in a vice and the handle was turning, slowly, slowly, the jaws threatening to crush her skull to nothing. She's heard that those who sleep whilst in custody are the guilty ones. The innocent can never rest: too terror-stricken. So she made a valiant effort to stay awake. She really did. But now it's too late. They have cameras in the cells and they would have seen her resting, her breathing slow and shallow, her face slack. She's annoyed at herself but can do nothing to rectify it.

They can keep her here for twenty-four hours without charge and if she had to take an educated guess, she'd say she's been here for around sixteen. But she has no way of knowing for sure. The cell is without a window so she has no sense of the time of day. Every hour that passes means she's one step closer to leaving. She's watched the TV programmes; she knows they'll need a watertight case against her for the CPS to authorize a charge.

And she really can't see how that's possible. It seems incredible to her that they found anything at all.

She wonders if they'll work all night. It seems cruel to ask that of an officer. How do they keep going? Do they have beds where they can take a power nap? And what about their children? Who tends to them if they're delayed at work, trying to prevent a murderer from being released because of a lack of evidence?

That's what she is now: a murderer. That's how everyone will think of her. Even if all this comes to nothing. They'll know she was a suspect. They'll know all about Ella and Pete and they'll say that it was some sort of sick love triangle. Only Carrie couldn't play by the rules of the game and so had to stick the knife in. Stick the knife in over and over until all of Ella's blood drained from her.

She thinks of Pete and Ella fucking.

She laughs. It's a hollow laugh.

Pete never really knew what to do with a woman. Didn't know which buttons to press. Didn't know how to get the right response. And yet he was never short of offers. This is something that's always puzzled Carrie. Why, when there was little in it for them, did these women continue? She couldn't understand it. But perhaps the bigger question was why, after all the porn Pete watched, was he still so completely inept? His mother always said he was a terrible student. She said he'd look at the blackboard and it just wouldn't sink in. Perhaps it's that, thinks Carrie.

The service hatch drops open with a clatter and Gillian Frain's face fills the gap. She looks tired. She ought to be allowed home. It's not right that someone is required to put this many hours in without a break. 'Your solicitor is here, Carrie. Do you want to get yourself together?'

Carrie's unsure what Gillian means exactly. Is she supposed to fix her hair? Touch up her make-up?

The service hatch closes and she waits at the door for it to be unlocked. Her triceps ache as well as the area in and around her armpits. She doesn't know if this is from being held up by the two officers who dragged her into the cell earlier, or if it's from Gavin's aqua-aerobics and all that arm circling. It crosses her mind that if she'd plumped for horse riding instead of that ridiculous class she could've cantered off into the distance at the sight of Gillian Frain and the other arresting officer. Too late now though. Too late for anything now.

Now

I T'S SATURDAY. TESS makes her way to the Midland Hotel in Morecambe to interview Steph Reynolds alone. Avril, unlike Tess, *does* have a life, and is attending a cousin's wedding somewhere in the Yorkshire Dales. She's keen for an update though and so Avril will call Tess – some time during the interlude that comes between the ceremony and the speeches, when the photographs are taken, when everyone would benefit from a lovely nap to keep them going so that they can make it through to the disco later – and Tess will report on what Steph has to say about Ella Muir's murder.

The Midland underwent a sympathetic renovation and re-opened its doors for business in 2008. It draws quite a crowd now, apparently, and Tess has had an itch to step inside since she returned to Morecambe. During her youth it was run down, 'haemorrhaging money' her dad used to say, and even the filming of Poirot within its walls didn't arrest its demise.

Tess circles the car park for the third time, looking for a space. She checks the clock. She's running late. A woman in a suit and killer heels exits the hotel and signals to Tess by waving her keys in Tess's direction. 'I'm going,' she mouths expressively and Tess presses her palms together and bows her head at the woman as if her prayers have been answered. She drives into the space, facing the hotel steps, and her phone rings. The car's Bluetooth connects and Tess hits 'accept'.

'Hi,' the voice says, a little unsure, 'it's Steph. I'm here but I'm nervous to go inside on my own. It's a bit fancy for me so I'll wait for you on the steps. If that's OK?'

'Sure.' Tess is reaching for her handbag in the passenger foot-well before grabbing her coat from the back seat. 'That's fine. I'll be with you in a minute.'

She catches sight of the girl on the steps with the phone clamped to her ear. She's clear-skinned and pretty. There's something familiar about her. Her hair is braided over the top of her head.

Tess freezes.

She stares at the girl.

'Fuck,' she whispers.

Frantically, Tess rummages through her handbag, trying to locate the letter given to her by Bill Menzies, the lawyer. She finds it and pulls it out. 'Are you still there?' Steph is saying via the car's Bluetooth, and Tess doesn't answer. She's unfolding the letter, examining the photograph. She looks between the hotel steps and the photograph in her hand.

'Fuck,' she whispers again. '*Fuck.*'

It's the same girl. How has this happened?

Tess scans the letter. Only this time she reads right to the end. All the way down to the name that she was too cowardly to read the first time around. 'Love Stephanie', it says.

Now there is no doubt. The girl on the steps is Tess's daughter. The girl with information about Ella Muir's murder is Tess's daughter.

Tess closes her eyes just as Steph's voice fills the car. 'Are you there?' she's asking. 'I don't know if you can hear me . . . I think we've been cut off. I'm going to call you back.'

Steph is now staring at Tess. From the steps, she's looking at Tess through the windscreen of the car, an expression of puzzlement on her face. She seems to know that this is the woman that she is supposed to meet.

Tess watches as Steph takes the phone from her ear and frowns. She taps it a couple of times and again Tess's car is filled with the sound of the girl, the sound of her *daughter*, trying to make a connection.

Tess can feel bile rising in her throat. Her hands are shaking on the wheel.

Can Steph hear the ringing phone inside Tess's car? She is looking in Tess's direction, no longer frowning, but now hopeful.

Is it you? she seems to ask.

Tess can't do this. She just can't. She's had no preparation.

Shit.

Tess moves her finger towards the screen. The ringing is now deafening. She can hardly think. She should go to her. She should go to her daughter, and yet she knows she can't.

Tess presses 'decline' and the ringing is silenced. She puts the car into reverse and locks her gaze on her rear-view mirror so she can avoid eye contact with Steph. She tears out of the car park like a madwoman, almost colliding with an elderly driver, who has to brake hard to avoid hitting her.

Then she guns along the promenade. And she can still hear the ringing. Only now she's not sure if it's for real or it's inside her head. It's ear-splitting. It seems to cripple her, and she has to pull over.

Tess puts her hands over her ears and waits, she waits for an eternity, until it stops.

Now

LYING ON HER bed, Tess stares at the ceiling. She's been here since yesterday afternoon and cannot get up. There's something sitting on her chest. It's a heavy, malformed thing that won't let her move. Every time she tries to turn on to her side, every time she tries to lever herself into an upright position, it shifts and she is again pinned to the bed. What is it, this weight, this entity, that won't let her up? And her dead mother answers, clear as day, as if lying right beside her. 'Shame,' her mother says, bluntly.

Tess tries to sleep. When she does doze she is released from the feeling and she can momentarily escape into her dreams. Even the dream of her mother dying is preferable to what she's experiencing right now. She wants to reach inside herself and rip it right out of her. She wants to fall asleep and never wake up.

Fucking Morecambe. She knew she shouldn't have gone back. It's such a small, hopeless town; of course she would meet her past there. What did she think would happen?

Tess had called her baby Angeline – after her mother, Angela. Steph's parents changed her name when they adopted her. Perhaps she was named after someone they also loved fiercely? Tess hopes so. She squeezes her eyes shut and finds herself thinking about the night of Steph's conception. She is standing at the kitchen sink, washing up, and her mood is black. Tina is getting ready to go to work and is applying lipstick, teasing and back-combing her curls to attain a fuller look, whilst admiring her reflection in the mirror by the back door. The mirror was hung there by Tess's mother, who told Tess a woman should always check her appearance before leaving the house because you never knew whom you were going to meet. 'Cheer up, it might never happen,' Tina says, pulling on her coat, and Tess gives her a look as if to say, *It already did*, but Tina is remarkably unperceptive when it comes to Tess's state of mind and so ignores the look, instead licking the lipstick from her teeth and calling through to Tess's dad who's watching TV in the other room: 'I'll be back by twelve, Barry! You'd better wait up for me!'

Tina slips out and Tess slams the saucepan down on the drainer, making the cutlery shake. She can see her own reflection in the kitchen window and she scowls back at herself. She hates Tina. But right now, she hates her dad more for bringing Tina into their home.

'You OK?' her dad asks. He has appeared in the kitchen without Tess realizing.

'Hmm,' she replies.

'You mad at that pan?'

'No.'

'What then?'

Tess shakes her hands dry and turns to face him. 'Is she living here now?'

'Tina?' he says and laughs awkwardly. 'I hadn't thought about it.' And then: 'No, she's not living here.'

'And yet she's here every day.'

Her dad starts to busy himself. He lifts the kettle, gives it a small shake and decides there's not enough water inside. He removes the lid and reaches across towards Tess. As the water cascades in, he asks her, 'Do you want one?' and Tess tells him she doesn't. He goes to the fridge and hums as he rearranges his beer on the lowest shelf before taking out the milk and sniffing the top of the bottle. 'This is yesterday's,' he says. 'It could do with using. Make yourself some cereal and use it up for supper?'

Tess doesn't answer.

'What?' he says, smiling. 'What's the matter?'

'Is she living here or not? I would like to know.'

Her dad puts the milk down. He looks past Tess and his brow is furrowed. 'Would it be a problem if she did live here?' he asks eventually, and Tess's eyes go wide.

'She's been dead a *month*!' she yells. 'My mother has been in the ground for a month and you want that woman here?'

'She cheers me up.'

'She's a fucking slut.'

'Tess—'

'What? She is. You know she is. Is she the best you could do? It's pathetic.' She glares at him, daring him to tell her to shut her mouth. And when he doesn't, when he looks back at her confused, not really sure what's happened, the tears pour out of her. 'You said we'd be OK. You didn't say anything about moving someone else in the minute she was dead. What is *wrong* with you?'

She's crying hard now and her dad sighs long and deep. He gets two cups out of the cupboard and drops a teabag into each. He then pours in the water and, as he's adding the milk, he says, 'It's not enough.'

'What's not enough?'

He hesitates. '*We're* not enough,' he says quietly. 'I need a companion. I need something else . . .'

Tess grabs her coat and flees.

The music is throbbing when she enters the club. The bouncers know her, they know she's underage, but she had sex with two of them the previous weekend (not at the same time) and so they don't ID her. Tess is alone. The girl she came out with has found a boy and has deserted her. Tess is angry, she's been angry since her mother died, and she wants to get drunk. She wants to drink until the clenching pain in her stomach is no longer there. Until the feeling that she can't bear to be inside her own skin disappears. She wants to drink until she feels desirable. And then she wants to have sex.

She buys a double vodka and lime, pulls down on the straps of the vest she's wearing so she's revealing more flesh and makes her way to the edge of the dance floor. She hates dancing. But she does like to watch. The DJ is playing 'Dirty Cash (Money Talks)', loud, and the floor is filled with young women. They're all a little older than Tess and they're dancing around their handbags, hands in the air, laughing at nothing, falling over each other's feet and then laughing some more. This is not a cool club. The women are not city women. This is a small-town, one-room club that people go to because there's nowhere else. The walls are black and the lights are harsh and the toilets are dirty. The men stand around the edge of the dance floor, eyeing what's on offer, and the women flash their skin and their eyes, they toss their hair and pretend not to notice they're being checked out. It's a mating display that is remarkably effective and if Tess is going to have any chance of ridding herself of this falling sensation beneath her ribs, she must join in with the spectacle.

But it's not easy for her. Her face, she knows, is set in a deep scowl and she is casting black looks at any man who is courageous enough to glance in her direction. So she goes back to the bar. She needs more vodka. The little she has inside her is not enough to change her mood significantly and so her only option is to have more. Tess checks her purse. She has fourteen quid and a few coppers. She'll need to keep aside at least three pounds for a taxi home or she'll be stranded, so that leaves her with enough for three more drinks. 'A double?' the barman shouts over his shoulder and Tess nods her head. He has sweat patches beneath each arm and on his top lip perches a moustache – a relic left over from the previous decade. He places the glass in front of Tess and adds a paper umbrella from beneath the bar. Then he looks at her as if he has bestowed the most unique gift. 'What's your name?' he asks.

'No,' replies Tess flatly, and she takes her drink to where she was a moment before.

There is a barricade of sorts around the dance floor. Something at waist height to lean against, to stand behind, a purpose-built structure designed to separate pursuant and prey. Tess isn't sure yet which category she falls into so she stays where she is. She swallows half her drink and her frown softens. She swallows some more and the rest of her face follows suit. She feels some pressure in the small of her back. A hand? A groin? Whatever it is its owner is not very subtle and this makes Tess smile. Her first smile of the week. She thinks about turning but she doesn't. She likes the brazenness of this person. Likes the way they're not pulling away when she hasn't reacted to their touch. She smiles some more.

The song changes and she hears a voice in her ear. 'Do you smoke?'

And even though she doesn't, she says, 'Yes.'

The palm on her back is removed and she is handed a cigarette and she turns, holding her hair away from her face as he lights the end for her. She inhales deeply and then blows away the smoke and when it clears she's able to get some sense of him. He's not great-looking. Who is around here? But he's taller than Tess and his skin is good and his eyes are alive and he doesn't look smarmy. He smiles at her, happy she's giving him the time of day, and Tess decides right then and there that he is the answer. 'Hello,' she says.

Now Tess wakes up with a jolt; her bedroom in semi-darkness. Is it morning? Or is it not yet night? She's disorientated. There's a banging inside her head but she can't remember drinking. She remembers going to bed. What happened before that? Oh, God. Steph. Now she remembers. Steph. At the Midland Hotel, she saw her daughter.

The banging resumes and it's only now that she realizes it's not inside her head at all but it's someone trying to get in. She pushes herself into a sitting position and swings her legs over the edge of the bed. She is wearing only one sock. She tries to stand but her legs feel unsubstantial, as if they can't take her weight and so she sits back down again for a moment. How long has she been in bed? She has no idea. Could she have been here a week and her muscles have atrophied to the extent that they no longer work?

'Tess!'

The sound of her name being shouted through the letterbox startles her. Come on, she tells herself. Move. Move yourself.

There is a band around her wrist which she uses to tie back her hair with. It leaves a hollow in the flesh where it's been cutting in. She stands. Her head swims a little but she's OK. She takes a step. She's still OK so she descends the stairs. When she walks into the front room, she sees the letterbox is open and a set of eyes is surveying her. She opens the door and the caller stands. 'You weren't answering your phone. I got worried.'

Clive.

'Where does Rebecca think you are?' she asks.

'The gym. Don't panic.'

'How'd you find me?'

Clive shrugs. 'Wasn't hard.' Tess holds the door wide. 'You look like shit, by the way,' he says, stepping in. He surveys the spartan space, the neatly kept living room without any real possessions in it, and raises his eyebrows. 'Been burgled?'

She walks through to the kitchen. 'Why are you here, Clive?'

'I called Avril. She said you were interviewing a witness alone yesterday and you'd not checked in with her either. You didn't answer your phone and I got worried. I'm allowed to be worried, aren't I?'

Tess pours red wine into two glasses.

'I don't suppose you've got any beer?'

'No.'

Clive takes one large swallow as if the wine is indeed beer and drains most of the glass. They sit at the table. 'They're resetting Avril's nose tomorrow so she won't be in,' he says. 'She said to tell you that if I got hold of you. Where've you been, Tess?'

'Nowhere. I've been here.'

She sounds unconvincing even to her own ears and it's clear he doesn't believe her, but Clive drops it. Whatever's going on with her is her business, she's told him this more than once, and he knows not to push.

'So how did it go with the witness, anyway?' he asks.

'What? Oh, she bailed. Decided she didn't want to talk after all. Turned out to be a wasted trip.' Her voice is level as she delivers this lie but inside she's screaming. She's back inside the car, the girl with the braided hair looking at her through the windscreen, looking at her as if to say, *Do I know you?* And Tess wants to reach out her hand through the glass and say, *Yes. Yes, you know me. Don't you remember?*

'Are you OK?' Clive's face is full of concern as he studies Tess from across the table.

'Course.'

'You look like you've been crying. I've not upset you, have I?'

'Just tired,' she tells him.

Now

THE FOLLOWING DAY, Tess stands in the conference room, ready to address Innocence UK. She has done this many times but today her game face has deserted her. And whatever zeal she usually possesses appears to have vanished. She stands in her tired suit with her tired face and the expressions on those reflected back at her tell her that they're aware something is amiss.

Tess tries to rally herself before speaking. 'So we can now cast doubt on the time frame the prosecution claims was adequate for Carrie to get to Ella's house, commit murder and get home again,' she says. 'Avril and I drove the route and when we repeated it in rush hour it would be almost impossible. I've also had word that Morecambe FC *were* playing at home that evening, in a cup game, so the streets would have been busier still.' Tess pauses. The panel are taking notes, jotting down the particulars. 'And then we have the witness, Mr Hurst, saying he saw Carrie get into her car directly after the murder. His statement should be straightforward enough to refute with a standard eye test. As long as it's not argued his sight has dramatically declined within the last four years, so I'll track down his medical records from the time of the murder just to be on the safe side.'

'I feel a "but" coming,' says Tom.

'Disappointingly, there are two,' replies Tess. 'The car captured on CCTV, the white Honda CR-V, was fairly rare. There are only seven in Lancashire, two in Morecambe, and one of those is Carrie's . . . Perhaps more worrying, though, is that when we interviewed Carrie again, this time pressing her a little harder, she admitted to following Pete Kamara four times when he was having the affair with Ella. This, coming from the woman who claims she couldn't care less who he was sleeping with . . . It was jarring to hear her admit that, to say the least.'

'Is it worth doing another psychological evaluation?' asks Vanessa Waring.

'I'm not sure. She's pretty strung out right now, her daughter's having the baby – in fact she must have had it by now – and all Carrie can think about is that she's not there with her. I've heard since our visit they've got her on some heavy-duty anti-anxiety medication. Would that affect the evaluation?'

Vanessa considers this.

'What's your gut instinct?' asks Clive.

'You mean, did she do it?'

'Did she?'

Tess thinks. If she had to call it one way or the other which way would she go? There's a collective gaze on Tess. They expect an answer. 'I'm pretty sure she didn't do it . . . but my gut's hardly going to impress the appellate court. We need more. We need another angle.'

Tom taps the end of his pen on the desk. 'Avril reported there's a friend of Ella's? Some friend who doesn't want to talk?'

And Tess feels her cheeks become hot. 'Oh, yeah, she was a no-show.'

'Is it worth contacting her again?' Tom asks.

'I don't think so.' Tess looks down at her notes and flips over a couple of pages. Can Tom tell she's lying? She thinks not, but she's reluctant to lift her gaze just in case. She takes her pen and crosses out a couple of words, frowns as if what she's looking at doesn't really make sense.

'OK,' Tom says, 'so, what next? I'm thinking forensics. Fran? Chris? Anything you want to chip in with here?' Tom looks at them both expectantly.

Fran Adler moves her reading glasses to the tip of her nose so she can peer at them from over the top. 'I think there's enough here to warrant requesting the forensic records. I'd like to see the reports that were *not* submitted in court. The reports we didn't get to see. And I wonder, do we retest the blood that was found at the scene? Make sure it's actually Carrie's? I'm thinking that if there's a chance it isn't, then we should go ahead and retest.' Fran glances at each member of the Innocence UK panel in turn to gauge their reaction.

From what Tess can determine no one is sure if this is a good idea. 'If we do retest and, again, it is proven to be Carrie's blood, surely that's more damning for her?' she says.

'But what if it's not her blood?' replies Fran. 'Or what if the sample didn't come from Ella's front door at all? There have been a lot of mix-ups, Tess.'

Tess concedes that there have. But still, it seems too great a risk to take. If they retest the blood and it is Carrie's they're basically agreeing that she was there in that house with Ella. That she murdered her. And that's bad.

Or . . . is it?

It's bad for Carrie, yes. But is it so bad for Tess?

If they retest and the blood is found to be Carrie's, they can abandon the case. No questions asked. There would be little value in going forward with it as they would be compounding Carrie's guilt. They could chalk it up to experience and move on to another prisoner who requires their help.

And Tess wouldn't have to think about it any more.

She wouldn't have to think about Steph.

She could shut off that part of her life and never revisit it.

Tess has never influenced the progress of a case for her own advantage and she wonders if she is capable of doing it now. *Am*

I? she thinks, the idea shaking her. She turns her attention to Tom. He has the final say. He's deep in thought, appearing to be weighing their options. Should she push to retest the blood?

'I'd be very interested to see the results of the fibre analysis,' says Chris Pownall from across the table. New to the team, Chris has spoken very little in these meetings so far, so it's a bit of a shock when he actually does. 'The fibre analysis wasn't submitted as evidence. Is that because it wasn't done, or is it because the police didn't like the result of it and decided not to make it available?'

Tom is nodding. 'Yes,' he's saying, 'interesting. Good call, Chris.' He turns to Tess. 'Let's delay any decision about the blood for now. I'm thinking it might be a good idea to abandon testing it completely. Just to err on the side of caution. Tess? Are you in agreement? Fibre analysis next?'

'Absolutely,' she says.

That evening, Tess flicks through a copy of yesterday's *Sun* as she waits for her king prawn dopiaza to be prepared. It's a quarter past seven, a busy time for the British Raj, and the open kitchen is all go. There are six chefs, as well as Rakib (who takes the orders on account of him having the best English), who addresses Tess as 'Mrs Tessa' – which she quite likes because she's never been married, nor is she ever likely to be. The chef in charge of the naan bread works a slab of dough between his hands and throws it against the oven wall before catching Tess's eye. He smiles shyly her way and Tess smiles back before returning to her newspaper. Customers who have placed their orders by phone come and go, the customers seated in the waiting area tap on their phones, and there is something gratifying about being here on a foul, rainy evening, some of the customers nodding in recognition to one another, some nodding towards Tess.

Tess thinks again about Kyle Muir's statement that Carrie Kamara is innocent. That they got the wrong woman. And the image of her daughter, standing on the Midland Hotel steps, all apprehensive and vulnerable-looking, slips into her mind's eye again. For the past couple of days, it's as if Steph is always there, waiting in the wings, waiting for a quiet moment in Tess's consciousness, or a break in her thoughts, so that she can slide into view.

Kyle said Steph knew things about Ella, things other people didn't. Well, *how* did Kyle Muir know this? How could he be so sure? Perhaps it was simply pure speculation on his part. Perhaps Steph knows nothing. And surely if Steph *did* know something relevant she'd have gone to the police at the time? Surely she wouldn't have sat back and watched an innocent woman take the rap for something she didn't do?

Tess consoles herself with these thoughts, these unanswered questions. They make abandoning her daughter outside the hotel a little easier to stomach.

'Mrs Tessa?' Rakib says. 'Your dopiaza is ready, love.' Tess stands. She collects the brown paper bag, encased in a white plastic bag in case of drips, and hands Rakib a ten-pound note. He whispers that he has hidden two poppadoms within her order, 'For your loyalty,' and Tess thanks him, even though she's quite sure every customer benefits from these complimentary extras.

She places the curry on the passenger seat of the car with the seatbelt wrapped around it protectively and sets off for home. As she drives, the gingery-garlic aroma fills the air and her stomach begins to complain furiously. She takes the twists and turns carefully, so as not to upset the dopiaza, and in less than five minutes, she arrives. Her mouth is watering as she takes the box of case files from the boot of the car, before grabbing her handbag and the curry, making sure to hold the plastic bag at arm's length so she doesn't get any turmeric-stained ghee on her coat. When she arrives at her front door, ravenous and eager to get inside, she finds it ajar.

Tess takes a step back and looks up.

Each window is in darkness. It doesn't appear as if anyone is inside. And yet she knows she locked it. Knows she would never leave the house unlocked. She's the type who must pull down on the door handle whenever leaving to check she really has the place secure.

She pauses. Thinks for a moment. Who else besides Tess has keys to this place? The owner? The letting agent? A previous tenant, who neglected to return a full set?

She thinks about the green car. The car she's seen in her rear-view mirror repeatedly, the car that switches lanes on the motorway when she does, the car that disappears when the driver realizes he's been spotted. Tess doesn't know anyone who drives a dark-green Subaru. She doesn't know anyone who'd want to follow her either. And she sure as hell doesn't know anyone who'd want to break into her house.

She pushes the door open a little. The lounge is in darkness, the kitchen beyond that is in darkness too.

It is conceivable that it's her landlord who has entered the house to check on his property. Check she hasn't sublet the house to an army of undocumented workers or turned the whole of the top floor into a cannabis farm. He is well within his rights to inspect his property. But he is supposed to notify Tess first. It's possible he forgot, she's thinking, pushing the door open a little further. But is it also possible he left his property unsecured as well? Tess thinks this is unlikely.

She runs her hand along the interior wall until she feels the switch beneath her fingers. She turns on the light. As she thought, the room is empty, so she deposits the box of case files near the front door and makes her way towards the kitchen. As she walks, she hears the creak of a floorboard upstairs, and she stops dead in her tracks.

Someone is in the house.

Unmoving, she listens. She listens and she waits. Whoever is up there is standing still also. Are they listening too?

Suddenly, she's raging.

Making quite a bit of noise, Tess struts towards the kitchen. She puts the curry on the counter and takes a glass from the cupboard, filling it with wine. She slams a few cupboard doors. Next, she turns on the stereo, making like she's settling in for the evening, before putting a plate in the microwave and pressing start.

Then, silently, she takes a long knife from the drawer.

She slips off her shoes and climbs the stairs, barefoot, the music from the stereo drowning out her steps.

Once upstairs, she checks her office.

Empty.

She checks the spare room.

Empty as well.

She pushes open her bedroom door and it's then that she sees a figure sitting on the bed in the darkness.

Tess switches on the light and for a second both Tess and her intruder are blinded.

When her eyes adjust, she sees a woman. A woman who is hunched over, a woman who appears to be incredibly sad.

Tess lowers the knife a little. 'What do you want?'

And the woman looks up. But it's as if she's not fully with it. She seems displaced, not quite lucid.

The woman says, 'You're older than I thought you would be.' Tess doesn't reply. 'And you're not as pretty as I imagined either.'

She has an odd, creepy air about her and Tess feels herself becoming progressively panicked.

'I told myself—' The woman's voice catches as she tries to speak. 'I told myself that if he was doing this then it had to be with someone younger. Someone younger and prettier must have caught his eye. I told myself he was flattered. But now I don't know what to think.'

Tess leans her weight against the wall and closes her eyes. 'Clive,' she exhales.

'Yes,' says the woman. 'Clive.'

'How did you know where I lived?' she asks Rebecca. Clive's wife.

Rebecca takes a tissue from her pocket and blows her nose. 'I hired someone.'

'Why?'

'I needed to know.'

'*What* did you need to know?'

'Who you were.'

Tess takes a breath as things start to make sense. 'Does he drive a green Subaru, by any chance?' and Rebecca nods. 'Is that how you got in here?'

'He helped me,' replies Rebecca. 'He used to be a security specialist or something. He's very serious, ex-military. He was kind of odd actually, seemed to want to take things a bit too far, but I needed to see where you'd been fucking my husband.'

It occurs to Tess to tell Rebecca that she has not been fucking her husband on the bed on which she now sits. That she hadn't even let Clive know where she lives. But there is no point. The woman is broken and angry and Tess being pedantic over the details of their relationship is not what she needs. 'So, what now?' Tess asks cautiously, aware that Rebecca is not exactly stable. Her uncertainty must show in her face because suddenly Rebecca flares at her out of nowhere.

'What?' she spits, rage flashing in her eyes. 'You think I'll hurt you? No, I won't hurt you. I want answers. I want to know why he wants *you*. I want to know how long. I want to know why.'

'I don't have answers.'

'Oh, don't play games . . . He never talked to you? He never said why he was unhappy at home? He never said you were beautiful? More beautiful than me? He never told you he liked screwing you more than he did me?' Rebecca's face collapses and she starts to cry. 'What did he want?' she whimpers. 'What did I do that was so wrong?'

'I'm sorry,' Tess says, but Rebecca doesn't hear. Tess thinks about approaching, putting her arms around Rebecca, but she senses this offer of empathy would not be well received either. For now, Tess has no option but to stand by and let Rebecca cry herself out. This is why she's so bad at relationships. A normal person would find the right words with which to comfort Rebecca, a normal person would not conduct affairs with married men so they could avoid entering into real relationships in the first place.

There is a change in the rhythm of Rebecca's cries and Tess senses she's beginning to taper off. Tess stands up straight, ready to take whatever Rebecca throws at her. Rebecca blows her nose again. She then takes a small compact from her bag and tidies up her make-up before pushing her hair behind her ears. She looks around the room as if seeing it for the first time. 'Our bedroom is so much nicer,' she says, bewildered. 'I made it so pretty. So much prettier than this.'

'I bet.'

'And we have such lovely kids.'

Tess smiles weakly.

'He does love us, you know,' Rebecca says.

'I know he does.'

Rebecca bites her lip and Tess wonders what she's going to say next. 'Why do you do it?'

'Why do I ...?'

'Do you love him? Is that it?'

Tess exhales. She *does* love Clive. But not in the way that Rebecca's thinking. She loves his wit and his charm, and she loves him as a colleague, and even as a lover. She loves him in that way you do when you really care for someone. In the way that you only want the best for them. But if she were to say this to Rebecca, she imagines Rebecca might feel the need to hit her.

'I don't love him,' she tells Rebecca firmly.

'But he loves you?'

'No,' Tess says. 'I'm a distraction, that's all.'

Rebecca sits quietly, taking this in. After a minute she gets up and tells Tess that she'd better be going. She apologizes for breaking and entering and says that in the heat of the moment it seemed a perfectly reasonable thing to do but she can now see that she was hasty.

Rebecca then asks Tess if she thinks she'll continue to see Clive and Tess tells her she won't. As soon as Tess says it she knows that she means it. She can't continue to do this. Not to Rebecca and not to Clive. Just because Tess is a disaster relationship-wise, that doesn't give her the right to drag them down with her. It isn't fair. Not on either of them.

'You're sure?' Rebecca asks warily.

'It's over,' Tess says.

'Really?'

'Really.'

Now

TESS AND AVRIL arrive at Morecambe Police Station. They park nearby and make their way to the entrance on foot. It is a truly awful building: a square monstrosity rendered in cat-litter grey, with a crazy collection of aerials on the roof. The windows are sad vertical slits and the whole thing looks as though it was put up in a hurry and has been lamented over ever since. Avril missed yesterday's meeting on account of having her nose reset and so Tess is doing her best to explain the reasoning behind requesting the fibre analysis records. She tells Avril that when two people come into contact, fibres from their clothes will be deposited on each other. So if Carrie really did murder Ella, there should be a record of the fibres from Carrie's clothes that were deposited on Ella's clothes, and vice versa. But these records were never submitted. (She does not mention Rebecca's break-in right now. In fact, she might never.)

Avril says, 'Yeah, but perhaps the records were not submitted as evidence because there *was* no transfer of fibres.' She says this reasonably, and Tess holds eye contact, waiting for the penny to drop. When it doesn't, Tess lifts her brows, as if to say, *And?*

'And what?' asks Avril.

'Take your time. Think about it.'

They push open the doors to the station and Avril stops dead in her tracks. 'If there was no transfer of fibres, then they were not *in* contact. No transfer of fibres means they did not meet and Carrie did not murder her.'

'Hurrah.' Tess smiles, glad that she's getting it. 'And if that evidence was not submitted at the trial, that means Carrie was convicted by an *omission* of evidence. Which is serious stuff. If the jury had been made aware that the two women had not come into contact that day, then they would've had no choice but to acquit Carrie.'

'Wow,' Avril says.

'Wow, indeed.'

They approach Enquiries and the desk sergeant greets them with a grin. He's mid-fifties, sweaty, leering, the aggravating type that Tess really hasn't time for today. 'Cheer up, ladies, it might never happen!' he says brightly, and Tess remembers her father's girlfriend Tina using the exact same phrase many moons ago. It pushes her buttons. Where do people get the idea that this is a useful thing to say? She could be here to report a rape. The desk sergeant looks at Tess. 'You know you'd be so much prettier if you smiled,' he says confidently, and so Tess fires back a wide, unhinged, maniacal grin in his direction. He flinches. Then frowns, unsure what on earth's wrong with this woman. 'What can I do for you?' he asks cautiously.

'We need to speak to DI Gillian Frain.'

'Can I ask what it's regarding?'

'You can, but I won't tell you.'

The desk sergeant disappears through a glass door behind him leaving Tess and Avril alone.

'How's your nose?' Tess asks.

'Not as sore as I thought. They've given me a ton of co-dydramol though, so it could be hanging off and I probably wouldn't notice. How does it look?'

Tess inspects as Avril turns first to the left, and then to the right. 'Beautiful,' she declares, and Avril gives her a look as if to say she's full of shit, but she smiles nonetheless. Then the glass door shudders open and a heavy-set woman in a V-neck jumper and ill-fitting slacks walks in.

'You were looking to speak to me?'

'Gillian Frain?'

'Yes.'

'Excellent,' says Tess. 'Is there somewhere we can talk?' Gillian Frain spreads her hands wide as if to say, *What's wrong with here?* 'It's about Carrie Kamara. We're from Innocence UK,' Tess tells her, and Gillian's expression darkens.

'Follow me.'

They make their way past the enquiries desk, through another set of double doors and along a corridor. Gillian's sensible plum-coloured Doc Martens squeak a little as she walks. She doesn't make conversation. She is late thirties and has that worn-out, frazzled look of a working mother of young children. They enter an interview room. 'Make yourselves at home,' she says, deadpan.

They sit down and once settled, Tess leans in and puts on her 'We're all friends here' face.

'As I understand it,' she says, 'you were the senior investigating officer when Ella Muir was murdered?'

'Yep.'

'Well, what we're really interested in is taking a look at some of the forensic reports.'

Gillian Frain keeps her expression intentionally neutral. 'That shouldn't be a problem . . . But you've already got access to the court documents?'

'Yes.'

'Well, everything's in there.'

A pause.

'Not everything,' says Tess. 'See the thing is – this is rather delicate, Detective Frain, so bear with me. You're aware, I'm sure, of reports in the press recently of police and prosecutors failing to disclose vital evidence?' Tess smiles sweetly. 'Now I'm sure this is not the case with your team, but you're aware of certain forces believing that the defence counsel is not really entitled to see *all* of the evidence?'

'That doesn't happen here.'

'I'm sure it doesn't. I'm sure you run a very tight ship.'

They share a strained moment of silence. DI Frain shifts uncomfortably in her seat.

'Were there any tapings done at all?' asks Tess. 'Any fibres taken from both the victim's clothes and the suspect's clothes at the time of the investigation to establish whether they'd been in contact that day?'

'I . . . I'd have to check.'

'We're very happy to wait.'

Gillian Frain walks out of the room.

'She's lying,' says Tess.

And Avril points to a camera positioned in the top right-hand corner of the room. 'Shhhh,' she whispers.

Tess looks directly at the camera. 'She's *lying*,' she repeats loudly.

Fifteen minutes later and Detective Inspector Frain is back. She is flushed and rattled. She doesn't sit down. 'So, the tapings *were* done.'

'Excellent,' replies Tess.

Frain hesitates. 'But the results were not made available to the defence.'

'Oh, that *is* a shame. What was the reason for that?'

'I don't know.'

'You don't know,' Tess mirrors back, flatly. 'Well, where can we get hold of the forensic report now?' she asks.

'I don't know that either.'

Four Years Ago

CARRIE'S WEIGHT IS supported by the plastic chair. The backs of her thighs have lost feeling and the knots of her spine are on fire. She has been in this chair for ever. She wants to get up but she can't. She must stay still, she must behave herself, she mustn't cause a fuss. She has pins and needles in her right foot. She circles it but it's not enough, so she slips off her shoe, folds her leg into her lap and rubs at the vulnerable area, the fleshy spot between ball and heel, with her thumbs. The criminal defence solicitor in the seat beside her pauses. He casts a critical eye over her foot and she lowers it. She slips her shoe back on, places her hands neatly in her lap, and keeps deadly still. 'Would you like me to go on?' he says, and Carrie tells him that she would.

She was brought from her custody cell by DI Gillian Frain and told that a solicitor had been appointed for her. He would go through the particulars of her case and advise her accordingly. She told him she had nothing to hide and was willing to answer any questions put to her by the police, but at this he shook his head as if she was woefully naïve.

'We will work on a prepared statement,' he said. 'This is the way to go. There is nothing to be gained by you defending yourself in a police interview.'

He is writing the statement out longhand, trying to capture Carrie's voice, trying to reproduce exactly what Carrie has told him, but in a way that doesn't raise questions. Carrie can see it's a skill he's developed over time. And she can also see why a pre-pared statement can be preferable to interrogation – less chance for slip-ups, less chance for her to hang herself by saying the wrong thing. But she can't help thinking that it's cheating. And Carrie doesn't want to cheat. She wants to come at this from a position of integrity. She wants to answer their questions so she can set the record straight.

The solicitor finishes the statement and asks that Carrie sign the paper on both sides as well as printing her name clearly and putting today's date alongside. 'Think we're all done,' he says and Carrie thanks him for his services. 'Don't thank me yet,' he answers gravely, 'thank me if they let you out.'

'If?' she asks.

'If,' he replies.

Carrie is returned to the custody cell where she is given a bottle of water and three Rich Tea biscuits. Shortly afterwards, she is shown to an interview room by a uniformed officer. He doesn't lead her there in the way DI Frain did – gripping her elbow, shep-herding her – he trusts that she's able to make it there on her own without incident. Carrie is not wearing her own clothes any more as they are covered with vomit. She's been provided with a pair of blue cotton trousers and a blue smock top. If you were to meet her on the street you might think she's making her way from the operating room, that she's wearing theatre scrubs. And for a second, Carrie allows herself to lapse into this fantasy of a dif-ferent life led. She could've been a theatre nurse – if she'd not left school at sixteen. If she'd not fallen in love with Pete she could've done all sorts of things. If she'd not fallen in love with Pete she would not be here.

'So, remember, don't answer any questions. They'll read the statement but then they'll try to get you to talk. You don't want to do that. Do you understand?'

'I understand.'

'Are you sure, because I'm not sure you're grasping the gravity of this.'

'I'm not to speak. I understand.'

The detectives file into the room. 'Have you had something to drink, Carrie?' asks Gillian Frain and Carrie nods. No speaking, she tells herself. 'Have you been offered a bite to eat as well?' Gillian asks next, and Carrie nods again. It's harder than she first thought.

Gillian places a laptop and a file on the table before introducing her colleague. 'This is Detective Sergeant Alice Goodwin.'

DS Goodwin seems nervous. Carrie wonders if this is her first murder case. Then she remembers that this is Morecambe and she's not living in some sprawling metropolis and she supposes this must be Gillian Frain's first murder case too. What if they screw it up? They must be under enormous pressure; they must be worried that this case will define their future.

Carrie's solicitor is reading from the prepared statement. The whole thing has started without her realizing because her mind is unfocused. What is he saying? That she remained home on the evening of Ella Muir's murder. That she watched *Escape to the Country* before preparing a meal for Peter Kamara and herself. Shepherd's pie. Did she really make shepherd's pie? She can't remember. She knows she doesn't like the sweet, fatty smell of minced lamb cooking in the pan, so she can't imagine that she made that. And yet her solicitor seems convinced. What else has she told him that can't possibly be true?

He finishes the statement and tells them Carrie won't be answering any questions and both detectives stare at Carrie impassively. She gets the impression they think it's a work of fiction.

Gillian Frain takes her time, but when she does eventually speak, she says this: 'I'd like you to look at these images, Carrie,' and she swivels her laptop around for Carrie to see. 'They're taken from a CCTV camera the evening Ella Muir was murdered. We believe this is your car, here, on your way to Ella's house. Take a note of the time at the bottom of the screen.'

Carrie squints at the image. No one has seen fit to provide her with suitable reading glasses yet. She had to sign and print her name on her statement holding the paper as far away as her arm would allow. It does *look* like her car on the screen. Yes, it definitely looks like her car. She starts to panic as Gillian Frain pulls the laptop around towards her, brings up another image, and turns it back to Carrie.

'We believe this is you on your return journey, after going to Ella's house.'

'I didn't kill her,' Carrie says in a small voice, and she receives a hard stare from her solicitor.

'I repeat, Carrie won't be answering any more questions,' he says.

Gillian Frain closes the laptop. 'We also have a witness who can place you at the scene.'

This news hits Carrie square at the back of the head. What witness? Who are they talking about? There can't be a witness. There *is* no witness!

She needs to get out of here. Carrie goes to stand and the detectives fly into action. 'You need to calm down, Carrie,' she can hear one saying. She's not sure which. She needs to get out while she still can. She doesn't know what she's doing with her hands or her feet but she can hear yelling, she can hear someone shouting, 'Calm down *now*!'

And then without knowing how it happens she has her face pushed to the floor. There is a knee in her back and the person is telling her to keep still. That she is only a danger to herself. She hears the sound of metal on metal and there's a sharp burning sensation around her wrists. She can no longer feel the knee in her back but she can hear ragged breathing all around her. They pull her to her feet and she's shocked to see the laptop on the floor along with a number of loose sheets of paper. Her solicitor is holding a paper napkin to the area above his right eye and a bright patch of blood is beginning to bloom through it. 'I didn't do that,' she says to him, and he tells her, 'Yes, you did. You hit me with the fucking laptop,' he says.

He's angry.

'We'll need to swab her,' she hears Gillian Frain telling her solicitor. 'We've found blood at the scene not belonging to the victim, so we'll need to swab Mrs Kamara for DNA.' And the solicitor tells DI Frain to do whatever the hell she likes. He's leaving. She'll need to get a new solicitor.

Now

'I DON'T UNDERSTAND,' Avril is saying. 'How do police records disappear? How is that even allowed to happen?'

'They just do,' answers Tess.

If Tess appears unmoved by Detective Inspector Frain's bombshell, it's because evidence does go missing, all the time, and forensic reports do somehow become unavailable – it's not exactly a rare occurrence. And yes, it's frustrating. Yes, she can understand Avril railing – Tess had the same reaction herself when she was a little greener – but there is little to be done.

'There's no point whining about it,' she tells Avril. 'We can raise the issue at the appeal – if we get one granted – but forget it for now because I have an idea.'

Tess is backtracking. She is pursuing a lead that is almost certainly not going to be fruitful, but the alternative . . . well, she can't think of the alternative right now, so she heads to the dealership.

The dealership is across town, situated at the edge of the White Lund Industrial Estate – north-west of the River Lune. If Tess had more time she would solicit Clive's services, ask him to call in another favour, gain access to the police records that she requires. But as it is, she's here, essentially on the doorstep, so she may as well get the job done herself. And besides, she doesn't like to abuse Clive's goodwill. She prefers to use him when there is no other viable alternative, partly because Clive is putting himself at risk whenever accessing information he's not legally allowed to access, and partly because she doesn't like to be beholden to him. She's not yet found the right moment to talk to him about Rebecca's visit and her promise to his wife that the arrangement she shares with him is now defunct, so she'd rather simply avoid him for the time being.

The car park is packed with Hondas large and small, old and new, and Tess finds a space from which she can survey the internal workings of the dealership unobserved. Avril goes to climb out but Tess tells her to stay put: 'The second they see us on the forecourt, there'll be a salesman sniffing round.'

'OK, but what are we actually here for?' asks Avril.

'I need an address,' she says, and points. 'From them.'

Tess keeps her eyes glued on the sales staff inside. From what she can determine there are two: both male, both mid-thirties, both with heavy paunches, both eager for it to be lunchtime. They move slowly around the showroom, killing time. If Tess were ten years younger, she might use charm to try to prise what she requires from them, but her days of petitioning using her sex appeal are well behind her.

Avril begins tapping away on her phone.

'Start the car again and take a left out of here,' Avril instructs.

'Why?'

'You'll see.'

Tess pulls out of the car park and when she returns, shortly afterwards, Avril has two large kebabs resting in her lap. One doner and chicken. One shish and doner. Avril gets out of the car and takes the polystyrene boxes along with her. 'Follow my lead,' she tells Tess, and she makes her way across the forecourt. She holds the door open for Tess, glancing backwards and quickly rearranging her features into that of a smiley, happy young woman, a woman who is about to present the most glorious gift. 'Gentlemen,' she says, upon entering.

Five minutes later they are sitting opposite Avril's new friend Alex. Alex who is eyeing the takeaway boxes, salivating, and who really can see no harm at all in looking up any white, limited-edition Honda CR-Vs that happened to be registered in the Morecambe area at the time of Ella Muir's murder. 'So there's one here that belonged to a Mr Peter Kamara,' Alex says. 'He bought that new from us in . . . let's see, it must have been—'

'Any others?' asks Tess impatiently.

'Just a moment. Yes. One more. Her name rings a bell, actually, not sure why.' Alex takes a pen from the grey desk tidy and writes the woman's details on a compliments slip: 'Melanie Phelps, 10 Shady Lane, Hest Bank'.

He hands it to Avril who bestows a beatific smile on him. 'Alex,' she says playfully, 'you really have been most helpful,' and she slides the kebabs across the desk towards him.

Ten minutes later and Avril pulls down the sun visor and checks her reflection in the small mirror. They are at Melanie Phelps's address. The white Honda is in the driveway. 'So, if Melanie remembers driving through Morecambe on the evening of Ella's murder, then it could have been *her* on the CCTV and not Carrie.'

'Exactly that,' replies Tess, and she feels a prickle of irritation as she knows what Avril is about to say next.

'Then why didn't we come to see her earlier?'

Tess looks out of the driver's side window. 'Other evidence needed checking,' she answers vaguely. What she doesn't say is that they are here because she has nothing else. They are here because she has run out of leads, options. What she also doesn't say is that Melanie Phelps attesting to driving in Morecambe on the night of the murder would, yes, be useful to their case, but in itself is not exactly earth-shattering evidence. For Innocence UK to approach the Court of Appeal they must have either strong new evidence, or a new legal argument. And Melanie Phelps is neither.

Tess bites down on her lower lip. She was expecting to find her *strong new evidence* courtesy of Stephanie Reynolds. Steph. What she didn't expect was for her past to come hurtling towards her, slamming into her like a high-speed train and derailing her thoughts, her *life*, in the way it has.

'Melanie's off out,' Avril is saying, nodding in the direction of Melanie's house. 'We need to move now if we're going to catch her.'

Tess rubs her face with her hands. The car smells of kebab. She wonders if she smells of kebab.

They approach the driveway; Melanie Phelps is loading three Staffordshire bull terriers into the back seat of her car. The dogs are giddy with excitement, their tales wagging, their big mouths wide open, smiling. Melanie picks up each dog in turn and kisses the top of its head. She tells them how good they are. How much she loves them. She calls each one puppy. She is not aware of Tess and Avril, lingering behind.

'Mrs Phelps?' Tess calls out hesitantly. She doesn't want to frighten the woman – absorbed as she is in her task – or the dogs.

Melanie Phelps spins around. 'Mrs? Not likely. I answer to Ms these days.' Her voice is coarse and gravelly. A smoker.

Tess steps forward and offers her hand. 'Tess Gilroy,' she says. 'I hope you don't mind but I got your name from the Honda garage. We're investigating a miscarriage of justice case and—'

'Honda? Those robbing bastards. Bet they didn't tell you they sold me a complete piece of shit, did they? This car's been back inside that garage more times than . . .' She looks skywards trying to find a suitable way to end her sentence, and when nothing is forthcoming decides on 'bastards' again.

Melanie is mid-fifties, blonde, brassy, with a row of capped teeth, and Tess likes her immediately. 'Two years old this car was when I bought it,' she tells them. 'Two years old. I thought

I was buying something reliable but I'd barely got it back here when it started dying on me.' One of the dogs starts to bark from the back seat. It's wearing a baby-blue fleecy jumper with small sheep dotted on it. 'Dixie!' Melanie yells at the dog, crossly. 'Stop shouting!' She turns back to Tess. 'She knows we're off to the beach – she's got no patience. What was it you wanted again?'

'We're investigating what we believe is the wrongful conviction of Carrie Kamara. You might remember her case. She was convicted for murdering—'

'Ella Muir. Yeah. I know Ella's mother, Sandra. She's a right little battleaxe. Not that she deserved to lose a child. No one deserves that . . . Do you know Carrie Kamara stabbed Ella over a hundred and fifty times?'

Avril coughs. 'I think it was a little less than that.'

'Was it? Whatever . . . Dixie! Stop picking on Miss Luna.'

'We're here because you drive the same car as Carrie Kamara,' explains Tess, 'your Honda. How long have you had it?'

'Five years. Biggest mistake of my life. Well, one of 'em.'

'Oh. OK, good. We're specifically interested in the night Ella was murdered – the eleventh of November, four years ago. There was some CCTV of what the prosecution believed was Carrie's car driving past the Eagle and Child pub around six o'clock. We were wondering if there was any chance that could have been you?'

'Me?'

'Yes.'

'Why would it be me?'

'Because . . . you might have been on your way to somewhere?'

Melanie seems put out. She's frowning. 'Who are you again?'

'We're from the charity Innocence UK. We look into alleged miscarriages of justice and work on behalf of those incarcerated to try to find out what really happened.'

'Well, I can tell you right now I did not murder that girl. No matter what I thought of her mother.'

'No, no,' says Tess quickly. 'You've got the wrong end of the stick. We're not for a moment suggesting you had any part in it.'

Melanie looks at Tess sceptically.

'What we're trying to find out is if it could be *your* car, not Carrie's, that was caught on CCTV. The prosecution claimed she drove past the pub on her way to Ella's house and then back again a little later after she killed her.'

'Why do you want to get her off?'

'We think she was wrongfully convicted.'

'Have you asked her?'

Had she?

Suddenly Tess can't remember. Yes. Of course she'd asked Carrie if she'd done it. She must have.

'I've always thought she was guilty as hell,' Melanie goes on. 'She's got that look. Sneaky. I think you can always tell.' She glances at the three hopeful faces in the back seat of her car. 'Now dogs, they *are* a good judge of character. Put them in a room with Carrie Kamara and you'd soon know if she was telling the truth. I had this guy round once, nice, decent, drove a Lexus, and when I went to put my hairspray on, Miss Shelby – she's the quiet one on the right – she barked at him so hard he locked himself in the understairs cupboard.'

'What had he done?' asks Avril and Melanie's eyes go wide.

'I didn't wait around to find out,' she says, as if this should be self-evident. 'I got rid of him.'

'So, the CCTV?' interrupts Tess gently. 'Do you think there could be any possibility that it was you in town that evening?'

'Possibility? Yeah. My mother lives a few hundred yards past the pub and I go round there each night and take her a plate of whatever I'm having. She starves herself otherwise and then goes pestering the doctor saying she can't put any weight on. She gave herself pneumonia last year on account of the fact she won't eat. Anyway, that's what I do. I go by there each night and make sure she's fed. Not that she appreciates it.'

Tess can feel her pulse quickening. This is it. This evidence will refute the prosecution's claims and they can prove the car was not Carrie's once and for all.

'What date did you say it was again?' asks Melanie.

'The eleventh of November.'

'Four years ago?'

'That's right.'

'Oh, no, then that couldn't have been me.'

'What?' says Tess. 'Are you sure? How can—'

'I was sunning myself in Benalmádena.'

Now

So now they wait. Tess and Avril wait at the local Wetherspoon's: the Eric Bartholomew it is named, in honour of the late, great Eric Morecambe, king of light entertainment, who was born here in Morecambe. Avril is wavering between the Whitby breaded scampi and the Mediterranean vegetable lasagne with a side order of chips. Tess won't be eating. She's too nervous to eat.

When Melanie Phelps told them the day before that it wasn't her driving after all, Tess was all out of options. And Avril had said, 'What now?'

Well, this was *what now*.

This pub.

This pub with its guest beers and its patrons who, with the exception of Tess, Avril and a couple of others, are all over the age of sixty-five, all thrilled to be ordering a hearty meal and an alcoholic beverage for less than a tenner. 'What are you fancyin'?' Avril asks, and Tess tells her that the teriyaki noodle dish is supposed to be good, but she doubts she'll order it. Her stomach is beginning to roil and there is a bitter taste in her mouth.

'Did you tell her one o'clock, or half past?' Avril asks.

'One.'

'She's running late then.'

'Yes,' replies Tess. 'She is.'

This wasn't what she wanted to do but her hand has been forced, so to speak. With the forensics a dead end and the Honda now a non-starter, she has no other choice. This is what she's telling herself as she sits here with her stomach in knots, as she glances at the door every two seconds, as she wrestles with her conscience because she knows this is wrong. It isn't the right way to do things. *It's wrong,* Tess. *Wrong.*

'Do you think that's her there?' Avril says, pointing to the young woman on the other side of the glass. The woman is finishing the last of her cigarette whilst scrolling through her phone at the same time.

'I'm not sure,' replies Tess, even though she is. 'I'll go and check.'

Tess rises and smooths the creases from her trousers, picks a few stray hairs from the lapels of her jacket, and then she heads for the door. Just before she opens it, she pauses in the entrance-way and there's a will-she-won't-she moment as Tess's nerves get the better of her. Her heart is in her mouth and she's not sure she can go through with it.

She takes a deep breath and presses on.

'Hello? Steph?' she asks the young woman with the pretty face and the braided hair.

'That's me.' Steph hurriedly extinguishes her cigarette. 'Sorry I'm late. I got held up.'

Tess smiles. 'Would you like to join us?' And she motions to Avril through the window. Avril is still studying the menu but now has her phone out and is tapping away on the calculator. She will be adding the calories of each dish to her daily running total, Tess expects, and Tess feels a surge of warmth for her colleague as she watches Avril frown and shake her head slightly, before running her finger down the menu another time.

They go inside. Tess sits beside Avril and Steph settles herself on the chair opposite. 'Can I get you something to drink?' Tess asks Steph. She is trying not to stare too much. She's trying to take in her daughter's face without freaking her out. She is quite lovely, and as Tess reaches for her own drink, suddenly she doesn't quite trust herself to pick it up without throwing it all over herself, so she quietly withdraws her hand and rests it neatly in her lap.

'Half a lager, please. Any type. I'm not fussy.'

Tess gets up and goes to the bar. She pays for the drink and returns. When she sits down, Steph says, 'So I was kinda depressed to miss out on that slap-up lunch at the Midland.' And Avril shoots Tess a sidelong glance as if to say, *What is she talking about? I thought she was a no-show?*

'Well, we're here now,' Tess replies weakly.

'Yeah,' Steph says, frowning. 'Here is definitely where we are.'

'Are you from Morecambe, Steph?' asks Avril.

'Born and bred.'

'What a coincidence,' she says, 'so is Tess.'

'Really?' and Tess can only nod her head in reply.

Now that this is really happening, she's finding it difficult to form words. It's as if the neural connections between her brain and her mouth have been severed and though she wants to answer, no words will come out. She smiles gawkily at Steph. They return to their menus and perhaps Steph is finding her awkwardness a little weird because when she speaks, she says this: 'So, do you want to talk about Ella or what? It seemed there was some kind of urgency the other day, so I was pretty surprised when you went ahead and cancelled on me.'

After Tess had fled the Midland Hotel car park, she'd sent Steph a lame text explaining that she'd been called away on an urgent matter. Really, it can't be helped, she'd said, and so on and so forth. When she thinks about this again now, she's even more ashamed. It was a shitty thing to do. Leaving the girl there without a proper explanation was a shitty thing to do.

'What can you tell us about her?' Tess asks, her words surprising her as they come out of her mouth in the normal way.

'What do you want to know?'

'Anything at all would be useful,' she answers, and she can feel Avril's eyes upon her. She's going around the houses. Being vague. She's not getting to the point, which is something she has repeatedly warned Avril against. Tess knows this and yet she is powerless to take charge of the conversation as she would do normally.

Her daughter has a row of freckles dotted across her nose. She has a small vertical scar between her eyebrows. When Tess held her as a baby she was unfreckled and lacked the scar. She wonders how old Steph was when these things appeared. Wonders whom she cried for when she cut open her lovely face.

Steph places her menu flat on the table. Her expression has hardened. 'You asked me here to find out what sort of person my murdered friend was? That's it? That's all you want to know?'

Tess again finds that words escape her so Avril steps in. 'We received some information that you knew things about Ella. This person said you knew things about Ella that no one else did. We're hoping you can talk to us about that . . . This person—'

'*What* person?'

'I can't say, I'm afraid,' replies Avril.

'OK, so *someone*,' Steph says, rolling her eyes, 'you can't say who, this someone says I know something, and you want to know what that something is? Have I got that right?'

Avril tells her that's right. 'To be honest, we're running out of leads. We've hit a bit of a dead end.'

'Well, she had a boyfriend,' says Steph. 'Maybe that's what this *someone* is referring to.'

'Yes. Pete Kamara,' says Avril.

'No. Another boyfriend.'

Avril tilts her head. 'She was seeing two people at once?'

'Yep. Ella was my boss at the café. She talked about her love life quite a lot. It passed the time.'

'Did these two boyfriends know each other?'

'I don't know.'

Tess leans in. 'Was this other guy ever investigated for Ella's murder?'

'I don't think so . . . his name was never mentioned in court, but I suppose he could've been.'

'Who is he?' asks Tess.

'Greg Lancashire,' replies Steph.

'Did you ever meet him?'

'I don't think she wanted me to.'

'Because . . .?'

Steph sighs. 'Because, frankly, he's a bit of a dick . . . He wanted to keep her to himself, he wouldn't let her see her friends. He's the jealous type – which *I* would've hated, but I think, in a weird kind of way, Ella liked? I think she enjoyed feeling important to him. She'd never had that before.'

'Is he married?' asks Tess.

'Divorced. Ella said she wouldn't go out with another married man. Not after what happened with Carrie.'

'Because she felt bad about the affair,' states Tess.

'No. It was more that when Carrie turned up at her door, threatening she had to stay away, she decided she didn't need that kind of drama in her life any more. She said she'd learned her lesson and wouldn't get involved with anyone married again.' Steph pauses. 'Bit too late by then though, wasn't it?'

Tess and Avril share a look. This is a very different version of events than Carrie's recollection.

Tess takes out her notebook. 'Do you know where Greg Lancashire is now?'

'Last I heard he was living on the caravan park 'cause his life had kind of gone to shit. When Ella was with him he used to be a mechanic for Jaguar Land Rover and he rented a nice little cottage with some land alongside in Carnforth. Ella liked it there.'

'What happened?' asks Avril.

'Greg's got a temper on him and he threw a torque wrench at some salesman's head so they had to let him go. I heard he lost his house after that 'cause no one would employ him, so he's like a self-employed welder now or something.'

'You never see him around?' asks Tess and Steph shakes her head just as Tess becomes aware of a large group of people making their way out of the pub.

The group filter past their table; it's clear they've all had a boozy lunch, and there is much laughter and bonhomie, everyone speaking a little too loudly, faces flushed, arms linked, and a woman who Tess assesses is not really a natural high-heel wearer trips over her feet, and Tess watches as she falls towards their table of drinks. This all seems to happen in slow motion and just as she's about to crash, perhaps resulting in her sustaining cut palms, perhaps even a bloodied face, she is caught from behind and pulled back to safety.

She apologizes profusely. And the man who caught her apologizes too. But then he stops. His eyes land on Steph and—

'Steph!' he booms. 'What are you doing here? How's your dad? It's good to see you, are you—'

And then his eyes alight on Tess.

It's Bill Menzies. The lawyer. The lawyer who has taken care of the affairs of Steph's family since the adoption and who hand-delivered Steph's letter to Tess. The letter informing her of Steph's adoptive mother's death.

Bill beams at both women. He stands back, puts his hands in his pockets, and rocks back and forth with a well-I'll-be expression on his face.

Bill can't stop smiling as he looks between the two of them. 'Bloody hell,' he says. 'Bloody *hell*. I can't believe you actually found each other.' He leans over and gives Tess's shoulder a firm squeeze. 'I never thought it'd happen. I never thought I'd see the day when the two of you made contact.' Bill shakes both their hands in turn, saying, 'Well, as you can see, this has made my year.' Then he decides that this occasion warrants a bigger gesture and he dips down, trying to hug/kiss first Steph and then Tess. 'Bloody hell,' he says again, quite overcome.

Bill tries to gather himself. 'Right,' he says firmly. 'Right. I'll leave you to it. You don't need me interrupting your big reunion.' He bows at the waist. 'Goodbye, ladies.'

And finally, he leaves.

Tess is afraid to look at Steph. But she does look and it's immediately clear Steph is poleaxed by this turn of events. Tess is unsure whether Steph wants to yell or cry. It's probably both. Steph stares back at her mother, hurt, disappointment and fury dancing in her eyes, and Tess feels skinless. Exposed. She can almost see Steph's brain running through what has just happened. What happened at the Midland Hotel too.

Suddenly her beautiful daughter looks so brittle she might crack into pieces.

Tess reaches out her hand.

And Steph looks down at it, appalled.

She flees.

Both Tess and Avril rush after her and when they get outside they see Steph's already halfway down the street, running. She is running as fast as she can to get away from Tess.

'Do you think you should go after her?' Avril asks.

And Tess thinks about this for a moment before heading back inside. 'We need to collect our coats,' she says.

Now

TESS IS TRYING to get hold of Clive. The sound of the dialling tone fills the car and Avril reaches forward to adjust the volume so it's less of an assault on their ears. Tess taps her fingers on the wheel impatiently. She has not discussed what happened earlier in Wetherspoon's with Avril. Nor is she likely to.

They hear a click as the call finally connects before there's a loud crack. This is followed by the sound of wind rushing, then a rustling, and then, finally, Clive's voice, which is faint, as if far away, saying, 'Bloody hell.'

'He's dropped the phone,' says Avril.

'Looks that way.'

After a few seconds, Clive's phone finds its way to his ear and he says, 'Miss Gilroy. To what do I owe the pleasure? Sorry about that, nearly dropped my phone in the bath. The kids have come home covered in paint.' Tess can now hear splashing and the lovely infectious giggle of a child. Oh, yes, she remembers, Clive's kids. Clive has kids. This is something she often forgets.

'I need an address,' she tells him.

'For?'

'Greg Lancashire. I think he's somewhere in Morecambe.'

'OK, I'll see what I can do, but Tess?'

'What?'

'When can I see you? I need you. I miss you. I know you saw Rebecca. We need to talk – I just need to—'

'Hello, Clive!' chips in Avril.

'Oh, Avril,' he says, embarrassed. 'Didn't realize I was on speakerphone.'

They end the call and head to the supermarket. Clive said to give him an hour to find Greg's details, so, short of anything better to do, Tess and Avril agree they may as well stock up on groceries as sit there in the car twiddling their thumbs.

The day is cold. Minus two. This is rare for Morecambe, as the moisture-laden air masses which regularly envelop the coast prevent the winter temperatures from dropping too low. Today though, the winds are coming from the north so there's a real bite in the air – which is just as well because, as Avril points out, it will stop their freezer stuff from melting in the boot.

Avril pushes the trolley while Tess throws the stuff inside. Tess's items are at the front, Avril's at the back. Tess picks up things in the fresh produce section that Avril has never seen before and marvels at Tess's ability to confidently deal with a small swede, a butternut squash and a globe artichoke. 'What do you do with that?' Avril asks, holding up the artichoke, and Tess tells her it's a little hard to explain. 'Is it like an avocado?' she enquires, and Tess tells her it is, sort of, because it's easier. 'I cut my palm open trying to get the stone out of one of those once,' Avril says. 'Never again.'

'The trick is to cut it into quarters, then the stone falls out easily,' Tess tells her, but Avril is shaking her head repeatedly whilst pulling a face to suggest that those who do partake in such business are taking an ungodly risk.

Tess is loading the groceries on to the conveyor belt when Clive gets back to her. 'OK, I've got it,' he says.

Tess hands over her debit card to the checkout assistant, a man of seventy-plus years with cloudy eyes and skin covered in liver spots. 'Go on,' she says to Clive.

There's a pause.

'Hello?' she says, wondering if they've been cut off.

'Listen, he's a bad lad, this Greg Lancashire . . . I'm not sure I like the idea of you going around there. He's got previous and I'm really not happy about—'

'I'm a big girl, Clive.'

'What if something happens?'

'It won't.'

She hears him exhale. 'Anyway, I need to see you,' he says. 'Why have you been ignoring my calls? Rebecca came home in a state saying she'd broken into your house. I went berserk. I told her she was insane but she's been doing all sorts of stupid shit lately.'

'Because she thinks you don't love her.'

'I do love her,' he says.

'Not enough. Not nearly enough. And she knows it. So she's going to keep doing stupid shit until you sort that out. She'll keep testing you and behaving like a madwoman, or a petulant schoolgirl, she'll keep crying for you to love her until she gets the assurance she needs. You need to either commit fully to her or walk away.'

'Do you want a bag for life?' asks the checkout guy.

'I'd like two, please,' replies Tess.

'Let me see you,' Clive says.

'I told Rebecca it was over between us, and I meant it. I can't keep doing it to her. It's not fair.'

'Please, Tess.'

'What's the address, Clive?' she says.

And she hears him exhale again. When he's sure she's not going to budge on either issue, he says, 'I'll text it to you.'

Ten minutes later they pull on to the caravan site. But this is no holiday park. These are long-term residences, home to Morecambe's most hard-up. The sky is almost fully black and as Tess drives along the track, which loops around the site, she's finding it difficult to make out the numbers affixed to the vans. It's not a nice place. After dark, this is not where you want to be. 'Seventeen . . . nineteen . . .' Avril reads the numbers aloud. 'Twenty-one. Here it is. Twenty-one, right?'

Tess stops the car and double-checks the text from Clive. 'Twenty-one,' she affirms. There is nowhere to park, so she pulls the car on to the grass in front of Greg Lancashire's home. They get out. Greg's caravan itself is in darkness, but from the light of next door's van, Tess can see it's in a bad state of repair. There's a layer of filth covering the entire fibreglass shell and one of the front window frames has come loose. Give the thing a firm pull and it would probably come off in your hand. 'I don't like this,' Avril says.

There are raised voices coming from the van opposite. Yelling. It's a man and woman. Husband and wife, by the sounds of it. '*You?*' the woman shouts bitterly. 'What are *you* gonna do? Don't make me laugh.'

'I'm warning you, lady.'

'You're warning me?' she says. 'You couldn't warn a fucking cat.'

Tess taps her key fob on the door of number twenty-one and almost immediately, it's opened. The inhabitant must have been watching Tess and Avril approach. She's a fragile-looking woman in her early twenties. She's rail-thin – her body is that of an eleven-year-old – and has a quilt draped around her shoulders for warmth. Tess can smell a musty damp odour coming from the girl. 'Hi,' she says, 'we're looking for Greg Lancashire?'

'Are you the police?'

'God, no,' replies Tess. 'I hate the police. We're with a charity that looks into miscarriages of justice. We have some questions for Greg. Is he around?' The woman shakes her head. 'Maybe you could help us, then?'

Inside, it's pretty squalid. Avril's eyes widen when the woman switches on a lamp and the full extent of the place is revealed.

Tess avoids Avril's gaze. Her own eyes are drawn to the tiles behind the cooker; they should be white, but it's as if someone has thrown a pan of soup against them and left it to dry. Tess's boots make a soft thwacking sound as she walks across the kitchen linoleum, which is sticky with grease, following the woman into the lounge area. A cat is curled up inside a cardboard box; she has four black-and-white kittens attached to her belly who are making tiny mewing noises. Across the back of the sofa area is a large, glass aquarium. But it has no water inside. When Tess sees movement in the lower left-hand corner, she realizes it's housing a snake. A big snake. She experiences a moment of horror as she looks from the kittens, so small that they can only be a few days old, back to the snake again. What if they feed the kittens to the—

'Sit down, if you like,' says the young woman.

Tess resists the urge to dust off the chair before perching. Avril, meanwhile, is hovering a couple of feet away, reluctant to sit at all. Tess glares at her. And Avril glares back, appalled that she's being asked to make physical contact with anything inside this hellhole. 'Do it,' mouths Tess, and Avril acquiesces, settling her bottom on to a ladder-back chair that seems to sigh under her weight.

'Are you Greg's girlfriend?' Tess asks the woman, who holds out her left hand to show a stupidly large, ostentatious ring.

'We got married last year.'

Tess smiles. 'Congratulations, Mrs Lancashire.'

Hearing 'Mrs' makes her go all coy. It's as though she's still a child pretending to be grown up. 'I'm Shannon.'

The snake moves and Tess flinches. She needs to get out of here. She is not good around reptiles. That said, she doesn't like to see any animals abused, and she's not sure that keeping a large predator inside a dirty glass tank is any kind of life for the poor snake. She wonders how Greg Lancashire would fare if he were kept inside one. 'Did Greg ever mention Ella Muir to you?' she asks Shannon.

'Just that he was with her for a while. It was big news around here so I knew about her being murdered.'

'What's he like?'

At this Shannon seems taken aback. As though no one's ever been interested enough to ask her a personal question before. Struggling to answer, she says, 'He's like . . .' and then she stops.

'Is he a good husband?' prompts Avril.

'Yeah,' she replies, firmly, as though persuading herself. 'Yeah, he's a good husband.'

'He treats you well?' asks Avril.

'I think so . . .?'

Tess smiles encouragingly at Shannon. 'Shannon,' she says, 'tell me, does he ever . . . does Greg ever get mad with you?' and Shannon looks towards Avril, quietly panicked. She seems reluctant to answer Tess's question but does not have the skill set to divert the conversation. 'Does he ever, say, stop you from seeing your friends? Stuff like that?' pushes Tess.

'Sometimes,' replies Shannon, 'but that's only because he's frightened I'll go off with another fella. He's very protective. He really treasures what we've got together, so it's only right that he gets mad. It's not because he doesn't like my friends or anythin'.'

Tess smiles again as though she understands. As though Greg's behaviour is perfectly reasonable. Every woman's dream. Then she drops her voice to just above a whisper. 'Does Greg ever scare you, Shannon?'

And Shannon drops her head. 'Now and again.'

'Does he ever hurt you?'

Shannon nods, head down still.

'Do you think Greg could be capable of *really* hurting a woman?' she asks. 'Say if he was more than angry?'

And Shannon looks up. 'Maybe.'

Now

'WHY THE HELL wasn't he investigated?'

It's the following morning and Tess and Avril are in 'Interview Room 3' with a defiant DI Gillian Frain. Gillian refused to see them initially, claiming, via the desk sergeant, to be up to her eyes in paperwork. So Tess issued a warning: 'Tell her to get down here or I'll pass on this information to the press,' and Gillian gave in. It was an empty threat but Gillian Frain was with them within moments and Tess made a mental note to use the bluff more regularly. The police's reputation is taking a battering in the British press right now, reports of non-submission of vital evidence being an everyday occurrence. DI Frain is yet to see her own name in the papers and Tess assumes she'd like to keep it that way, hence the reason she's with them now.

'He was not investigated,' DI Frain replies to Tess's question, 'because, as I explained, we didn't know about Greg Lancashire's link to the victim at the time of the murder.'

'You didn't know because you didn't bother to look. All that manpower at your disposal and he didn't even crop up? It's taken me no more than a week to find the connection between Greg Lancashire and Ella Muir and there is only one of me.' Tess sees Gillian eyeing Avril. 'She's a trainee.'

Tess pushes a picture of Carrie Kamara across the desk. It's Carrie as she is now. Not the Carrie Gillian would've known from the trial and the months preceding the trial. Carrie's scalp is visible through her stringy hair. Her skin is grey and hangs loosely from the bones of the skull. She's looking at the camera but her eyes are empty. She has a beaten-down, helpless expression, and if you had to guess her age, you'd put her somewhere around mid-sixties. 'This woman is dying in there. Do you understand that? She's dying. She's losing the will to live in prison and all because you were too lazy to do your job.'

'A jury of twelve people convicted Mrs Kamara.'

'Because you told them what to think!' yells Tess, and Gillian Frain looks away. 'You provided a witness who said Carrie was at Ella's address, a witness who wouldn't see a waving hand in front of his own face. Your CCTV evidence was sketchy at best. You didn't submit the fibre analysis. Oh, and guess what? Ella Muir had a real nasty bastard for a boyfriend. A guy who gets violent if his girlfriend tries to have a life of her own. Looking at all that evidence, I can *totally* see how you had no option but to charge Carrie Kamara.'

'As I said, *twelve* people convicted Carrie Kamara—'

'Oh, fuck off with your twelve people.'

They make their way to the breaker's yard where Greg Lancashire is currently employed. Tess is still fuming. How is it possible that DI Gillian Frain, as senior investigating officer, with all the resources at her disposal, didn't think to interview Ella Muir's closest friends? If she'd interviewed Steph, she'd have been aware of Greg Lancashire right from the start, and instead of making all the evidence she collected fit her hackneyed hypothesis of Carrie Kamara being responsible for Ella's death, just because she thought Carrie had some sort of jealous grudge, she'd have realized that Ella was engaged in an abusive relationship. Which is a massive red flag if ever there was one.

'I don't think we should go,' Avril is saying as the satnav tells them to take a right in one hundred metres.

'Of course we should go.'

'Greg Lancashire is dangerous.'

'He's only dangerous if you're sleeping with him. We're not sleeping with him.'

DI Gillian Frain had argued that Carrie Kamara's statement – which they believed to be fantastical – along with her behaviour in custody, had added weight to the evidence that they already had against her. She said they'd had no option but to class her as their primary suspect and once the Crown Prosecution Service authorized a murder charge, yes, naturally all other investigative leads were terminated. 'I don't know what else you would have expected us to do,' she said reasonably, and Tess opened her mouth to argue but found, for once in her life, she had no argument.

What else could DI Frain have done? She had a suspect. She had evidence against that suspect. She had motive. A witness. She had the suspect's blood at the scene.

And yet.

And yet Tess is still furious. If they'd only interviewed Ella's friends and co-workers fully there would've been doubt in their minds. And they would have acted on that doubt and pursued more leads. Which would have taken them to Greg.

They pull into the breaker's yard. It's a pretty big operation: cars stacked on top of each other, the whole place overflowing with scrapped vehicles. Near the entrance is a wrecked police car, its roof torn clean off.

Tess and Avril approach a decrepit prefab office that displays the sign: 'RECEPTION'. A light rain is starting to fall and the sky is heavy with cloud. Tess's heels sink into the earth and she looks up to the sky, trying to establish how much daylight is left. Half an hour? Certainly no more than an hour. Tess mounts the steps to the office and sticks her head around the door. Inside is a man with a large, lumpen body. He's slouched over some sort of ledger, anachronistic in the computer age, and appears to be adding numbers to a column in pencil. Pencil, the tax avoider's friend, thinks Tess. He doesn't look up and so Tess knocks politely on the inside of the door. 'Greg Lancashire?' she asks. And the man waves in the general direction of *out there somewhere.*

They walk between the stacks of cars. Avril is grumbling, saying that she doesn't think he's here, but Tess presses on regardless. She has the bit between her teeth now and she must speak to Greg Lancashire, at least to exclude him from this if nothing else.

Long shadows are cast from the stacks of cars. As the temperature starts to dip, there is an audible groan from the contracting metal. They continue to walk and Tess knows how vulnerable they must appear in their heeled shoes, their handbags swinging gently at their sides.

'What are we even *doing* here?' Avril says and Tess is starting to wonder the same thing herself. They could disappear from here and no one would know. There are no cameras. No people around. This place is kept purposefully shut off to watchful eyes.

'I really think we should call it a day,' Avril says.

'I think we should too but what about Carrie?' And when Avril looks sceptical, she adds, 'We're her only hope, Avril.' Reluctantly, Avril nods her head in assent. 'Come on, we'll try the next row of cars and if he's not there, we'll catch him at home early tomorrow morning.'

They set off and before the next corner they hear a noise. It's a sound Tess recognizes. A blowtorch. Tess quickens her step, turns right, and there he is.

He's squatting beside the wheel arch of an old RAV4, safety goggles in place, absorbed in his task. He looks to be around mid-thirties and is wearing well-worn jeans, a jacket, Adidas three stripes, and a red leather apron to protect him from stray sparks. He looks to be the kind of guy who can handle himself.

He is unaware of their presence and so Tess takes the opportunity to survey him for a moment. He has a strong jaw and prominent cheekbones, emphasized by his dark-blond hair which has been cut exceptionally short around his ears. He must have been squatting for a time but it seems effortless. He's flexible, agile.

'Greg Lancashire?'

No response.

She moves closer and shouts above the noise of the blowtorch. 'Mr Lancashire?'

Greg cuts the gas and lifts his goggles, smiles. He looks Tess up and down. 'Who's asking?'

He's still smiling and Tess makes the split-second decision to go with it. She threads some stray strands of hair behind her ear, crosses one foot in front of the other, and adjusts her expression to appear available and girly. 'You're a difficult man to track down, Mr Lancashire. I'm Tess Gilroy and this is my colleague Avril Hughes. Pleased to meet you.'

'Greg,' he says, standing, and puts the blowtorch on the bonnet of the car.

For a second it seems he's delighted to have company. But there's something just a little off. Something not quite right about the guy.

'What can I do for you?' he asks.

'We spoke with your wife yesterday.'

'Oh yeah?'

'Did she mention it?' asks Tess.

'She didn't actually. Must have slipped her mind.'

'Well, we're investigating a possible wrongful conviction and I wondered if you'd be able to answer a few questions.'

'Don't see why not.'

Tess turns to Avril and Avril steps forward, smiles at Greg. 'You were in a relationship with Ella Muir?' she says.

'Yeah.'

'What was she like?' she asks.

'She was beautiful.'

'Can you tell me a little bit about your relationship?'

'Well, I was fucking her,' he says and he holds Avril's gaze.

Tess steps in. 'You were never questioned by the police, as I understand it.'

'Nope.'

'Why was that?' asks Tess.

He laughs. 'Er, because I didn't do it? They caught who did it straight away, didn't they? Besides, I had an alibi.'

'Where were you on the evening of the murder?'

'That's none of your business, *Tess*.'

Tess tries to smile as though she's enjoying this game they're playing, but there's a steeliness in Greg's eyes. A rigidity to his jaw. Tess shifts her weight to her other foot. Suddenly she's uncomfortable. Uneasy. Greg's expression seems to conceal something, something else: a kind of deep loathing, perhaps? Tess decides to soft-pedal. 'We're just trying to find out anything we can that might help our client,' she tells him. 'She's doing fifteen years in prison for a crime she didn't commit.'

Greg lets out a long low whistle. 'Then I'd say you've got your work cut out.'

'We have. It's certainly not an easy case to prove, I'll agree with you there . . . Can you tell me a little more about Ella?'

'I loved her.'

'What else?'

'She was funny. She liked life. She was a happy girl and you don't meet many of those around here. That's why she wasn't short of male attention.'

'Did that ever make you jealous?' asks Avril.

He shrugs. 'Not really. Like I said, I was the one she was sleeping with.'

He turns to Tess and she nods in agreement. Makes like she can totally see his point, to keep him on side. She's not sure whether to push him further; she senses a charge in the air, an electricity around Greg that wasn't there a moment ago. 'Did you ever . . .' she says, hesitating, wondering if she should continue to press. 'Did you ever *hurt* Ella?'

'I loved Ella. I told you that.'

'Yes, but sometimes love can be hard, Greg. Sometimes when you really love someone emotions can take over and things can get—'

'What are you suggesting?'

'Just that relationships get heated. People – both men and women – can get physical and strike out when they're not really meaning to, and I'm just interested if this ever happened between—'

'You're not listening to me,' he says between his teeth. 'I *loved* Ella. I *still* love Ella.'

'I hear you and I'm sure that's true . . . It's just that we were told Ella was seeing two different men at the same time. And I wondered . . . Well, I wondered how that affected things? Were you aware Ella was in a relationship with another man at the time?'

Out of nowhere, Greg grabs Tess. He seizes her by the throat and pushes her up against the RAV4.

'Don't say that,' he whispers.

'I'm sorry, I—'

Tess tries to pull away.

'Don't say that.' His face is inches from hers.

'I didn't mean to upset you, I was just—'

'Why are you here?' he demands.

'To help my client,' Tess manages weakly.

'I don't think so. I don't think you're telling me the truth. I think you think I did it.'

'I'm here to find out what happened.'

Tess tries to pull away again but he's got a strength she can't match.

'I loved Ella.'

'I know.'

'I would never hurt Ella.'

'I know.'

Tess's throat is burning and her lungs are on fire.

'Do you?' he yells at her. '*Do* you!'

Tess tries to nod.

Then, incredibly, Greg picks up the blowtorch with his free hand. He picks it up and holds it close to Tess's face.

'Christ, no. *Don't,*' she begs, panicked, totally staggered at how things have escalated so quickly.

Greg flicks on the flame and Tess hears Avril let out a yelp from behind her. 'What do you want?' he demands.

'Nothing. Please. I don't want anything.' Tess's legs are weak. The heat from the flame is unbearable.

'You want me to confess?' he shouts. 'You came here thinking *I'd tell you*? That I'd tell you I did it?'

Tess can't answer.

'I loved that girl!' he yells again, and Tess can only hope that someone hears. Can only hope Avril is trying to get her phone out of her bag and is calling the police.

Tess's skin is on fire. The pressure on her throat is making her eyes bulge. Her body starts to quake. 'I loved her,' Greg says, weaker now.

But Tess's skin is starting to cook.

'Please,' she tries, desperate.

'I really loved her,' he says. And he is crying.

Now

TESS LIES SUPINE, her head unsupported. Even though he wears a mask, she can feel his breath seeping through to her skin. It's not unpleasant though. It's comforting. Like a soft breeze.

Now he's irrigating the burned skin with saline solution that comes ready prepared in a plastic pouch and this is *not* pleasant. It feels as if he's taken a flat blade to her cheek and is slicing away the upper layers of her flesh. She whimpers and he hushes her gently. The saline solution runs down her cheek, on to her neck, and gets lost in her hair. 'Let me get some tissue for that,' the medic says absently, and he begins dabbing at the area behind her ear.

It's the same doctor who attended to Avril's broken nose. He works methodically, with care. He is late forties, greying at the temples, and has dark soulful eyes. The rest of his face is obscured by the mask. 'This might hurt a little,' he says, and in her peripheral vision she sees the glint of polished steel as it catches the light, and what follows is a piercing white-hot pain, deep within her cheek. There are two metallic fragments lodged inside the burn, the burn which was inflicted by Greg Lancashire, and they have to come out. Tess assumes it was she who transferred the fragments. After Greg released her, she'd steadied herself on the bonnet of the car he was working on, fighting to get some air into her lungs; and then, when Tess and Avril fled, she remembers touching her face as she couldn't be sure if Greg had wounded her or not.

She wonders if Pete Kamara knew about Ella's relationship with Greg Lancashire. It would certainly give him a motive to kill her. She also wonders if she should press charges against Greg Lancashire tonight, or if it will wait until tomorrow. She should do it tonight. She *will* do it tonight. Just as soon as—

The medic is using tweezers and more saline solution to try to dislodge the splinters. 'Almost there,' Tess can hear him saying, 'if you can just hold on a bit longer for me.' She's not sure she can. Her eyes are brimming with tears and her hands are clasped together so tightly she's losing feeling in her fingers. She could do with a piece of wood to bite down on. A shot of morphine. Someone to pin her to the bed.

And then it's over. He's telling her it's over and she'll need to keep the wound covered. He's telling her he'll prescribe a course of antibiotics and she'll want to visit her local surgery to have it checked within forty-eight hours. 'Luckily it's only a surface wound, but if you find yourself feeling feverish or just generally unwell, come straight back to A and E.' He removes his mask and gathers up the rubbish from around her: the empty saline pouches, the packets containing the sterile dressing, the blue tissue he used to mop up the liquid from around her head, and he bundles it all up before tossing it into the non-hazardous waste bin. Then he raises the top half of the bed, bringing her into a sitting position. 'OK?' Tess nods her head weakly. 'Dizzy?' he asks.

'No.'

He looks at Avril sitting beside the bed and Tess thinks he will advise Avril to drive home. But he doesn't. Instead, he looks back at Tess and hesitates before speaking. Whatever he is about to say can't be good because gone is the empathetic expression, gone is the smile from his dark, lovely eyes.

'You know if you're going to keep attacking each other like this,' he says sternly, 'I'll have to file a domestic abuse report.'

He's not joking. He thinks they're a couple.

He thinks they're a couple who are trying to kill each other.

Tess looks at Avril expecting her to at least crack a small smile, but Avril's still too annoyed with her to speak.

'You could've got yourself killed,' Avril says later in the car on the way home.

'Yeah, well, I didn't.'

'You could've got *me* killed.'

'I didn't do that either.'

Avril turns her head away in disgust and stares out of the window. Tess stops the car. 'OK. Say what you need to say.'

It takes Avril a moment to get her words lined up but when she does she says this: 'I just don't see why we had to go and talk to the guy when we knew he was dangerous. What was there to gain? You should've told the police what you knew and let them deal with it.'

'The police are not interested in Greg Lancashire. And they will remain not interested in him until Carrie's conviction is overturned. *If* her conviction is overturned. Only then will they revisit the case and look into potential suspects.' Tess takes a breath. 'Answer me this. Do you think Greg Lancashire is capable of violence against Ella Muir?'

'Yes! *Of course* yes. That's not what I'm saying. I'm not refuting your motives. I'm simply trying to be sensible in our approach and I think the way you went about it was . . . well, it was stupid.'

'I repeat: the police won't be interested in Greg Lancashire until Carrie is acquitted. But you *know* this, Avril. At least now *we* know what he's capable of. We know he's volatile, we know he's capable of extreme violence, and so we can keep digging.'

Avril is not convinced. Tess puts the car into gear and rejoins the flow of traffic. They're almost at the turning for the motorway slip road before Avril speaks again. 'Do you always put yourself at risk like this?' she asks. And Tess tells her she doesn't. 'So why now? Why this case?'

'Because I know in my heart Carrie didn't do it.'

'*How* do you know that? I mean, how do you know for sure?'

'I know because she wouldn't leave her daughter all alone in the world. You've seen the bond between the two of them. That mother wouldn't leave her daughter no matter what.' Tess accelerates up the slip road and knocks the car into fifth as she joins the motorway. Checking her mirror, she sees she's clear to pull across both the inside and middle lanes, overtaking a Royal Mail lorry which itself is overtaking a caravan.

'You mean like you did with Steph?' asks Avril.

Tess glares at her, shocked.

'What?' Avril says. 'You think I didn't work it out? That guy in Wetherspoon's gushing over you two finding each other again . . .? And the girl looks just like you, Tess.'

Tess swallows.

'She even talks like you and walks like you,' Avril goes on, 'which is pretty remarkable when you think about it. It just goes to show that the whole nature-versus-nurture debate is—'

'Stop talking.'

Not one person in Tess's everyday life knows that Steph is her daughter. It's her secret. Hers alone. Tess is suddenly filled with a fear that's as close to terror as she's ever felt. She never wanted this aspect of her life exposed. Certainly not for someone like Avril to be allowed to speculate upon.

'Has she been trying to contact you?' Avril asks. 'Has she been trying to track you down, is that it? Is that why you moved away from Morecambe? Is that why you're always moving house? Why you don't tell anyone your address? In case she turns up on your doorstep?'

Tess keeps her eyes fixed directly ahead. The glare from the headlights on the other side of the carriageway is aggravating her already sore eyes but she doesn't blink. She dips her foot on the accelerator and the needle moves from eighty to eighty-five, ninety.

'Why didn't you want to see her?' Avril presses.

'I just didn't.'

'Yeah, but—'

'Am I interrogating you about *your* life? Am I asking you why you felt the need to invent a whole fucking person? A mother-in-law? I made a mistake and I didn't want to think about it again. And yes, maybe I didn't want her turning up at my door, mad at me, holding me accountable, wanting answers . . . And I sure as hell didn't go telling you about it so you could bring it up every five seconds.'

'Perhaps you didn't want everyone to know what happened.'

'So? Perhaps I *didn't* want everyone to know. So what? Who walks around saying, "Oh, yeah, me too . . . I gave a baby away when I was younger." No one *does* that! We move on and we keep it to ourselves . . . Don't go making out like there's something wrong with me. I'm not the first woman to make that choice and then bury it. That's how people get though *life*, Avril.'

Avril is quiet.

They drive on for a time. Tess thinks maybe she might have screamed at her a little *too* hard. She glances sideways and sees Avril is taking a boiled sweet from her handbag. She unwraps it carefully before popping it inside her mouth. 'Well, why change things now?' Avril says quietly. 'When it's all working out so well for you.'

Now

IN FRONT OF the bathroom mirror, Tess tentatively eases the edges of the dressing away from her skin. Beneath, the wound from the blowtorch is raw, open and weeping. An orange-yellow liquid seeps down her cheek, a liquid that doesn't appear entirely of human origin. Tess winces and hurriedly presses the dressing back into place, smoothing down the edges of the surgical tape. Now she wishes she'd not looked.

She heats a cup of milk in the microwave and carries it up to the home office. She is unable to sleep. She tells herself this is because of the burn – no longer is it simply painful, it's now starting to itch and throb, which is why she'd decided to see what was going on under there. She yawns. Checks her watch. It's 1.43 a.m. She really needs to sleep. But she *can't* sleep. She tells herself it's because of the case. Tells herself it is definitely *not* Avril getting inside her head about Steph. About the choices Tess has made. The way she's lived her life.

Before going to bed, Tess had received a text from Melanie Phelps – the woman who, like Carrie, owned a white limited-edition Honda CR-V at the time of Ella's death, the woman they were hoping could have been driving past the CCTV cameras on the night of the murder. Melanie had told them it couldn't have been her driving because she was on holiday. And having no other options left, this had prompted Tess to arrange a second meeting with Steph, which led to the discovery of Greg

Lancashire's involvement with Ella, which led to her daughter fleeing Tess's presence in the pub when she discovered her mother's true identity, and which also led to the burn on Tess's face.

Tess read the text.

You won't believe this but the friend who was dog sitting while I was in Spain says she used my car a couple of times! Wish she'd told me sooner! It could have been her on CCTV? Hope this hasn't put you out much?

'No, it's hardly put me out at all,' she'd said after flinging her phone across the room.

She sips her hot milk now, surrounded by papers, files, maps, photographs. She has all of this great evidence, evidence that should cast doubt on Carrie's conviction, but is it enough? She had been hoping for so much more. She sifts through the crime scene photographs and reminds herself that it's not her job to find out who did this to Ella. They might never know who did this to Ella. All she needs to do is present enough new evidence to convince the appellate court to retry the case. So she'll stay inside this room till she finds it. She tells herself that the reason sleep is evading her right now is because she's so dedicated to her job that she really won't rest until Carrie Kamara is released from prison.

Is it working? she thinks. Is it possible to pull the wool over your own eyes?

Tess picks up her phone. She needs to keep busy. She goes to dial before considering the time. It's now 1.54 a.m., not really the hour for business calls, so she puts the phone down. It will have to wait until tomorrow. But tomorrow she's presenting her findings to the Innocence UK panel, so she picks up the phone again and dials.

It's answered by a sleepy-but-trying-to-force-himself-awake Clive. 'What's happened?' he asks.

This is typical Clive. Years of working as a detective have made him feel indispensable and he is assuming that the only reason she is calling after midnight is because she has an intruder and/ or she requires assistance because her safety is compromised. She can picture him, hastily shoving one leg into a pair of jeans, hopping around the room with his phone to his ear, swiping the change from the bedside cabinet, striving not to wake Rebecca.

'You know you said Greg Lancashire has a criminal record?' she says. 'Well, do you think you can get access to his police file and bring it with you to tomorrow's meeting?'

There is a long pause. 'It's two o'clock in the morning.'

'Can you get it or not?'

Clive sighs. 'Probably.'

She cuts the call and strikes through the third item on her to-do list, which she's noted as: 'Greg's previous'. Numbers one and two have already been dealt with and number four is not exactly pressing: 'Update social media'.

Tess is responsible for the social media accounts of Innocence UK and though she can see the very real need to keep people updated and aware of their services, the progress of particular cases, she resents the drain on her time. She opens her Twitter account and scrolls through her timeline. A couple of years ago, Tom employed the services of a young digital media strategist to advise them on their social media platform. Tess had been dead against it. 'We can't get through the correspondence we already get,' she'd argued, but she'd been overruled. This was a way, Tom said, to get information out there in one easy click. 'You can reach thousands of prisoners instead of replying to each one individually. Honestly, Tess, this will free up so much of our time, you won't believe you ever doubted it.' Tess can believe she doubted it because she still does. She doesn't believe she reaches the people who need reaching this way, and instead her notifications are cluttered with true-crime fans looking for their next project, as well as random lonely people from all four corners of the earth, looking to interact with someone, anyone, who is willing to listen.

Tess runs down her notifications – there are over a hundred – and clicks on the heart icon of each message to indicate she 'likes' what they've written. Then she goes back to her timeline. There are other charities besides Innocence UK who investigate wrongful convictions and they are far more present on social media than Tess is. Tess follows them and feels a general irritation every time they post success stories or promotional material to make their companies look good. She can't bring herself to unfollow them, though, because that would mean denying herself a certain masochistic pleasure that comes from reading about what these people she doesn't actually like get up to. One company – which is essentially a group of solicitors touting for business, masquerading as do-gooders who work tirelessly on behalf of victims of miscarriages of justice – are at a charity function in their best clobber. Tess rolls her eyes at the pictures. These are her competitors and just look at them. All red faces and pulled-in guts. Holding champagne flutes aloft, celebrating the release of – when Tess looks into it – someone who is clearly guilty but they've managed to get off on a technicality. She huffs at the screen and closes the page. She's being uncharitable. She knows this. These people are just trying to do a job, as is she. So why does she find them all so very annoying?

Perhaps it's because she doesn't like herself so much right now. Perhaps faffing about on social media when you're trying to avoid feeling the one thing you can't avoid feeling will make you uncharitable and mean. Perhaps she should simply look in the mirror and acknowledge that luring your daughter to a Wetherspoon's pub while neglecting to tell her that you are the person who abandoned her, you are the person who let her down most in her life, is not the way any decent human being should behave.

Now

THEORETICALLY, MIA COULD visit Carrie every week if she wanted to. Visits need only be pre-booked in advance by telephone and it is not difficult to arrange. In an ideal world that's what would happen. Weekly visits would keep Carrie going. She could cope with prison life if she knew she had them to look forward to. But weekly visits are now impossible. The journey from Morecambe to Styal Prison takes only one and a quarter hours by car. But Mia doesn't have a car right now. And the journey from Morecambe to Styal using public transport can take as much as three and a half hours each way – something that Mia was accustomed to doing *before* she had the baby, but not something she can do so easily now.

Today, a friend of Mia's has kindly brought mother and baby to Styal. A friend who, during their visit, plans to hit the charity shops of nearby Wilmslow, where, she says, the rich mothers and footballers' wives of south Manchester donate their children's designer outfits. Two weeks ago, she found a Dior christening gown for twenty-eight pounds, which she promptly sold on eBay for eighty.

Carrie starts to cry when she sees Phoebe. It is the first time she's seen her granddaughter in the flesh.

'She's put on point two five kilos,' Mia tells Carrie proudly.

Carrie doesn't know how this translates into pounds and ounces but cradles Phoebe in her arms and kisses the top of the baby's head. Carrie inhales her scent. She wants to absorb the child. Never wants to let her go.

Mercifully, Mia has been blessed with a 'good' baby. Phoebe rarely cries, she sleeps for six hours at a time, and when she is awake she is remarkably amenable. Carrie shudders to think what the alternative would have spelled for Mia. What could have been. Carrie had lain awake many nights during Mia's pregnancy, worrying about Mia, worrying about her emotional state, worrying what would happen should she be dealt a baby that needed so much more from her than she was able to give. Particularly because Mia is on her own.

Mia made the decision not to tell her baby's father about the pregnancy, which was not something Carrie condoned, but something she had had to stay quiet about to keep on good terms with Mia. Mia was adamant she wanted to do it all by herself. 'Why make life so hard?' Carrie had asked. She was thinking about the financial implications as much as anything else, but Mia had argued the boy in question was 'a slut', 'not to be relied upon', and she certainly didn't want to have him in her life for the next however long if she had the choice to keep him out of it.

'I passed by Ella Muir's house yesterday,' remarks Mia now, brightly. She is rooting around inside the nappy bag, looking for a bib. She pulls out a packet of baby wipes instead and uses one to wipe Phoebe's chin.

'What took you over to that part of town?' asks Carrie, trying to keep her voice level, trying not to show the alarm she's feeling inside.

'Oh, I don't know, I was taking Phoebe for a walk and she was sound asleep, so I just kept walking. I had my music on and the sun was out. I found myself there by accident.'

'By accident,' Carrie repeats back, flatly. She looks over her shoulder to check if any of the prison officers are within earshot.

'Well, maybe not *entirely* by accident,' Mia says impishly. 'I knew where I was going. I think I kind of wanted to see the place again? See what it's like during the daytime? It's not changed that much,' she says. She puts the baby wipes away. 'You know what, it's actually not a bad little street. I got chatting to another mum pushing a buggy there and the rents are really reasonable – what with it being over that side of town. For another hundred a month more than I'm paying now, I could afford a two-bedroom terraced. I might see if I can go on the housing list.'

Carrie surveys her daughter. She seems perfectly calm. Perfectly together. Perfectly reasonable.

'Perhaps that's not such a good idea,' Carrie suggests gently.

'No?'

'It might look a little . . . *odd*.'

'Odd? Really? D'you think so?'

'Maybe.'

'Oh, OK,' Mia says, not at all put out. 'It was just an idea. I'm thinking ahead really, to when Phoebe gets older. We're fine sharing one bedroom for now, but I can't stay there for ever. We're going to need our own space. Especially when *you* come home,' she adds, smiling. 'We're definitely going to need more space when that happens.'

Carrie tries her best to smile back. 'Yeah,' she says. 'We will.'

Now

TESS STANDS NEXT to the whiteboard. On it she has written a list of Greg Lancashire's previous crimes and alleged crimes:

1. Handling of stolen goods
2. Battery
3. Detention of woman against her will for unlawful sexual intercourse
4. Possessing a controlled drug

'He was charged with numbers one, two and four on the list. Not enough evidence for number three . . .' She lets the words hang. The panel jots down Greg's criminal record. And Tess wishes she had more to give them. She goes on to say she's been trying to make contact with the woman who could have been driving Melanie Phelps's car on the night of the murder, but as yet has had no luck. Her calls have remained unanswered.

'Is it enough?' asks Tom, gesturing to the whiteboard.

'I don't know,' Tess replies.

Addressing the panel, Tom says, 'So, thoughts? Do we take more time? Go at this again, or do we hedge our bets and present Carrie's case to the Court of Appeal now?' Tess looks around the table. They're undecided. They're aware that they're lacking the one good piece of evidence that would swing this for them. But they're also cognizant of the fact that they can't throw unlimited resources at this. There comes a time when they have to make the leap and go with what they've got, so that the case can be moved forward, or so they can put their resources into helping the next victim of an alleged miscarriage of justice, rather than continue flogging a dead horse.

Dr Fran Adler asks Tess if she sees any advantage in going through the evidence again. Would there be any merit in exploring avenues she may have missed? Fran asks, and resignedly, Tess tells her that this is all she has. She can try for more but she's not hopeful. 'The blood's still a problem,' Fran says, biting down on her lower lip.

Tess moves away from the whiteboard and retakes her seat.

'I don't want to retest the blood,' says Tom firmly. 'Let's keep it as low-key as possible, to be on the safe side. We'll put it down to an anomaly, and if they argue the point, we'll go with the "mistreatment of forensic materials" angle. Who knows, the fact that they lost the fibre test results might highlight the incompetence of the investigation and it could go in our favour.' Tom looks around the room. 'I vote we present to the appellate court now.'

Tess looks around the room.

'Show of hands?' Tom says. 'Those in agreement . . . ?'

He gets the vote.

As Tess is packing up her belongings, she feels her phone vibrating inside her trouser pocket. She takes it out and looks at the screen. 'Stephanie Reynolds' is the caller. Steph.

After taking off from the pub, her daughter now wants to speak to her?

Tess's mouth goes dry as her thumb hovers over 'accept'. She looks up. There are still three or four people in the room. They're discussing Carrie's chances, wondering if this will be an Innocence UK success story or one of their few failures. Clive catches her eye. He lifts his finger to his face. 'You OK?' he mouths, referencing the burn on her cheek.

Tess nods.

He motions taking a drink. 'Time for a quick one?' he mouths and she thinks, yes, she'll have a drink, but that is all.

'Two minutes,' she mouths back and Clive nods before shrugging on his coat.

The phone feels red-hot in Tess's hand. She never expected Steph to try to make contact. Not now. Not after watching her flee after discovering Tess's real identity.

A few years ago, a young woman on probation for drugs offences confided to Tess about her baby's acid reflux. Her baby would not stop crying and the mother described herself as 'not coping'. She described feeling powerless, sleep-deprived; she talked about feeling so desperate, so on the edge, she worried she might hurt her child. Tess went home and immediately googled the condition and what she read stunned her. She realized she might have given her own baby away because of this self-same illness, an illness that had gone undiagnosed, an illness that was often considered a precursor to shaken baby syndrome, such is the despair experienced by the parent. If Tess had had her own mother there, perhaps she'd have got through it. Some moral support might have changed the outcome completely.

Tess looks at the phone and reflects that Steph must really hate Tess for what she did the other day. Hoodwinking Steph and concealing from her who she really was for the sake of Carrie's case. She must hate Tess and that's why she's calling, to tell her as such, to scream at her, now that the shock has worn off.

Well, Tess doesn't need to hear her say it out loud. She knows it was inexcusable. She knows she doesn't deserve any kind of mercy from this girl.

So she presses 'decline'. She presses 'decline' and slips the phone back inside her pocket.

Avril approaches and asks Tess what happens next. 'What do we do now?' she asks.

'We prepare,' replies Tess.

'Prepare, how?'

'The technical work is over. This moment, this decision to present to the appellate court, is what we've been working towards. Go home, Avril. Go home and get a good night's rest. Because tomorrow is when the real work starts.'

Five Months Later

CARRIE IS WAITING. She has spent a lot of time waiting, at the mercy of other people, things, events that have been outside of her control, and she wonders if she will spend the next eleven years of her life waiting. Perhaps her prayers will be answered and she can stop waiting. She has no way of telling. Today, she admires the tulips outside C wing which she planted last September. They are in full bloom and she's quietly pleased with the way they turned out.

Before her incarceration, Carrie would merely tell Alan, their odd-job man, what she wanted where, with vague instructions of how she wanted the overall effect to look. Alan wasn't a gardener as such, more like one of those practical men who can do a bit of everything, so if she found a damp patch on the spare bedroom wall, or if she ordered IKEA furniture for Mia's bedroom that Pete couldn't be bothered/didn't know how to assemble, or if they were going away for a long weekend and the cat needed feeding, it was Alan they called upon.

She wonders if Alan is still around. The cat isn't. Luigi had curled up on Carrie's knee and when she'd gone to gently nudge him on to the sofa, she'd realized he'd very considerately died on her. Which had been one less thing to worry about at the time because Pete had never liked the cat and she'd worried what would become of him should she be going to prison. Pete said he wasn't a cat person, 'Can't stand them,' but Carrie knew this was nonsense because his mother had always had cats and he'd mentioned an inquisitive Siamese he'd been particularly fond of as a child. What Pete *couldn't* stand was the fact that their cat wasn't interested in *him*, and Pete, being someone who needed to be centre of attention at all times, found this rankled.

She'd buried Luigi herself. Being by the coast, the soil was fine and sandy and it wasn't a hard task. She'd been released from police custody earlier that day after being held for twenty-four hours. She'd been sent home in a taxi whilst they awaited the results of the DNA test. If her DNA matched the blood they'd found at the scene, she'd be rearrested and charged. When she got out of the taxi and put her key in the front door, she'd found Pete waiting for her on the other side of the door. 'If you're staying here, I'm not,' he'd said simply, and he'd disappeared into the bedroom, banging cupboard doors, flinging clothes into suitcases. He'd left without saying goodbye and the next time she saw him was at the trial.

A prison officer heads out of C wing now carrying a large stack of toilet rolls and a dustpan and brush. 'Any news?' she asks, and Carrie replies she's heard nothing as yet. 'Takes time,' says the prison officer, and she tells Carrie they all have their fingers crossed for her.

Carrie smiles.

The psychiatrist working for the prosecution had claimed Carrie was a high-functioning psychopath and Carrie had worried upon entry to Styal Prison how this would affect each prisoner's view of her. She worried they would try to knock it out of her. That the head of the prison hierarchy would arrange for her to be beaten into submission. She worried the prison officers themselves would keep order using a system of brutality. Her first night inside the prison she stuffed her pillow into her mouth so her frightened sobs would not be heard by her cellmate.

But none of what she'd feared occurred. Not even close. In all the time she's spent with this ragtag group of women she has not witnessed one episode of physical cruelty; in fact, she's not witnessed anything but support, and a camaraderie she's not sure she'll ever experience elsewhere. Even the prison officers, who must have their own ideas about who is guilty and who is not, seem to take great pains to make each offender feel as if what got them into this mess was probably not entirely their own doing, and, more likely, the product of circumstance. When this particular officer, the officer with the toilet rolls, tells Carrie she's rooting for her, Carrie believes her.

But the wheels of justice turn slowly. And it's now been months since she was visited by Tess Gilroy, Avril Hughes and a solicitor she'd not met before by the name of Tom Robinson. They would need to prepare for the meeting with the appellate judge meticulously, Tom informed her. He explained that it was his job to ensure that all of Tess's and Avril's findings were documented correctly, to ensure there were no questions raised by the judge that could not be answered and backed up with evidence. He seemed rather young to have a position of such responsibility and doubt must have registered on her face because Tess leaned forward, squeezed her arm and said, 'Tom has a brilliant mind, Carrie. You are in very capable hands.'

Before leaving they asked that she be patient. No news means good news and all that. They told her that if they were not in touch she was not to worry, it was simply that these things had a habit of taking three times as long as anyone wanted them to, but it was the system they were stuck with, and railing against it didn't do anyone any good.

She wasn't sure if it was a good sign or not but both Tess and Avril appeared to have aged somewhat in the time since she'd last seen them and when she'd commented on this – covertly, of course, saying they both looked a bit tired – Avril explained that getting all their ducks in a row, so Carrie had the best possible chance of an acquittal, had been, at times, 'challenging'.

So now Carrie waits. She waits and watches her perennials emerge from the soil and she gets some satisfaction from being able to see the cycle of life in action as opposed to watching it on a TV screen. She lives for the phone calls and visits from Mia and baby Phoebe. She listens to Mia recount her struggles and the moments of elation that come from being a new parent, and though her heart feels as though someone has it between their hands, and they are wringing it, twisting it, she smiles at her daughter, and she coos, and she delivers the advice Mia needs to hear – softly, softly – and she hopes, as she waits, she hopes that one day she'll have her two girls to herself, and that no one will be limiting their time together. No one will be checking the baby's nappy for contraband, and no one will remove Phoebe from Carrie's arms when their time is up.

TWO GOLDFINCHES AT the feeding station are spitting seed from their beaks on to the ground. Tess watches from the kitchen window. They have been at this for a full five minutes now, ejecting nine-tenths of what they peck, and sometimes Tess wishes they would be just a little more grateful. Sunflower hearts do not come cheap and this wanton disregard for her feelings goes on most days. If the robins and tree sparrows were not there to forage for cast-offs, Tess might stop putting seed out for the birds altogether.

Tess is nervous. Today they will hear whether Carrie's case will progress to the appellate court. She tries to keep busy. Tries not to check her phone every five minutes. She has another case to be getting on with, another mountain of paperwork to get through – it's a further murder case, a 37-year-old man imprisoned for killing his boss, and again the boxes are stacked from floor to ceiling in her office, and again her back is complaining after carrying the said boxes from her car. Her full attention should be on this new case but it's not.

Avril is on standby. They have agreed that the minute they find out they will travel to Styal Prison to let Carrie know in person. Carrie does not know that today is the day, but they have warned her that if she sees their faces in the visitors' area, she must not automatically assume it is good news. Good or bad, they will be there either way.

Tess takes a shower. She blow-dries her hair and applies a little make-up – just enough to combat the grey pallor of her skin. She's never found a lipstick that suits her but she goes through the routine of swiping it across her mouth, pressing her lips together twice, checking the result in the mirror, before removing it again. She opens the bedroom window and sticks her hand out to test the air temperature. It's dry but there's a slight nip in the air so she selects a short-sleeved shirt, a sweater that she can slip off if it gets too warm, and pairs them with some navy cords. She goes downstairs, makes herself a cup of hot chocolate, and waits.

The call from Tom comes in at 9.37 a.m.

By eleven fifteen they are at the prison.

As Tess suspected, the day has now warmed, and she takes off her sweater and leaves it on the back seat. The other side of the chain-link fence, women prisoners sit in groups on the grass. Some are plaiting each other's hair; some are lying down, propped up on their elbows, their faces angled towards the sun. The scene takes Tess back to high school, when the first glimpse of summer had them rolling down their socks and rolling up their sleeves in an attempt to absorb any scrap of sun they could before the afternoon bell went, signalling their return to class.

Tess casts around the visitors' room but cannot see Carrie. She and Avril have been granted permission to visit Styal out of the usual visiting hours, which are between 2 and 4 p.m. each day. The visiting room is empty, save for a prisoner pushing a Hoover around at the far end. The prisoner wears an orange tabard and a pleasant expression that suggests she seems to obtain some small satisfaction from her work. Tess and Avril nod in her direction. The woman cuts the power and asks them if she's OK to continue or, if they're holding a meeting, would they like her to finish this later? Tess says it's no trouble. They can do what they need to do whilst she continues with her work.

At eleven twenty-six Carrie enters the room. She keeps her eyes on the floor and, as she walks towards them, she looks rather odd: she's neglecting to swing her arms in the usual fashion, instead keeping them pinned to her sides. Tess can also see Carrie is biting the inside of her cheek and has lost quite a bit more hair since the last time she saw her. Tess swallows. She needs to do this right. She can't imagine how Carrie is feeling right now. She can't imagine the toll this has taken, not simply on her body but, well, on everything.

How do you go from complete freedom, freedom to go wherever you like, whenever you like . . . How do you go from having money in your wallet, a car in the driveway, from a safe, warm home, from making your daughter's breakfast each day . . . to this?

Tess has worked with criminals her whole life, she knows what makes them tick and from her early days as a probation officer she saw what set them apart from the rest of society, and she knows Carrie is not of that ilk. Carrie doesn't have the icicle in the heart, the misguided self-belief, the deluded certainty that she is intelligent enough to outwit the system.

Carrie shuffles towards them and both Tess and Avril rise.

Tess came across a poll recently. What's worse: a guilty person being acquitted or an innocent person being incarcerated? Over 95 per cent of respondents thought it far worse that an innocent person could be sent to prison for a crime they did not commit.

Tess smiles at Carrie. 'We have a court date,' she says.

MORE TIME PASSES, and when Carrie's case eventually reaches the Criminal Court of Appeal, Carrie is another dress size larger, has developed Type 2 diabetes, and is now fully in the thick of the menopause. Baby Phoebe can feed herself with a spoon, is eager to start walking, and can point to pictures of animals whilst making the correct sounds: moo, meow, baa, woof, neigh, cluck.

Yesterday, Carrie was brought to the Royal Courts of Justice in London where the Court of Appeal is. She has never been to London. Why not? she wonders now. She's never been a big one for musicals, so perhaps it's that.

Today, in the holding cells below the court, she is dressed in a plum-coloured suit from Debenhams and a pair of court shoes with a block heel from Clarks. These items were picked out for her by Tess and paid for by Innocence UK. Tess also arranged for a hairdresser to visit Styal Prison in the week preceding, and Carrie's hair has been cut and highlighted. The hairdresser showed her how to backcomb the roots on the crown of her head (where she is thinning the most) and fix it with hairspray so her scalp is less visible. Tess also provided Carrie with some basic make-up essentials: blusher, mascara, a golden-brown eye shadow that has the surprising effect of making Carrie's dull blue eyes shine and appear almost aquamarine in colour. If the appeal goes her way she will buy more of this eye shadow and wear it every day.

Two Lady Justices and one Lord Justice will hear her appeal. She has met her barrister only once but Tess told her not to be concerned by this, he has been very well prepped and it's quite normal. Innocence UK have a lot of faith in him and Carrie should be very optimistic. 'If the appeal process has got this far,' Tess said, 'there is good reason to be hopeful, as many, many are dismissed in the early stages.' Still, Carrie is not allowing herself to hope. Not yet. She has had her hopes dashed too many times and will not put herself through it again. Whatever the outcome of today is, she knows she will have conducted herself with dignity, and she will have spoken the truth. Those are the only things she is in control of.

At 10.15 a.m. she is led from her cell. Her stomach is in knots and a cold layer of sweat sits between her shoulder blades. It all comes down to this, she is thinking, as she enters the court and her gaze immediately lands on Mia. Mia has made the trip to London without baby Phoebe – something which they discussed at length. Mia was not ready to spend a night away from Phoebe yet but agreed the court was no place for an infant. As Carrie takes her seat at the front, she looks behind momentarily. Tess, Avril and Tom are also in attendance. They are seated on one of the pews to the left. The place is rather church-like: there is a lot of wood panelling and it has the sombre, reverential atmosphere of a place of worship. At the front is a raised platform where the judges will hear the case. As they make their entrance, everyone stands, and it's now that something odd happens to Carrie's awareness. As she rises, the world tilts and blurs. And the only thing she can see in front of her now is Ella Muir's face.

Ella was pretty: great big eyes that took up most of her face like a Disney princess. It's been a long time since she's thought of Ella. Within this whole process Ella got lost somehow. She became irrelevant and Carrie wonders, glancing behind her at Ella's family, how they're doing. Will they ever feel normal again? Will her mother ever wake and feel light, hopeful, glad to be alive? Carrie supposes not. Ella's mother is in her own kind of prison and Carrie knows that if she were forced to choose between her incarceration, and what Ella's mother has been forced to endure, she would repeat her imprisonment in a heartbeat.

She can hear her barrister speaking as if from another room. He is Welsh but his accent has been anglicized and as he begins running through the facts of the case she sees a blur of images: Richard Burton playing Hamlet, Anthony Hopkins in *The Remains of the Day*. 'No reliable witnesses,' he is saying, 'no weapon, nothing in fact to place Mrs Kamara at the home of Ella Muir on the day of the murder. Yes, she'd been there before, we don't dispute that, Mrs Kamara herself has never disputed that . . .'

When Carrie had rapped on Ella's door that day she hadn't known how Ella would react. Sure, she'd unnerved Ella in the café that day, but that was Ella's place of work. This was her home. Her turf. Carrie had seen Pete disappearing inside on the few times she'd followed him, but she hadn't seen Ella up close since the café, and when Ella opened the door, Carrie was a little taken aback by just how beautiful she was. She looked so different when she was relaxed. When she was waiting for Pete to arrive, presumably.

Carrie had stammered through her first few sentences, the power she'd felt in the café that day deserting her, and she was unable to keep eye contact with Ella. When her nerves did finally settle, and she was able to take a proper look at the girl, what was reflected back at her was sympathy. Ella felt sorry for her. And it was this more than anything which had caused her to become unmoored. Caused Carrie's veneer to crack.

Her barrister pauses to take a sip of water. He is not a young man. He is tall and rangy with a long nose and hooded eyes. In his wig he appears rather villainous. 'And when looking at the time frame offered by the prosecution,' he says, 'it's very hard to see how one could do all that they're suggesting and *still* get home in time for Mrs Kamara's husband's return at . . .' His voice becomes faint again as she thinks about Ella's face. This time she is seeing the crime scene photographs she saw at the first trial where Ella is dead-eyed and lifeless. Her skin is the colour of ash and the essence of her, that thing which must have caught Pete's eye, is long gone. She wonders if Pete has ever got over the loss of her. He claimed she was the love of his life. He claimed he was going to marry her. Maybe he would have.

One of the Lady Justices is turning the page of the pamphlet she has been provided with as the barrister continues his address. Each judge remains impassive, even though the barrister has now become rather impassioned in his delivery. They seem unmoved by his words but if he has noticed it does not affect his perfor-mance. 'Which brings us to', he says authoritatively, 'the disposal of, or the disappearance of, vital forensic evidence. Evidence that could have proven Mrs Kamara had *not* been in physical contact with Ella Muir at all. Why has this evidence been disposed of, you might ask? Well, we may never know the answer to that. What we do know, however . . .'

What do they know? Carrie thinks, amused.

They don't know anything.

They think they know but they don't. Carrie knows. Carrie knows what happened that day at Ella's house. Carrie knows everything.

INSIDE THE COURT waiting room the air is heavy and thick. There is an urn of tea, a large jug of orange squash, and a plate of shortbread fingers on a table next to the door. Tess pushes the remains of a shortbread finger inside her mouth, thinking that this set-up is not unlike when she gives blood. After donating, she has to sit at a table with a group of strangers as a nurse watches over them to ensure they replenish their fluids and eat at least three flavourless biscuits. This is to prevent them from passing out at the wheel on the way home. Here, instead of a nurse, there is a kindly lady. She is forcing tea and shortbread on the unsuspecting, telling them it's a while yet till lunch, and they don't want to get light-headed while court is still in session. Tess supposes there must have been some recent fainting episodes as refreshments were not available the last time she was here.

She glances to her left. Mia is sitting alone, tapping away on her phone. She's had to leave her baby with a friend and Tess knows Mia's not comfortable with the arrangement. Mia confided that she has little Phoebe practically Sellotaped to her throughout her day. Watching Mia now, it crosses Tess's mind that the reason she's fought so hard for Carrie is because Mia reminds her of her young self. Mia is bringing up a baby girl, alone, just as Tess did, without the help or assistance of her mother. And so far Mia's been OK. But what happens when things are not OK? What happens when things are not OK and there's no back-up? Perhaps it's been this thought that has unconsciously driven Tess forward.

Avril nudges Tess's arm. 'Imagine if she gets to walk out of here with her mother,' she whispers, gesturing to Mia. 'Just imagine.'

Tess checks her watch. The judges have been deliberating for close to two hours now and they can only wait. She thinks about Carrie in the bowels of the building, alone, with nothing to do except contemplate her fate. Will she spend her fifties locked up? Tess can't call it. For her, this is the worst part of the job: bringing a case this far and then watching the absolute devastation on her client's face if it doesn't go their way. It is an appalling way to end a project. And there is nothing she can say to help. There is no *We'll appeal again* speech. Because they won't. This is the end of the road as far as Innocence UK is concerned. The prisoners are on their own and must lodge future appeals from their cells, filling out the forms themselves, unless they have the funds to employ a solicitor to do it for them. And Tess hasn't yet met anyone who falls into that category. So she tells them she's sorry. She tells them she did her very best. And then she says goodbye. Later she will take the train home and she will pour herself a large glass of red wine, and as she drinks, she will reflect on this strange business in which she finds herself, all the while hoping the next case will turn out differently.

'They're ready for you.' An usher has entered the room and is holding the door wide. Silently, they gather up their belongings as the kindly tea lady tells them not to worry about the rubbish. 'What I'm here for,' she sings happily.

As they file out, Tess avoids Mia's eye. This is on purpose, as she finds it's best to start disentangling herself from the victim's family before they hear the final outcome. She's sending a silent message to Mia, letting her know that Tess's role is now over. She can do no more and what lies ahead is out of her hands. Tess had a client hang himself after the appellate court ruled the original verdict was to be upheld a few years ago, and she knew his family blamed her because they shouted it right into her face. Tess was required to attend the inquest and his daughter spat at Tess, telling her she was not fit to do her job, and after that Tess consciously put some distance between herself and members of the victim's family. She hopes Mia will be able to hold it together. They're on different trains home, at least. An hour apart.

It was the first thing she'd asked Mia about when they'd entered court this morning.

IN THE GLARE of photographers and camera operators and reporters, Carrie looks like a startled fawn. She is trying to smile but she's almost scowling because she can't cope with the attention and the noise. Her skin is flushed and her eyes are darting left to right, left to right. 'Carrie! Smile for us, Carrie!' shouts a reporter, and Tess can see she's completely overwhelmed and has no idea what to do about it. This should be a joyous moment, her moment of vindication, the moment when she gets to stick it to all the doubters. But Tess can see that all that Carrie wants to do is to become invisible.

'How do you feel, Carrie?' they ask.

'I feel . . . grateful,' she manages to stammer.

'What will you do with your first night of freedom?'

Carrie looks over to where Mia is standing, along with Tom, Tess and Avril. 'I'm going to go home. I'm going home to be with my family. That's all I want. It's what I've dreamt of.'

'Do you have anything to say to people like yourself, people who are victims of a miscarriage of justice?'

Now Carrie does manage to smile. Shyly, she answers, 'Write to Tess Gilroy,' and Tess watches as the cameras pan across to where she's standing. She'll never get used to this – being in the spotlight – but it's part of the job and so she nods her head, acknowledging Carrie's remark, Carrie who has tears in her eyes and is looking at Tess as if she owes Tess her life.

'You OK?' Tess mouths.

'Happy,' she mouths back.

Tess gives Mia a gentle nudge: 'Go and be with your mum,' and they watch as mother and daughter hug on the steps, both crying, both still looking so unsure, as if this could all be a mistake and any moment Carrie will be led away to the back of a police van, whereupon she will be driven north and returned to Styal Prison.

'Can't believe they didn't raise the blood issue,' Tom says under his breath, still smiling gamely for the cameras.

'Neither can I,' whispers Tess.

'Why didn't they?' asks Avril.

'Probably because they're obligated to consider each piece of evidence equally,' suggests Tom. 'In contrast to juries, who, as we know, will ignore each piece of evidence in favour of DNA.'

'Still, though,' says Tess.

'I know,' says Tom. 'Still.'

There is a general kerfuffle amongst the journalists and camera operators as they quickly try to move from their position. The Muir family is now exiting the court and Avril looks away when she catches sight of Ella's mother, Sandra, the woman responsible for her broken nose.

Ella's brother, Kyle, takes a step forward from his family and waits until a camera operator signals he's ready for him to start speaking. It's an awkward moment and Tess can feel a collective holding of breath as the camera guy fiddles with his equipment, leaving poor Kyle in limbo, not sure what to do with his hands as he waits. Finally he gets the thumbs up and Kyle speaks directly into the lens without blinking. Later, Tess will watch this on the ten-thirty local news bulletin and wonder how Kyle got through it so convincingly. She wonders if he will ever air his doubts to his family that the wrong woman was charged. 'We are very disappointed with the result here today.' Kyle speaks confidently and assuredly to camera, without the need to read from notes. 'My sister Ella deserves justice for the terrible crime inflicted upon her and we . . .'

'Come on,' Tess says to the others. 'We don't need to stay for this.' It feels in bad taste, like gloating, and she can feel Ella's mother's eyes upon her, boring into her, blaming her.

She suggests to Tom and Avril that they should perhaps head to the station right away to determine if they can board an earlier train. It could get messy if they find themselves heading home together with the Muirs.

A FEW DAYS LATER and Tess is busy removing all traces of Carrie Kamara's case from her home office when she hears the knock on the front door. She ignores it and continues with her task: unpinning photographs from the noticeboard, removing the maps, the CCTV images. She could have done this earlier, much earlier – as soon as they got the court date – but she's superstitious. Her first case involved a nineteen-year-old boy who had been imprisoned for shooting an elderly woman in a bungled burglary. It had not gone their way; he was still inside. Tess had been convinced that the court would find him innocent, convinced they'd see he'd been shafted by his friends, and so she'd filed away everything she had on Clayton Kells as soon as she got a court date. Never again. Her complacency still haunted her. She knew there was more she could've done. Knew, if she'd not moved on mentally, she could've spotted something essential, perhaps when sitting in her office, daydreaming, thinking about something else entirely. He was twenty-seven now.

Tess runs the cloth over her desk and the top of the filing cabinet. The room is thick with dust and she feels a tingling in her nose, a scratching at the back of her throat as the particles become airborne. The room is a disgrace. She should really get into the habit of cleaning the office once a week but knows she never will. Mid-case, cleaning is as far down her list of priorities as it can get.

She hears the knocking again, and, 'What?' she says aloud, irritated. It's seven forty-five on Sunday evening. Who makes social calls at this hour?

Tess stomps down the stairs, cloth still in her hand, and opens the door. Standing on the step in the rain is Steph.

Tess's mouth drops open.

She isn't quite sure what to say so she doesn't say anything. She leaves the door wide and turns, walking into the kitchen to rinse her cloth. As she turns off the tap, she's aware of Steph's presence in the dining room. Steph is dripping wet. Tess grabs the roll of kitchen towel and hands it to her. She knows she's supposed to ask Steph why she's come here, but she can't bring herself to do it. She's not sure she wants to hear it. Not sure she can hear what her daughter has to say.

'Sorry to turn up unannounced,' says Steph.

'That's all right.'

'Thought you might bail again if I tried to get you to meet me somewhere.'

Tess takes a breath. Would she have bailed? Maybe. Probably. 'I understand you must be pretty angry with me.'

'I'm not angry.' Steph dries her face and neck with the towel. She doesn't remove her coat. Tess asks if she can get her a drink, anything to eat, and Steph says she's fine. 'I hear Carrie's free.'

'Yeah.'

'Must be nice to sleep in her own bed again.'

'She missed her family terribly,' says Tess.

'Do you think I was some help? In getting her out, I mean.'

Tess thinks about Greg Lancashire. He'll be appearing at Lancaster Magistrate's Court soon to answer for burning Tess's face at the breaker's yard back in November, but Tess has also heard he's been interviewed by detectives twice since Carrie was freed – about Ella's death. The case of Ella's murder has been reopened and Greg is now a suspect. 'I'm sure you helped Carrie a great deal,' Tess tells Steph.

Steph smiles. 'I'm glad it all worked out.'

'Yeah. Me too. Sure I can't get you something to drink? I was going to put the kettle on. I've been cleaning . . . I'm not much of a housekeeper and my throat is parched from all the dust. I've got a ton of boxes up there that need moving and quite frankly the place is a health hazard. I really should be more organized. I ought to be better at—' She's rambling. Tess knows she's rambling but she seems powerless to do anything else.

'Why didn't you want me?'

Tess closes her eyes briefly. When she opens them again she sees Steph is looking at her so earnestly. How does she answer this? How does she answer this *adequately*? She can't. 'I did want you,' is all that she can say.

'OK, so why didn't you *keep* me?' Steph asks, and Tess is back to that night. The night of . . .

Her baby is crying. Of course she's crying. Her baby is always crying. It's 5 a.m., the country is asleep, and Tess has not had more than fifteen minutes' rest. Her daughter is in her crib, drawing her knees up to her chest, and is not just crying, she's yelling as though Tess is stubbing cigarettes out directly on her flesh. Tess can't bear it. She knows Angeline is suffering but she's done everything she can think of. Everything any reasonable person could be expected to do – and more. She has changed Angeline's nappy; this has had a negligible effect – in fact, if anything, it's made matters worse. She has walked around and around the basement flat, Angeline pressed against her shoulder, Tess gently tapping her daughter's bottom in rhythm to her steps. She has tried to feed her. Oh, has she tried! She has moved Angeline from one engorged breast to the other, she has propped her up on pillows, held her beneath her arm like a rugby ball; she has even tried to breastfeed her infant whilst on the move. She has tried Angeline with formula milk from a bottle, with a dummy, with another expensive pacifier which claims to prevent orthodontic problems; she has given watered-down juice from a cup, a teething biscuit. She has stood in the shower holding Angeline. She has bathed her – which Angeline hates; she screamed whilst she was in the water, screamed whilst Tess towelled her dry, screamed as their neighbour rapped on the wall because her own toddler's bedroom is on the other side and Angeline is keeping her boy awake too. She has called her doctors' out-of-hours service. She spoke to a woman who, between the screams, asked if Tess's baby had a temperature: no. She asked if her baby was floppy or unresponsive: clearly no. She asked if her baby was vomiting: no. And so the woman concluded that, even though this was obviously very distressing indeed, Angeline did not warrant a home visit from a doctor, and she encouraged Tess to contact her surgery after 8.30 a.m. to discuss a visit from the health visitor.

Tess has played soothing music. She did this whilst rubbing her baby's back with a circular motion. She has played music with a reggae beat, which someone suggested to her as the bass can give comfort to distressed babies by mimicking the mother's heartbeat. She has played pan pipes of the Andes, nursery rhymes, garage. She has dressed Angeline in a snowsuit and bonnet, strapped her into her pram and walked the streets of Morecambe, with the wind howling and the rain hitting her face. All of this and her baby continues to cry.

Now Tess is in the bath with her head beneath the water. She opens her eyes and imagines she's drowning. She *wants* to drown. She wonders if she holds her breath for long enough will she simply lose consciousness? She doesn't have any drugs in her system. No alcohol either. The death will be recorded as unexplained. Misadventure. No one will know she did it on purpose. That she did it to escape.

What would happen to Angeline if Tess were to die? Tess is past caring. Someone would take her. Someone with more skill, more knowledge than Tess would look after her well. A phrase keeps popping into Tess's head. She doesn't know where she came across it. *You have everything your baby needs.* Perhaps Tess made this phrase up? Or else she dreamt it. She has nothing her baby needs. Her baby needs so much more than she is capable of giving.

Everything Tess gives Angeline, Angeline rejects. She rejects it as though, to her, it's polluted. As though she knows Tess is all wrong. Perhaps Angeline's not even Tess's baby? Perhaps there was a mix-up – some traumatized woman did not like the look of her own baby and switched her, and now this woman's baby knows that Tess is an imposter. Knows her milk is unmatched for her needs, knows she doesn't smell right.

Tess lifts her head an inch. Another inch and her ear will make contact with the air. Once out of the water, Tess will know for sure that Angeline is still howling, and the sound will hit her solar plexus like a punch. This is how it is now. If Tess is not suffering because her baby is crying, she is suffering because she is anticipating her baby crying.

Her insides hurt. She feels wounded in there as if she's been hit by a car; she feels raw, as if she's drunk a bottle of bleach. She wonders if the damage is permanent. Will she ever recover? Will it ever stop?

She lifts her head and shockingly there is no sound. Silence. And it's exquisite. She should get out of the bath, dry herself off and climb into bed as fast as she can. She needs to make the most of this silence so she is strong enough to deal with the onslaught which is sure to come within the hour. But she doesn't want to move. This is the first time she has taken a bath when Angeline has not lain on the changing mat beside her, her tiny head a hot ball of fury, and Tess has had to bathe in less than two minutes flat.

A minute passes and she wonders if Angeline has stopped breathing. Babies do that around this age. Their mothers put them to bed in good faith and, some time during the night, a switch is flicked, and the infant's lungs fail to inflate. She wonders if there is a way to do this without anyone knowing. Is there a way to make it *look* as if her child has succumbed to the mystery that is SIDS without anyone suspecting? Or, to take it a step further, what if she *were* to go in there and gently hold a pillow to her baby's face? What if she were to admit that she did it? Because who kills their own child? Only a crazy person. Could she endure being put away for being a crazed baby killer? Would it be harder than this? Could anything be harder than this?

She climbs out of the bath. Her whole body hurts. Her skin is milky white, her breasts covered with a map of blue veins. She hears the cries begin and her right breast leaks milk. The milk runs over her belly and all the way down the inside of her leg. Tess is filled to the brim with nothing her baby needs. She tells herself not to cry. She is braver than this. Her mother raised her to face her problems head on; she raised her to be strong.

She misses her mother.

Tess pulls out the plug. The yells are not yet at full volume as she dries off her legs, as she pulls on her dressing gown and wraps her head in a towel. When she gets to the crib she sees Angeline has been sick. There is not a lot. Just a small circle next to her ear and a patch on her babygro. It's beginning to dry. She must have made herself sick through crying earlier before passing out. 'Hi, poppet,' Tess says and, on hearing her voice, Angeline's arms start to flail. Her head turns from side to side and she kicks her feet. Tess leans over and picks up her baby. She is tightly packaged. She is a neat little bundle of ripped muscle. At two weeks old she could flip herself over from back to front and now at seven weeks she can push herself up on to her hands. She has worked every muscle in her small body to the extreme.

The constant crying has made her staggeringly strong. Tess wonders if she's possessed.

She makes soothing noises as she changes Angeline's nappy on the bed. 'I know, sweetheart, I know,' she says as she dresses her in a fresh babygro. It's the nicest one she has. It's from Marks & Spencer and is pure white with silk piping around the collar. Angeline fights with her. She draws her little fists into her body and Tess has to unhook them as her daughter screams furiously at her. 'Let me dress you,' Tess hisses between her teeth and she pulls at Angeline's arm, knowing she's hurting her, but something has snapped inside Tess.

Her baby cries even more as she becomes rougher, pulling at her daughter's limbs, her expression stern and unsympathetic. Tess has been overtaken by something, she doesn't know what, but it feels primitive. It feels like a release. Angeline cries harder as Tess brings each press stud together. 'Stop crying,' she says flatly, and Angeline is now coughing between sobs. She might be sick again. But Tess doesn't care.

When she's finished and her baby is clean, as good as new, Tess lifts her up high, so she's face to face, and she pauses for a moment. Then she throws her baby down hard on to the bed, as hard as she dares.

The room goes silent.

And Tess's mouth drops open.

Has she killed her?

Tess leans over. Angeline is still breathing. It's the shock of the fall that's silenced her. Angeline takes a couple of big breaths before flinging her arms out wide and inhaling deeply, ready to let out a fresh yell, and Tess sinks to her knees. She covers her ears with her hands. She has nothing left.

Packing the nappy bag with everything she can find, Tess is on autopilot. She can no longer hear Angeline's cries. She pushes her daughter into her snowsuit and fixes her bonnet on her head. Then she walks out into the street in her dressing gown and flags down the only passing vehicle. It's a Ford Transit and in the front seat are three men in paint-covered overalls. 'What's the matter, love?' the driver asks, and Tess hands him her baby.

'Take her,' she says. 'Please. Just take her.'

It's only when she gets back inside the flat that she realizes she forgot to kiss her goodbye.

Afterwards, she will call 999 and admit what she has done. And there will be social workers, doctors, a community psychiatric nurse – all kind people who tend to Tess, who tell her that they understand how she got to this point. These people really do seem to care. They try to persuade her to take Angeline back. They ask her to try again, just once more, 'With support, this time,' but Tess knows, ultimately, she'll be on her own. She tells them she can't. It's too big. Too much. And so there is the adoption process, during which she will opt never to see Angeline again. She will never completely cut ties with Angeline's family's solicitor – Bill Menzies – for reasons she still doesn't fully understand. But she will never see her baby.

Tess looks at the young woman sitting in front of her now and she doesn't know what to say.

'I was eighteen,' Tess stammers, 'I really wasn't equipped to—'

'I'm not mad about it, by the way,' Steph says. 'I have a great life. You totally made the right decision. I just want to know why.'

Why.

This is the thing Tess can't say out loud: *Because I couldn't trust myself around you any longer. Because the thought of going to prison for killing you sounded like relief.*

'What about my father?' asks Steph and Tess is suddenly thrown.

'Who?'

'My dad. Who was he?'

'Oh,' answers Tess, 'he was no one.'

'*No one*,' Steph mirrors back, flatly.

'Well, not no one, but you know what I mean.'

'No. I don't know what you mean.'

'He was . . .' Tess tries to cast her mind back. She casts her mind back to that night and there is nothing. Nothing at all.

'You don't have to tell me. Not if you don't want to. I understand if you don't want to tell me.'

'It's not that,' says Tess.

'Do you even know his name?'

Tess shakes her head and Steph tries to be brave here, really she does, but tears have unexpectedly sprung, and she has to look up to blink them away. Steph came here looking for answers but . . . 'I tried to find you, you know,' she says. 'I tried so many times to find you.'

Tess can't look at her. 'I know. Bill Menzies tried to pass on your messages; he really went out of his way to track me down and let me know that you were looking.'

'So you just didn't want to meet me?' she cries. 'You didn't even want to see what I looked like? You didn't want to check I was OK?'

'I did but—'

'Why wouldn't you see me?'

'I couldn't.'

'I wanted to see *you*. I wanted to tell you it was OK—'

'I'm sorry, I just couldn't.'

'I wanted you to see who I was. I wanted to tell you about my life. Who I am. What I'm planning to do. I wanted you to know about me! I wanted you to look at me!' Steph stares at her mother, waiting for an explanation, and Tess can only hang her head. Why did she run? Why did she run from this beautiful girl? She had no real reason to and yet she did. She's been running from her for her whole life.

Steph tries to gather herself. 'All right,' she says, defeat evident in her voice. 'OK. I don't know why I needed to come here but I did. And I'm going to leave now.'

Steph stands and she waits. She's waiting for Tess to persuade her to stay. Hug her. Something. Anything. But Tess cannot move.

Steph looks at her mother before heading to the door. When she's there, she turns around. 'What was it?' she asks quietly. 'What was it about my father that made you choose *him*? There must have been other boys around.'

And again, Tess's face falls. What she has to say is not what Steph wants to hear. Frantically, Tess searches her mind for a story. A story that will work. That's what her daughter has come here for – to hear the story of her life. Something that will make sense of things, something to tell her who she is and help her find her place in the world. But Tess doesn't have a story to give.

'There was nothing about him,' Tess begins. 'I wanted a baby. I was young and immature and lonely and I thought a baby would be the answer. He was next to me by the dance floor, and I was midway through my menstrual cycle, and I knew if I was going to get pregnant, I had to have sex right then. I had to have sex that night.' Tess looks at her daughter apologetically. 'There was nothing special about him. Nothing at all. I'm so sorry. If it had been a different night, he would've been a different guy.'

Later, in her dressing gown, after Steph has left, Tess is chopping carrots into strips in the kitchen. It's dark now and when she gazes outside it's her own reflection she's faced with. She finds it hard to look at herself so she looks away.

When she's finished prepping the meal, she puts the knife down and heads upstairs to the bathroom. Sitting down to urinate, she sees her underwear is stained with blood. 'Great,' she says.

She stands, grabs a fresh pair of knickers from the clean pile of laundry on the landing, and returns to the bathroom to search for a sanitary towel.

Fixing the pad in place, she frowns. And it's then that an alarm goes off inside her head.

What if . . . ?

No.

No, that would be impossible.

Would it?

Maybe not impossible.

Maybe it could be done.

In fact, it could be done if—

Suddenly, Tess is running. She's running downstairs, frantic-ally searching for her phone.

Tess finds the phone next to the sofa and begins scrolling through, looking for the right contact. She presses 'call'; it rings three times, and goes to voicemail. 'Shit.' She redials and this time she leaves a message. 'Mia, it's Tess Gilroy. Call me when you get this. It doesn't matter what time. Call me. It's urgent.' Then she's scrolling again, looking for the next contact, cursing herself, for in her state of anxiety she keeps overshooting. Did she list Fran under D or F? She can't remember. She finds her under F.

The call connects. 'Dr Fran Adler speaking.'

'Fran, it's Tess—'

'Oh, Tess, hi. I don't have my glasses on so I couldn't see who's calling.'

'Listen, we need to retest Carrie Kamara's blood.'

'The blood. Why the blood? And why now?'

'Tell me, is it possible?'

'Well, yes, it's certainly possible,' Fran says. 'I requested a sample when we requested the forensic records, so I have it at the lab. What exactly are we looking for?'

'Menstrual blood.'

Seven a.m. the following morning and Tess finds Fran Adler hunched over her workbench inside the forensics lab. Fran wears a white lab coat, protective goggles, navy woollen tights and lime-green Crocs. It's a combination Tess has not seen before. Tess hovers impatiently nearby.

'Do you know we only began testing for D-dimer recently?' Fran says absently as she works.

'You say that as if I'm supposed to know what D-dimer is.'

Fran stops and looks up. 'It's a protein. It's the protein which differentiates menstrual blood from peripheral blood. It's now a necessary and routine test performed in rape cases.' Fran has a pipette in her right hand and is transferring fluid from one test tube to another. 'The presence of blood after a rape signifies trauma, but of course, in the past, defendants argued that the victims were merely *menstruating* when there was blood present, and that the sex was consensual. We needed a way to tell the difference between the two, between menstruation and trauma.'

'When did the test become routine?' asks Tess.

'Two years ago.'

'So, after Carrie was incarcerated.'

'Indeed.'

'But,' Tess says, feeling a little sick at what she's about to say next, 'if we at Innocence UK had tested the blood back at the start, when we took the case on, wouldn't we have found the presence of menstrual blood?'

Fran shakes her head. 'As I said, we only test for it in rape cases. As far as we knew, this was a blood smear from the suspect who killed Ella Muir. No rape involved.' Fran puts a stopper in the test tube. 'So this test would never have been performed, but my question is this, Tess: what do you plan to do with this information? If indeed the sample is found to contain menstrual blood?'

Tess moves closer. 'The way I see it, there are only two people who could've planted Carrie's blood in Ella's house. Her daughter, Mia – which is highly unlikely because she loves her mother deeply and would not want her imprisoned – and the other is—'

'Carrie's husband.'

'Yes,' she says. 'Pete Kamara.'

Fran jiggles the test tube before feeding it into the haematology analyser. Tess asks her how long it will take. 'Couple of minutes,' replies Fran. They wait. Tess paces the lab. It feels like the longest two minutes of her life. Driving here today she told herself she was losing it. Only a crazy person would come up with this. Pete Kamara would not have actually gone through with the act of killing Ella Muir before planting his wife's blood at the scene, would he?

Tess is not sure which way is up any more.

The machine starts to beep repeatedly and Fran wanders over to it. It spits out what looks like a till receipt and Fran takes this to her workbench where there is an anglepoise lamp. Fran takes her reading glasses from their case and puts them on. Tess watches as she runs her finger down the slip of paper. Tess can't tell from Fran's posture what's written there.

Fran straightens. She removes her glasses and returns them to the case. She turns around. 'Well, clever old you, Tess.'

Twenty minutes later and Tess is switching lanes again. Someone is sitting in the middle lane of the M6 doing eighty so Tess undertakes on the inside. She has become *that* driver. The one she hates. The impatient, aggressive driver who could cause a crash. But she doesn't care. 'Oh, come *on*,' she yells at the windscreen as her phone begins to ring. It goes to her car's Bluetooth. It's Avril. The morning traffic is thick and heavy but no one seems in a particular hurry to get where they need to go. She switches lanes again.

She picks up the call. 'Avril, you need to get hold of Mia and Carrie right now,' she says, bypassing the niceties. 'I've tried and tried but there's no answer.'

'Let me get this straight, you think Pete Kamara planted her menstrual blood? So it looked like Carrie killed Ella?

That's so gross. What sort of sick human being do you need to be to—'

'Call them. Call them now.'

'I *have* called them. It went straight to voicemail. How did Pete Kamara even plant the blood anyway?'

'Fran Adler reckons the blood smear documented in the report could easily have come from a used sanitary towel.'

'Eww. So he took it with him *on purpose*? Like he put it in his pocket on the way to kill Ella? Jesus. That's so gross. Who even does that?'

'Call them again. Keep calling until you get an answer. And contact the police. Tell them to get around to Mia's. They need to warn Carrie that she's still in danger. Let them know what's going on.'

'Why? Do you think he's going to do something stupid?'

'I think,' Tess says, 'I think he really, really hates his wife.'

Tess is *sure* Pete Kamara is capable of doing something stupid. In fact, she's kicking herself now for underestimating him. He came across as a buffoon and so she treated him as such. She can hear her own words of warning inside her head. Words she spoke to Avril: *Here's something you need to know about people who commit premeditated murder . . . They're cold-blooded individuals who do not operate like the rest of us. Do you think those individuals are capable of elaborate lies to cover up their crimes? Do you think they're able to hoodwink well-meaning individuals such as yourself?*

She pulls on to Mia's street. Carrie has been staying here with her daughter. She's one of the lucky ones. She has somewhere to go. Most women leaving prison have nothing and they end up walking straight back into the abusive relationships that landed them in prison in the first place.

She gets out and crosses the road. The curtains to Mia's flat are pulled closed. A black bin bag has been torn apart by the gulls and its rubbish is strewn around the door and down the steps. Tess presses Mia's doorbell and as she waits she glances behind her. There is no sign of Mia's car. She recently bought a small, battered Citroën but it's not here. She presses the bell again and raps on the door with her knuckles. Where are they?

There are no signs of movement from within and it occurs to Tess that she might be too late. Tess is now pretty sure Pete Kamara butchered one woman. A woman he loved. What is to stop him from doing the same to his ex-wife and daughter? His granddaughter?

Tess knocks again and this time she hears footsteps. Someone is coming down the stairs. Tess squats and opens the letterbox. 'Mia?' she calls out. 'Mia, it's Tess. Can you open the door?'

A neighbour emerges from the house next door. She's wearing pyjama bottoms and a pink hoodie. Her hair is newly washed, the ends dripping; it's leaving damp patches above her breasts. She scowls at Tess. 'I've a husband asleep in here after a night shift.'

Tess straightens, realizing the footsteps she heard were coming from the wrong property. 'Sorry. Do you know where they are?' she asks, motioning to Mia's flat.

'Who?'

'Mia and her mother.'

'I've not seen Mia for a couple of days. The police were round here as well ten minutes ago banging hell out of that door. My husband's trying to sleep.'

'Do you know where they could be?'

The woman is less than impressed: 'We're not exactly close,' and Tess hears a baby howling from inside. The woman glances behind her. 'Gotta go,' she says and retreats, slamming the door.

Tess calls Mia's mobile again and, as it rings, she puts her ear to the glass to determine if Mia is in fact inside.

There is nothing.

Four Years Ago

I HATE MY WIFE.

I hate my wife.

I hate my wife.

Pete Kamara sits on the edge of the marital bed, the chanting inside his head getting louder. He gets up and paces. He can't believe what she's done. He can't believe Carrie has done this.

She has shit all over his life.

He has just spoken with Ella and she told him it's over. And no, she won't change her mind. She's done with married men. She's done with *him*.

The reason? There was no reason. None that he can make sense of anyway.

Carrie had been to see Ella and asked her to . . . What were the exact words Ella used? She said Carrie asked if she could be more discreet. Asked if they could conduct their affair on the QT. She said people were talking and it was embarrassing for both her and Mia.

'Then let's be more discreet,' Pete said reasonably to Ella. Discreet? He could easily do discreet. How hard could it be? 'Let's get a hotel for the night,' he said. 'I'll take you away. Let me spoil you the way I want to. We can go for the weekend. We can go for a week. Whatever you want.'

And this was when she told him the news. 'That's not what I want,' she said carefully. 'It's tricky . . . but I think I'm . . .' and Pete

274

thought: *What? What are you thinking?* 'I'm actually seeing someone else,' she said.

Gut-punched, Pete nearly dropped the phone.

'You can't be,' he replied weakly, and she told him she was sorry, but she was.

'What's his name?'

'It doesn't matter.'

'What's his *fucking name*?'

She wouldn't tell him.

Instead she said: 'Listen, Carrie coming around here made me realize that I'm not cut out for this. It's not right. I didn't understand that at first. I got caught up in what we were doing . . . I got caught up in *you*, Pete. But it can't go on. You've got a family. I never told you this but Carrie visited me at work as well as at home. She brought your daughter with her. It was mortifying. But anyway, besides all that, I'm so much younger than you are and—'

'You're not that much younger.'

She paused then. Seemingly to collect her thoughts. He could hear her breath and it sounded heavy; she sounded like a toddler with a blocked nose. Did she have another cold coming on? he wondered. She could be a bit of a baby when she was feeling out of sorts and Pete would have to minister to her like a parent. He'd spur her on, energize her, or else she'd stay in bed for days. Ella was immature and it was this childishness that Pete had found so unexpectedly alluring at the start. Her youth was intoxicating, even when she was being puerile. *Especially* when she was being puerile – because he knew he simply needed to gain the upper hand and she would do exactly as she was told. She could be so beautifully pliable and it was such a turn-on. She loved to mould herself into whatever he needed her to be and, after Carrie, it was pure novelty. And so he *knew* that whatever she was about to do next he could talk her out of. That's how they worked. That's *why* they worked.

'I don't love you any more,' she said simply.

And he laughed. From shock. Because honestly, it was hysterical. 'Aw, don't say that, love.'

'It's true.'

'You don't mean it.'

'It is true, Pete. Carrie made me realize—'

'Carrie? What did *Carrie* make you realize?'

'She made me realize that what we were doing was pointless. I mean, come on, really. Where is it going? You're never going to leave her. She told me about your arrangement. She said you had to stay until Mia gets to—'

'I am going to leave! Of course I'm leaving. I just need more time.'

'You're never going to leave, and I don't think I ever really wanted you to leave . . . It was all a game. A lovely game.'

'A *game*.'

'OK, maybe not a game. But you know what I mean. It was never going to be more than—'

'Who is he?'

'It's not important.'

'I want to know. I *deserve* to know. What is it? Why do you want him? What?' He laughs. But it's a maniacal laugh. 'Is he better in bed or something?'

Ella didn't answer.

'You little bitch,' he whispered.

An image of the two of them screwing crashed into Pete's head and he cut the call, staring at the phone in his hand. On the underside of his wrist, the tendons were standing proud of the skin. And he'd started to sweat. He needed to calm down. He needed to get his shit together. His thoughts were ricocheting around inside his head. Don't do anything rash, he cautioned himself. Don't do what you want to do and go over there.

And that's when he made the decision that he would remain here. He would remain on the edge of this bed until he could think straight.

That little bitch.

That little bitch.

Twenty minutes later and the words are deafening but it's the images Pete's having a harder time dealing with: Ella laughing; Ella lying on her back, another man's head between her legs; Ella lounging on the sofa, her feet in some guy's lap; Ella, Ella, Ella.

He wants to weep but he's too angry to weep.

He pictures them together. And the thought of someone else inside Ella turns his stomach. Suddenly he feels he might vomit. In a rush, he moves from the bed to the bathroom. He crouches in front of the toilet and rests his elbows on the rim. Heaving, he thinks of Ella's creamy skin. Her glossy hair. Her big, expressive eyes.

That little bitch.

His stomach is empty but he continues to gag. He gags until there is nothing left except the hot sting of humiliation. Then he stands. He washes his face and lowers the toilet seat, sits down upon it to try to recover. But the images of Ella are still coming and they make him want to tear his skin from his flesh. How could she do this to him?

A thought occurs: if he could just see her, she would come back. If she would only listen to what he has to say, he could persuade her, he's sure of it. He'll make her see that Carrie has planted this doubt for her own reasons. Carrie wants Pete for the sole reason of making Mia feel at home in the world. To keep a lid on Mia's *anxiety*, which seems to escalate the second her home situation isn't exactly as she likes it. Well, Pete's very sorry, because you know who else is anxious? The whole fucking world.

He'll go to Ella. He'll go to her house after Ella finishes work and he'll make Ella see that this is a mistake. There is no need for this to end. He will leave Carrie and they'll start afresh. Mia doesn't need him now. Mia is grown and this arrangement they have, this stupid, futile arrangement he and Carrie have for the sake of Mia's mental health, can finally come to an end. Mia is almost an adult. A woman. She can take care of herself for a change.

Yes, he will go there. And Ella will reconsider.

And if she doesn't? Well, he'll . . .

What?

What will he do?

All at once, he's not sure what he'll do. He can't consider failure as an option. Ella will relent because she has to. Because for him to live knowing she is sharing her life with someone else is simply illogical.

He washes his face again and brushes his teeth to get rid of the sour taste inside his mouth. He regards himself in the mirror. He turns one way and then the other. He sucks in his paunch, lifts his chin a little to tighten his jaw, and for the first time in his life he's not altogether confident in what he sees reflected back.

Is he too old? Too old for Ella?

Is it possible he might *not* persuade her? Could she reject him for a second time?

Pete glances down at the small steel pedal bin beside the sink. Carrie has neglected to push her rubbish in properly – again. There is the candy-pink edge of a sanitary pad wrapper peeping out at him from beneath the rim. He presses the pedal with his foot and stuffs the contents deep inside. 'Filthy cow,' he says when his fist makes contact with the used pads. Why can't *she* be more discreet?

Carrie used to flaunt the fact she was menstruating so he'd stay away from her in the bedroom. She used it like a banner so he wouldn't approach.

His toes slip off the pedal.

'I hate my wife.'

He says it again.

Except now something is forming in the recesses of his brain. Something that could be useful. Something he thinks might just take the pain away. Something like payback.

His toes move back towards the bin. He depresses the pedal and the lid springs open. *Surprise!* it seems to say.

He reaches inside and rummages around. His fingers landing on the prize after only a moment. He unwraps it. There is plenty of Carrie's blood for him to work with.

'Fuck you,' he says, smiling, grabbing a change of clothes to take with him. 'In fact,' he says, 'fuck both of you.' And he's down the stairs, grabbing the long-bladed knife Carrie uses for carving the Sunday roast, before getting in his car and heading back to the office.

He'll only have an hour to kill until Ella gets in from work.

Now

THE LIGHTS TURN to green and Tess's foot hits the gas. She can feel the blood pounding in her temples as she overtakes an old guy in a hat. He sounds the horn as she pulls in in front of him, her bumper way too close to his. She doesn't look in the mirror. He'll be yelling at her. When she gets the opportunity, she overtakes again. And again. She does this until she reaches P. J. Kamara Estate Agents, Sales & Lettings.

There are two cars parked at the front. She blocks them in and runs from her car. 'Where's Pete?' she says breathlessly, flinging the door open.

Pete's sour-faced assistant, June, is dealing with a young couple. She gives Tess a cursory glance before ignoring her. She is standing by a wall of photographs, starter homes, enjoying the power she wields. 'But if you *were* wanting that extra bedroom . . .' she is saying to the couple. 'How much deposit did you say you had again? Eight thousand. Hmmm.'

Tess takes a step inside. 'Where is Pete Kamara?' she repeats.

'Now this one is a very pretty dwelling. And there's no chain. The owner's gone into a residential home so there is some cosmetic work to be done. How do you feel about a project?' The woman now turns towards Tess. 'I'm sorry,' she says, 'you are?'

Tess covers the floor between them in two strides. She gets between Pete's assistant and the young couple, gets right up into the woman's face, forcing her against the wall. 'You know who I am,' she whispers nastily.

'Home,' the assistant says. 'He went home.'

Tess takes a step back. 'You were Pete's alibi? Remember that?'

'Of course I remember that.'

'You said he never left the building.'

'He didn't.'

Tess turns and heads to Pete's office. June calling out from behind, 'You can't go in there!' Tess ignores her protests and flings open the door. She stands in the centre of the office and looks around. Does a full three-sixty. And at first, she doesn't see it. She doesn't see the slightest of bumps in the plasterwork. She doesn't see it because there is a filing cabinet and a potted palm in front. She walks to the wall. Runs her fingertips over the paint. 'There used to be a door here,' she shouts to June and June doesn't answer.

Tess goes back through the main office. 'There was a door. Leading directly from Pete's office to outside.'

June's face has lost all its colour.

'Did the police interview Pete in here or in his office?' asks Tess.

'In here.'

'So they wouldn't have seen the second entrance?'

June is quietly stricken as she now realizes what she has done.

'When was the doorway bricked up?' asks Tess.

'A couple of years ago.'

'*Why* was it bricked up?'

'It was never used.'

Tess shakes her head. 'You stupid woman.'

Five minutes later and Tess turns into Pete's street. Immediately she sees Mia's small Citroën parked outside his house. Which means Mia's inside. Probably Carrie too. She pulls in behind it and gets out. A hundred thoughts crowd her head. She should call the police. She should wait for them to arrive. But approaching the house, there are no signs of life. The place is eerily quiet. Is she too late?

She peers through the front window. Everything seems in its place, as if there's no one at home.

The front door is shut.

She tries the handle.

It opens.

She steps inside and still there is no sound. Slowly, she moves from room to room. Her heart is in her mouth as she checks the two reception rooms at the front. Both are empty and there are no signs of a struggle.

She pauses at the foot of the stairs. Thinks about going up. She listens.

Silence.

She presses on towards the back of the house. The door to what can only be the kitchen is shut.

Again, she listens.

Waits.

And it's as she's pressing down on the handle that at last she hears a cry.

A baby's cry.

Tess bursts into the kitchen. She looks around and her mouth drops open. What greets her there is devastation. There's blood. A lot of blood. Everywhere. And lying in the middle of it all is Pete Kamara.

Mia is standing over by the French doors which lead to the conservatory, holding her baby, jiggling her up and down. And sitting on a chair at the kitchen island is Carrie. There is a long-bladed knife next to Carrie and she looks at Tess. 'Hey,' she says, softly, as if she somehow expected to see her. There is blood spattered on Carrie's face, on her bare arms, in her hair.

'Hello, Carrie,' Tess replies.

Tess's eyes drift to Pete. Blood is blooming through the front of his white shirt. He is lying flat on his back on the tiled kitchen floor, his right foot hooked behind his left knee. His eyes are open, his skin is still a good colour, and if you were to take away the blood, you might assume he was faking.

Tess leans against the wall. Her legs are suddenly weak as though they may give out at any second. She takes a couple of breaths, tries to regroup.

'It was self-defence,' Mia states curtly from the other side of the room. There is a forthrightness to her tone, a take-no-shit attitude, that is unusual for Mia. Tess glances at the body. It doesn't *look* like self-defence. 'He came at her with a knife,' Mia adds. 'She had no option but to respond.'

Tess walks around the body. She can't see another knife. 'What knife?' she asks, and Mia shrugs as if to say: *Whatever.*

Tess squats down. She's pretty certain this is not self-defence. 'I need to call the police,' she says, and no one speaks. 'Carrie, do you get what I'm saying, I need to call the police?'

Carrie nods. 'It's OK. Call them.' She's distant, trance-like, and Tess isn't sure if she comprehends what's going on.

Tess takes out her mobile and hesitates before dialling.

She can't believe Carrie has done this. After all they've been through to get her out of prison. Why would she do this?

'Did he attack you?' Tess asks quietly, and Carrie says that he didn't. 'What then?'

'I had to,' and for the first time Carrie looks at Tess straight in the eye. 'I had to do it,' she repeats, holding Tess's gaze, willing her to understand.

'*Why* did you have to do it?'

'There was no alternative.'

'Because you knew he'd set you up?' asks Tess.

'Yeah.'

'The blood,' Tess says. 'You knew he'd planted it.'

'Yeah.'

'When? *When* did you know?'

'Not at first,' Carrie explains, 'not when I was arrested. Not even during the trial. But . . . later. Pete came to see me a few months after I arrived at Styal. He wanted me to make things right between Mia and him, and when I refused, when I told him only he could do that, he got nasty. He said I was poisoning Mia's mind against him. He told me I'd poisoned *Ella's* mind against him.' Carrie pauses. And then: 'He killed that girl because he couldn't stand the thought of anyone else having her. She'd started seeing another guy and he blamed me for that. He blamed me for warning her off. She'd told him she didn't want to play around with a married man any more and he blamed me. And so he put my blood in her house so I'd take the rap. He hated me so very much for influencing Ella.'

'So why not tell someone?' Tess cries. 'Why not tell *me*? Why make us go through all that? Through the whole appeal process when there was no guarantee it would go your way?'

Carrie swallows. 'I needed you to get me out of there,' she says quietly.

'I *could* have got you out of there. No problem at all. Why did we have to go to the appellate court? Why spend all that time and resources when—'

And then it dawns.

Tess closes her eyes. 'If you'd told me about the blood, Pete would've been arrested and charged.'

'He'd be in prison,' says Carrie.

'And if he was in prison, you couldn't get to him, could you? You couldn't kill him if he was locked up?'

'No.' Carrie smiles sadly. 'And we had to kill him. I'm afraid we had to redress the balance.'

We? thinks Tess. *What does she mean, we?*

Tess looks over to Mia and Mia turns away. She is cradling her baby against her shoulder and Tess almost laughs.

She's been had.

Not for the first time, she's been led a merry dance by a prisoner, but she's pretty sure this is the *first time* a prisoner's family has got the better of her.

Carrie watches Mia softly sway her baby and she remembers meeting her for the first time back in November of last year. The tears, the pleading, the whole I-need-my-mother routine. Was that real? Some of it. Most of it, maybe. Mia simply neglected to make Tess part of the bigger picture. The one in which she gets her mother back and together they execute her father.

'Mia?' Tess says.

'What?' she snaps.

'Are you OK?' And Mia shrugs. This is a very different Mia from the one who played along with their plan all this time. The weeping, oh-so-vulnerable Mia. The wide-eyed innocent who'd lost everything. This Mia is tough. This Mia has a steeliness to her gaze. Her spine is straighter. She stands as though she owns the room.

But she's also scared. She's scared because she doesn't know what Tess is going to do about this.

Tess walks over to the body and surveys the scene again. The two women watch her carefully. She bends over and looks at Pete closely. Poor Pete. He still looks a bit of a dick even in death.

'Now would be a good time to find that knife he came at your mother with,' she says to Mia as she straightens. And Mia is nodding. Tess tosses her a tea towel. 'Use that to pick it up.'

'What, now?'

'*Yes*, now.'

Her strength of tone makes Mia flinch and she springs into action. With the baby on her hip, Mia grabs a knife from the knife block and deposits it by her father's hand.

'Now give that back to me,' Tess says, meaning the towel.

Mia tosses it to Tess who stuffs it inside her handbag. There follows a moment of silence when all three women regard one another.

'Ready?' asks Tess.

'Ready,' they say in unison.

'Well, you'd better hold your nerve, ladies,' she says, and she dials. 'Yes,' she says when the call connects, 'Police . . . Hang on,' and she looks to Carrie: 'What's the exact address here? They need the house number.'

Twenty minutes later and a black coroner's van is parked in the driveway. Tess takes a bottle of water from her handbag, removes the cap and drinks it down fast. The detective in front of her is keen to do things correctly. He's young. He's nervous. And Tess is thankful for small mercies. A more seasoned pro would watch Tess a little more closely. They might linger a while longer, watch her walk to her car, see if she can keep going with the I'm-rather-shook-up routine. This guy has asked Tess the same question twice already, and she knows he's too focused on his own performance, too eager to come off as someone who is capable of the role he has been allocated, to doubt the information she is feeding him.

'Perhaps if we'd all got here a few minutes earlier, this tragedy could've been prevented,' Tess is saying, adjusting her face into a mask of solemnity, and the young DC bites down on his lower lip. *Is she blaming the police for this?* he's thinking and, not sure of the protocol with such an accusation, his instinct is to try to wrap things up and take advice from someone in seniority. He tells her he thinks he's got everything he needs for now, but would she be willing to pop into the station at some point to give a full written statement?

'Absolutely,' she says.

Epilogue

TESS JOINS THE morning traffic and is heading to Manchester. It's early. A new day. Tess has her notes in order and is ready to present her findings of her current case to the panel. Back in Morecambe, Pete Kamara's body is still the property of the coroner. There will be no funeral yet, not for some time, and Tess wonders who would attend even if there was, now that the word is out.

'Pete Kamara murdered Ella Muir?' people are asking one another, aghast.

Followed by: 'His poor wife. His poor, poor wife. Going to prison for all that time. For something she just didn't do.'

Tess flicks through the channels on the car's digital radio as she battles through the Swinton Interchange. She settles on BBC Radio 3. She's not really a fan of classical music but the *Today Programme* is not what it once was, and the loud, faux-upbeat manner of the DJs on the other stations has started to set her teeth on edge. She can't seem to do 'happy' today. Scrap that, she can't do happy at all right now – she is listless, unmoored, and she doesn't know what to do about it.

Tess has done her job. She has done her job well. Carrie, the innocent, incarcerated client, is now free. And Tess is ready and prepared to move on to the next person requiring their help. Trouble is, she's not sure if she wants to help right now. Not sure she can. She can't say exactly why that is, she just knows that what once got her excited, what once got her out of bed in the morning, suddenly doesn't.

She arrives at Innocence UK. She's pleased to see her peers and they are pleased to see her. She receives congratulations; they're in a celebratory mood, they've bought flowers, they want to buy her lunch, they want to know what was the thing, what was the magical moment, that led to Tess requesting a retest of Carrie's blood? 'How did you make that leap?' they ask, eager to pick her brain.

'I don't know,' she answers truthfully, and they are deflated. They try not to show it, but they want to know: *Why aren't you jubilant?*

Yes, Tess. Why *aren't* you jubilant?

It was a defining moment in her career, the kind of moment she dreamt of, and yet it all feels a bit flat somehow. Meaningless.

Perhaps her feelings of apathy towards her job are merely the beginnings of a midlife crisis. Perhaps she's longing for something that doesn't exist and she simply needs to have an unsuitable affair . . . colour her hair pink . . . get a tattoo . . . have her forehead Botoxed.

'Tess?'

Clive is saying her name.

'Tess, love, are you OK?'

Is she OK?

Gradually, she becomes aware of her surroundings and realizes they are expecting her to speak. All eyes are upon her as she stands, laser pen in hand, the new client's name and main points of his case summarized and projected from her laptop on to the large screen over to her left.

'I'm not sure,' she answers.

'Would you like a glass of water?' asks Avril.

And Tess tells her she wouldn't.

'How about a whisky?' says Clive, and she tells him she doesn't want that either.

'I think,' she says, feeling unsteady, feeling unsure all of a sudden, 'I think I really need to go,' and she picks up her laptop, packs up her case notes, and she walks out of the door.

When she gets to the lift, Tess hears Clive calling out her name from behind. 'Tess!' He is running along the corridor. It's rather comical. Tess hasn't witnessed Clive sprint before and he has a unique style: knees brought up high, arms flailing across his body. He arrives at her side, his breathing laboured, saying, 'Christ, I'm unfit. Where're you off to? Aren't you well?'

'I'm fine.'

'So why the big exit?'

'I just felt like I had to get out of there.'

Clive's breathing steadies and he regards her, his face full of concern. 'What's going on?'

'Nothing's going on.'

'Is it what happened with Pete Kamara? I heard it was a proper bloodbath in there. Maybe you're traumatized.'

'I don't think so.'

Clive leans his weight against the wall. 'I heard they're still trying to find a way to charge Carrie.'

'Yeah. I heard that too,' replies Tess.

'I don't reckon she'll do any more time inside though.'

'No?'

'Her lawyers are claiming self-defence. That's correct, isn't it?' And Clive looks at her, one eyebrow raised.

'Well, he has killed before, Clive. Remember?'

'That's what I thought you'd say.' Clive is smiling as though to indicate he is sceptical about the official reported version of events. 'I doubt they'll put her away again,' he is saying. 'She's done, what? Three? Four years? Plus the year she did on remand before that for a crime she didn't do. I think she'll walk . . .' and Tess is nodding. 'But then I think you already knew that, didn't you, Tess?'

She looks at him a little guiltily.

'So, what now?' he asks.

'I need to go.'

'Go where?'

'There's something I need to do.'

'Will you be back?'

'I should think so. I just need to sort something out.'

The lift arrives and the doors open. Tess steps inside and turns around to face Clive.

He seems sad. 'I don't suppose you've time for a quick fuck . . . ?' he asks hopefully. 'For old times' sake?'

And Tess smiles. She hasn't.

The following day, Tess reflects on her decision to back up Carrie's story of self-defence. As she waits, she wonders: would she make the same call given the chance again?

Pete wouldn't be any less dead, no matter what Tess told the police, and so the real question is: does Carrie Kamara deserve to return to prison on a murder charge?

Some days Tess thinks yes, but more often than not she thinks no.

Tess *does* wonder, however, what was it exactly that made her compromise her own integrity in that way? Up until now, Tess has always sought and reported the truth, no matter how damaging for the client.

Why did she help Carrie and Mia construct a credible crime scene? Why not simply walk out of there and leave them to deal with the mess on their own? As she sits on this bench, her gaze resting on the café opposite, Tess can come up with only two plausible explanations: her drive to reunite mother and daughter was stronger than her urge to tell the whole truth, and, in this instance, her own sense of justice was *less important* than the truth. Tess wonders if this will continue. Will she continue to be swayed by her emotions or was it a one-off?

She glances at her watch. It's close to four and she has been waiting here for a couple of hours, but she doesn't mind. The weather is still balmy, there is a gentle breeze coming off the sea, and the pedestrians who pass by are genial. They smile at Tess. They nod. *Hello,* they say. *Good afternoon. I wonder when this weather will finally break?*

Tess continues to wait. She can wait here all day. She has nothing at all to do except to be here.

Tess did consider setting her thoughts down on paper. She even went so far as to buy a fountain pen and a stack of thick, creamy, luxurious paper. Her plan was to lay it all down for Steph to read: how Tess knew she didn't deserve to be a part of Steph's life after the way she'd treated her; how not revealing her identity was both ridiculous and gutless; how Tess ran from her daughter for all these years because allowing her in, letting that particular door swing open, might unleash a tidal wave of emotion in Tess that she wasn't prepared, or equipped, to deal with.

In the letter, Tess would also explain what she'd learned from all of this: that she is not the principled, honourable person she thought she was. That she'd built a life around the importance of those traits, but she'd never been put to the test, and it was only when Steph appeared that she realized she was just as fallible, just as reluctant to face up to her own weaknesses, as the next person.

Yes, Tess thought, she would transcribe these discoveries, commit them to paper, and Steph would have a letter, something she could return to again and again when she needed questions answering about her mother. Her birth mother.

But then Tess became cognizant of the fact that writing a letter was, in itself, an act of extreme cowardice, and so she decided she must travel to Morecambe in person instead.

On her way here, she'd allowed herself to indulge in one small fantasy. The itch was there again, the itch to move address – that was nothing new – and she knew it was almost time for another relocation, only this time the itch felt different. It wasn't compelling her to flee, to leave, *run, run away*, it was propelling her towards something. Towards someone.

Could she relocate to Morecambe? Could she come home, back to the place of her birth? Perhaps Morecambe itself might be too close for comfort for both parties – but Lancaster? Heysham? Grange-over-Sands? Tess fingers the details of the five cottages to rent inside her handbag that she picked up from the letting agency earlier. She could easily commute to Manchester from any of them. Each is available to rent from the beginning of next month, and she will look at them more closely this evening – depending on what happens next.

At four twenty, the door to the café opens and Steph comes out. She has a long-handled broom in one hand and from the back pocket of her jeans she withdraws a packet of cigarettes. She pauses to light one, and then leans her weight against the stone brickwork of the building, inhaling deeply. She seems tired. As though it's been a long day. She angles her face up towards the sun and closes her eyes.

Tess feels a deep longing inside her chest to approach, but for now stays where she is. She doesn't want to spook her daughter. Or would it be more accurate to say she is too nervous to approach? Tess's heart flutters like the wings of a trapped bird and just when she thinks this might not have been such a good idea after all, Steph's eyes fly open, as if she's heard a phone ring, or has remembered something she must attend to.

Steph catches sight of Tess. And there's a pause, a moment of confusion as if she's trying to place the forty-something woman opposite, but Tess knows that can't really be it. And so the frown on Steph's face makes Tess's heart beat more wildly, and she wonders if she should abort, if she should walk away now, before any more damage can be done.

Steph walks towards her.

'I knew you'd be back,' she says.

Tess is mildly stunned. 'You did?' She's thinking: *How could you know when I didn't know myself?*

And Steph smiles. 'I tend to have that effect on people.'

Tess looks up at Steph and is struck by her daughter's strength, her playfulness, her faith in herself. She's struck by her lack of judgement.

'Come on,' Steph says, 'I'll get you a coffee. You look kind of thirsty.'

Author's Note

I have mostly stayed faithful to the geography of Morecambe, Lancashire, but to make the story work, on occasion, I had to invent things. I'm afraid the Eagle and Child pub, for now, only exists in my imagination. Also, in the interests of telling a compelling story, I was forced to simplify the appeals procedure considerably.

Acknowledgments

Thank you, Frankie Gray. Thank you, Jane Gregory.

Thank you, Stephanie Glencross, Amy Hundley, Tash Barsby, Richenda Todd, Vivien Thompson, Hayley Barnes, Ella Horne, Richard Shailer.

I am also immensely grateful to my wonderful family and friends who supported me throughout the writing process.